# ALSO BY THE AUTHOR

FRANCES MACARTHUR

# I'LL BE PLAYING
# SOLITAIRE

To Ros
love
Frances

ISBN: 1522905677
ISBN 13: 9781522905677

# ACKNOWLEDGEMENTS

I dedicate this novel to my wonderful friends.
When someone you love very dearly, dies,
it is said that you find out who your true friends
are. Mine have all been true friends, many from a
distance by phone and email.

I want to mention in particular: Alan, Andrew
and Cynthia who rescued me the first Christmas
and ensured, generously, that I went back to Penang
with them the following year: Anne whose texts
kept me sane throughout the awful first months:
Archie, my friend since childhood, who tells me
off when I need it: Irene, busy running round
corners but who will do anything to help me; Julia
who sadly lost Neil, her husband, recently; Kay in
church who gives me good advice: Leela who as
a fellow writer keeps my nose to the grindstone:
Morag who got Ivor and me together many years
ago and came back into my life to comfort and
encourage me: Nancy who acts like my mother and
feeds me beans on toast and last, but definitely not
least, Tom, the lovely Sassenach from The Wirral

who came into my life in August 2014 and bears the brunt of my scattiness and stupidity!

Many others have done their bit to restore me to normal living. I can't mention them all but they will know who they are.

# CHAPTER I

"**D**ammit! I won't go into a nursing home, Robert. You can't make me."

"I think you'll find we can, Mother. In fact, that's the car pulling up now."

It was with a sense of complete frustration that Adele Stevenson found herself being pushed out of the door of her house in Giffnock, in her wheelchair. She was a slightly built, snowy white-haired woman in her nineties.

"Don't make a fuss, Mother. So undignified," commented Matthew Stevenson, her younger son, coming out a black Mercedes.

"So, not even a taxi-driver I can tell the story to, I see. Your own car."

Matthew, slimly built with abundant fair hair, came round to manoeuvre her out of the chair and into the front seat then he opened the capacious boot and put in a large suitcase and the wheelchair and got into the driving seat.

"See you there, Robert," he called to his brother.

The car purred discreetly away from the kerb, followed by the shiny, dark blue BMW belonging to Robert, a portly figure, almost completely bald. He was accompanied by his wife, Margaret, a slight woman with greying fair hair and an apologetic air.

"Robert. Do you think you're doing the right thing?" she questioned, timidly.

"She's spending a bloody fortune, keeping that house with a gardener and home help," he growled.

"But will a nursing home not be as expensive, dear?" said Margaret.

"My father put the house in his children's names years ago, remember, so when it's sold, the three of us get the cash from the sale. He left mother a tidy sum and that, plus what the state contributes will pay for her in the home. They'll take her pension of course but that won't affect us. Matt and I are going to apply for power of attorney as well, once mother's safely ensconced in the home so we should be able to make use of the large amount father left her. She has no use for that now."

"Pauline will be furious when she finds out," ventured Margaret.

"Yes, but by the time she finds out, when she gets back from her painting holiday in Cornwall, it'll be a fait accompli, won't it?"

"What if Kim and Lucy come to visit their grandma and find her gone?" persevered his wife.

"It's hardly likely. They went off to Spain last Saturday. I chose this time specially. Give me some credit and stop wittering on."

By this time, they were driving up the tree-lined driveway which gave the nursing home in Netherlee its name, so he scowled at his wife who lapsed into her customary, submissive silence.

The Mercedes had pulled up smoothly at the door which opened and a woman in an old-fashioned matron's outfit came down the short flight of steps to the car.

Robert got out of his car.

"Stay in the car, Margaret," he ordered.

He walked up to the matron and put out his hand.

"Robert Stevenson, Mrs Smith," he said. "My mother's in the other car."

Matthew came round to help him get his mother out and into her wheelchair.

"I don't know who you are," said Adele, "but you need to know right now that I've been brought here under protest, kidnapped from my own home. I want to be taken home right now!"

"Come on, Mother. You can't keep changing your mind, you know. You agreed to come here and I'm sure once you see your lovely bedroom you'll be quite happy. I showed you the brochure remember?" said Robert, smiling pleasantly.

"No you did not! I'm elderly but not senile. This is all your idea, your's and Matthew's."

Robert sent a rueful look towards the matron and she smiled back. Matthew had spent quite a long time, a few weeks ago, telling her about his mother who was in the first stages of dementia and had the doctor's letter confirming that. His mother had never seen the brochure and had never agreed to come into the home but matron need never know that. Their GP had asked Adele a few questions and she had got the date wrong as she always did and didn't know the prime minister's name so he had agreed that she was in the first stages of dementia. Young Dr Fraser was a member of Killermont Golf Club where Robert was captain.

"I'm Mrs Smith. My husband and I own Tall Trees and I am also matron," said that lady.

Another, younger woman joined them. She patted Adele on the shoulder and welcomed her to Tall Trees. She took the handles of the wheelchair and pushed it up the ramp at the side of the steps. Matron, Robert and Matthew followed them into an expensively-furnished hallway. There was a large rosewood table in the centre. On it was placed a beautiful arrangement of roses.

"There are lovely flowers in your bedroom too, Adele," said the young woman. "And my name's

Sandra, short for Alexandra. I'll be your special nurse."

"And I, for your information, am Mrs Stevenson, short for...Mrs Stevenson. Who gave you permission to use my Christian name?"

"Chosen name, my dear," corrected Mrs Smith. "We don't say Christian name here as we have an Asian woman staying with us."

"Well I am a Christian...so Adele remains my Christian name but you needn't concern yourself with it as you will call me Mrs Stevenson until my daughter comes and takes me out of here!"

By this time they had all squeezed into the lift which moved silently upwards, one floor. The doors swished open and the little group filed out. One room door was open and Sandra propelled the wheelchair towards it.

"Isn't this a lovely room, Mrs Stevenson," said Sandra, brightly, wheeling her charge in.

"It's OK but my living room at home is larger and better appointed."

At this moment a man appeared in the doorway. He told the visitors that he was matron's husband and he helped Robert to transfer his mother from the wheelchair to a Parker-Knoll armchair. Matron gestured to the others and they left the room.

On her own, Adele's aggressive mood evaporated and a silent tear trickled down one cheek. She punched her knee with one hand and grimaced as the action hurt. Looking round, she saw a nicely-furnished room with a single bed in one corner, its coverlet matching the material and design of the curtains. The room had two empty bookcases, a table and two chairs, a television set, wardrobe and a two-seater settee. A door which was ajar slightly, looked as if it led to an ensuite bathroom. Her glance took in the view which was of large trees and an immaculate lawn. On the lawn an elderly woman was sitting on a rustic bench, knitting something in white wool. As she watched, a man walked up to her and said something. The woman laughed. A dog had appeared beside them, a golden retriever. It licked the woman's hand and she patted its honey-coloured head. It was a peaceful scene but it did not bring peace to Adele.

Her hands clenched on her lap. She looked round the room again. The TV had a large screen and what was probably one of those new-fangled DVD machines, she surmised. Eagerly she looked round for a telephone but there was not one and she had never managed to get used to a mobile, unfortunately, in spite of her granddaughters trying to persuade her to have one.

"I wish I had one now," she spoke out loud into the empty room.

There was a red cord hanging on the wall beside her and she pulled it. Minutes later, the door opened and Sandra came in, smiling.

"I see you've found the cord to call for me," she said.

"Yes. I want a phone brought to me...please," said Adele

"You'll have access to a phone once you've settled in," said Sandra, gently. "We don't put phones into rooms right away in case residents worry their relatives when they feel strange at first. Now can I get you a nice cup of tea and a biscuit?"

"No, damn you, I don't want a nice cup of tea and a biscuit. I want out of here!" Adele shouted.

Her shouts brought Matron, and Sandra held the old woman still while she gave her an injection. In a few minutes, Adele Stevenson was asleep in the chair.

"Poor old thing," said Sandra sympathetically. "Dementia is such a cruel illness."

"Yes," matron agreed.

She glanced out of the window and, seeing her husband, she knocked and waved. The dog looked up in her direction and wagged its tail.

Matthew, Margaret and Robert went for lunch. Margaret sat silent as her husband and his brother had a celebratory whisky and congratulated themselves at having brought off the transfer of their elderly mother to a nursing home.

"Now I need to set the selling of the house in motion," said Robert.

"What do you expect we'll get for it?" asked Matthew.

"I would think, quarter of a million, at least," was his reply.

"So eighty thou each," Matthew said, grinning widely. "And we've done mother a favour. She'll be well looked after and when she's, shall we say, less sharp, we can transfer her somewhere cheaper."

Margaret said nothing. She knew that they would have a fight on their hands when their sister arrived home.

# CHAPTER 2

Pauline Macartney was in her element. Sitting on a cliff above Treen Beach in Cornwall, she was painting the scene but had been distracted by watching people wending their way down a narrow path to the beach. Having been down herself, she knew that the last part of the descent was difficult and this last group of holidaymakers did not all look up to the task. There was a mother and father with three children but one child was only small. The group reminded her of her own family, two elder brothers and herself, the youngest, and she knew what would happen when they reached the rock-climbing part of the descent. The father would climb down expertly as would the two teenage boys. Mother would wait behind for the young girl and would criticise her husband for not finding out about the difficulty of the climb down before leading them on this trip to the beach. The small girl would state bravely that she could manage, egged on by the taunting comments from the two boys who would be ready to blame their young sister if they had to abort this outing.

Pauline knew something else that the family did not know, namely that Treen beach was a nudist beach, not really suitable for this family. She had gone down there some years ago with Stewart, her husband and their twin daughters, then only ten years old. They had been staying in a caravan that year. They had not realised that there were nudists on the beach until she had wandered down to the water's edge, passing a quite elderly couple. She had greeted them cheerily and been surprised when Stewart had asked her on her return to their towels, what she had thought of them. He had laughed at her and told her that both people had been in the nude. She had not noticed. Kim and Lucy had noticed of course and found it all hilarious, especially when the man had tried climbing the cliff behind them.

A seagull circled noisily above her head now and she watched as it flew off in the direction of Logan's Rock, reputed to have been rolled down by some drunken sailors who had been forced to get the huge rock back into its original position. She and Stewart had once climbed to the top, no mean feat, and they had photographed each other. She could still remember Stewart silhouetted against an azure, cloudless sky, his yellow sweater and red cap, a vivid contrast to the blue.

She added a few touches to her painting, then sat back and reached for her basket which contained the sandwiches she had prepared that morning. The smell of pickle reached her nostrils. She glanced at her watch and was surprised to see that it was already early afternoon. Stewart would be joining her shortly. He had gone into Penzance and had promised to meet her on the cliff top. He was a writer, having retired very early and had made a start on a Cornish crime novel. He would sit beside her and write until it was time for them to gather their belongings and make for Treen Inn for an early evening meal.

"She always spoils everything!" said a grumpy voice and along the top path came the family she had spotted earlier.

"Stop it, Derek! I won't tell you again. You were Rose's age once yourself. We can go along in the car to Porthcurno Beach and swim there."

The woman smiled at Pauline as she passed, shepherding the little group. The young girl's eyes were wet with tears and Pauline felt such sympathy with her that she heard herself telling the family that the beach was disappointing at this time of day with the tide quite far in and going out quickly. The woman sent her a grateful glance and the child smiled timidly. The little line was soon out of sight.

Pauline's mind went back to a day when she and her parents and two brothers had gone to the carnival in Glasgow's Kelvin Hall and she had been terrified on the ghost train. Her two brothers had taunted her, Robert, the eldest being the worst. She had cried then and Matt had joined in, calling her a cry-baby and what had been a looked-forward-to afternoon out, had deteriorated into a slanging-match between her parents as her father had sided with the boys, saying that she had to grow up and her mother had protected her and called them bullies.

"You're miles away," joked a familiar voice and she looked up to see Stewart, his fair hair tousled, standing beside her. He sat down at the foot of her folding chair and looked up at her canvas.

"That's really coming on, love. What would you say? Two more days' work?"

"Yes, that's about right, darling. Did you get what you wanted in Penzance?"

"Yes, more paper and some beer and two bottles of wine for you. Oh, I got some of that marvellous chocolate nougat we both love. Do you want some now?"

"Yes please."

They shared a bar, knowing that it would spoil their appetite later but not being able to resist this sumptuous Cornish confectionery. With that and cream teas and the sitting around painting and writing, they were both piling on weight but neither cared. Pauline was what she called, 'happily rounded' and Stewart was a bean pole who could take extra fat

"Before I left, I told Peter and Barbara that we wouldn't be back for a meal tonight. Was that right?" Stewart asked, between mouthfuls.

"Yes. I'm glad that you remembered. We decided last night that we would spoil ourselves with a Treen Inn meal."

"I thought I'd remembered right."

Stewart was notorious for getting swept up in his novel-writing and forgetting arrangements, so he sounded quite smug. He brought out his notepad and a pen.

The light was beginning to fade behind Logan's Rock when Pauline took a final look at her painting and told her husband to finish off what he was writing. He straightened, grimacing at the stiffness. His previous work as a surgeon had weakened his back, one of the reasons he had given up in his late forties.

As a young surgeon, in the 1980s, he had performed an operation on the then Pauline Stevenson, saving her right leg after she got it snared in a trap on her grandparents' estate in Perthshire. She had been rushed back to Glasgow, to Canniesburn Hospital. Stewart had come in to see her in the ward the day before she was transferred to Ross Hall at her father's insistence and he had promised to visit his patient there.

Despite their different ages, Stewart being almost eight years younger than Pauline, they had grown to love each other. Arthur Stevenson had been against the marriage but Adele had taken to Stewart right from the start and had managed to talk her husband round.

Stewart helped his wife to her feet and stood while she circled her right ankle a few times to get life back into it. She packed up her basket, he added his notebook and pen to its contents and they made off, in single file, along the path, turning their backs on Logan's Rock and taking the path through the cornfield, a path well-worn by holiday-makers. Stewart had dropped Pauline off in the car park at the other end of the path and he had parked on his return from Penzance in the shade of some trees so the car was stuffy but not too hot. The journey to Treen Inn was a very short one and soon they were seated in the snug bar, in the window seat, with a pint for Stewart and a vermouth and lemonade for Pauline. They had looked at the menu on the way in and ordered two ploughman's meals.

The pub was quiet, only themselves and one other couple drinking there but they knew from experience that it would soon fill up and if they were lucky there would be a sing-song.

"Do you remember the first time I had bed and breakfast with Peter and Barbara?" Pauline said now.

"Do you mean the Cornish pasty meal?" Stewart asked, grinning.

"Yes."

"The night before when you and your friend, Jean arrived, Barbara gave you bacon and eggs so you thought the meals would be small. You had a huge cream tea the next afternoon."

"That's right and when she put down our plates that second night there was this pastry thing, no potatoes, no vegetables..."

"And then you discovered that all the veg and potatoes were inside the pastry and you couldn't even manage half of it."

"So we gave half of each to our dogs!" laughed Pauline. "Then the next year we came, they told us that we'd been the only people ever to finish off one of Barbara's home-made pasties," she finished off.

Their meals arrived and they tucked in hungrily, in spite of their afternoon nougat. The pub was filling up with a mixture of locals and tourists and they heard one man asking why there was a notice on the door saying, "No Irish".

The landlord informed him that last year there had been Irish navvies working on the roads and that they had caused trouble in the Inn one night.

"You could be had up for racism, surely, mate," said the man who had asked the question.

"I'll cross that bridge if I come to it," was the laconic reply.

"Excuse me a minute, Stewart. I'm going outside to phone Mum," said Pauline. "If I remember correctly, the reception is useless in here."

She returned some minutes later, looking puzzled and a bit anxious.

"No answer. Wonder where she is?"

She ran her fingers through her curly, greying brown curls.

"Bridge night?" queried Stewart.

"No. That's Wednesday and anyway Agnes who usually takes her, was going away this week so I think it was cancelled."

"Look don't start worrying. You left your mobile number. One of your brothers would have rung you if anything was wrong," Stewart reassured her.

Thus it was that Pauline drifted off to sleep that night in her husband's arms, blissfully unaware that in Glasgow, her mother was spending the night in a strange bed.

# CHAPTER 3

Sandra Keith, helped by another, young, female nurse called Julia Harrison, put Adele to bed on her first night in Tall Trees. The old woman had tried to resist being wheeled into the dining room at 5.30 for her evening meal but Sandra had been adamant that on this first night, she ate with the other residents, telling her that in future she would have the option of eating in her room.

"I want you to meet everyone tonight," the young nurse had told her. "All the others, with the exception of Martha, and Shahida on fasting occasions, choose to eat in the dining room every night."

There were three round tables in the dining room. Each table had a differently-coloured tablecloth and Adele was wheeled to the blue-covered one.

"Suits my mood," she thought bitterly. "Though black might be better!"

There was only one person at the table, a gentleman with thick, snowy- white hair whom she would have taken for a military man had it not been for the fact that he was rather slouched at the table.

"Excuse me not rising, madam," he said courteously as Sandra manoeuvred Adele's wheelchair into position across from him. "I have Parkinson's Disease which makes me rather wobbly at times."

He held out a hand across the table and rather reluctantly, Adele shook it. He told her that his name was Frederick Graham, "Fred to my friends," he had added.

"My name is Adele Stevenson but I doubt if we'll get to know each other as I intend to leave here as soon as possible."

The meal had progressed in silence, Fred being too intent on managing his cutlery and Adele being in no mood for small talk. It certainly was a delicious meal, smoked salmon to start with, chicken in a tasty sauce and a light soufflé dessert, followed by coffee and chocolate mints.

As the coffees were placed in front of them, Fred found his voice.

"I apologise for saying nothing throughout the meal. I hate to make a mess and this dratted disease makes my hands shake so I have to concentrate."

"Have you had it long?" asked Adele.

She had been determined to remain silent and disapproving but it was difficult not to talk to Fred. It was not his fault that she was here, after all.

"About two years now. I came in here last December. My dear wife died in 2002 and my daughter and son-in-law live in Singapore. My grandson lives in Newton Mearns and visits me every week without fail. We play bezique or chess together."

"Bezique! I've never met anyone else apart from our family who could play that. Arthur, my late husband and I played it a lot. My children learned how to play but never have the time and my granddaughters would call it old-fashioned," she laughed.

"We must have a game," Fred said, delightedly.

"Well, it will have to be soon as I plan to get home as soon as I can," Adele reminded him and his face fell.

"Tonight?" he asked eagerly.

"Oh no. Not yet."

Adele saw his disappointed expression.

"I need to think, tonight," she added.

After their coffees, Sandra wheeled Adele back to her room, asking her if she would like a drink brought to her and telling her that there was a bar of sorts in the communal sitting room, just along the corridor. Adele asked for a small brandy and sipped it slowly once Sandra had helped her into her armchair. She had declined the offer to wheel her along to the sitting room to meet the other residents whom she had seen at adjacent tables in the dining room although she was curious about a younger man who appeared to be only in his late forties, early fifties. It seemed to Adele that the carers assumed that she was wheelchair-bound which was not the case. She could walk quite well as long as there was furniture to hold on to but she had reached the conclusion in the afternoon that it might be wise to keep this fact hidden right now.

Taking another sip of the 'amber nectar' which was her nickname for her favourite drink, she tried to work out when her daughter would be returning from Cornwall and came to the conclusion that she might have another week in the nursing home. She had remembered that her granddaughters were also away, in Spain, so it was no good trying to contact them, even if she could remember their phone numbers.

She rose from her chair and walked over to the window. It had been a glorious August day and it was a beautiful evening. Mr Smith was working on a rose bed. The dog lay near him. It was a peaceful scene and Adele could almost feel her tense shoulders relax.

"Probably the effect of the brandy," she muttered to herself.

She heard a knock, then the sound of her door opening and turned round, frowning at having been caught standing unaided but it was not one of the nurses. It was a tiny, Asian woman.

"I don't know your name, just that you're new here so you won't have ordered a newspaper or TV guide. I brought you my paper. I've already planned my viewing for this evening."

Adele walked slowly across and took the paper from the woman's outstretched hand.

"That was kind of you. My name's Stevenson. Adele Stevenson. You are?"

"I'm Mrs Mohammed. Shahida but I prefer to be called by my surname."

Her friendly tone robbed the words of any standoffishness and Adele replied in quite a friendly tone that she too wanted to be called Mrs Stevenson.

"But I hope to be away from here soon," she added, thinking that these words had almost become a mantra.

"I wanted to stay at home too but I kept taking blackouts and my children don't live in Glasgow and decided that they wanted me somewhere where there would be twenty-four hour care. They meant well but it is not usual for a Muslim to be in care. The extended family is the norm for us. I myself took care of my parents."

"How many people are living here?" Adele asked her.

"There are seven of us now that you are here: four women and three men. The woman whose room is in between ours, Miss Cowan, seems to have no family. No one visits her. I hardly know her though I have lived next door to her for some months now. Still that suits me. I am a private person."

She turned to leave.

"My family all live in Glasgow," said Adele, bitterly. "They just don't want me living with them. Well, my sons don't and my daughter doesn't have the room. Anyway I am still perfectly able to look after myself. I will be leaving here soon."

The woman had turned back towards her and a look of disbelief flitted across her face. She turned away again to leave the room and Adele's explanation of being brought here under protest, fell on a closing door. She looked at the newspaper in her hand. It was already turned to the TV page.

At home she would have happily spent the evening watching TV in her cosy sitting room but now she wished she had not repulsed the offer of her dinner partner, to play cards. She had said that she wanted to think and going back to her chair, she sat down, placing the paper on the floor and resting her head on the brocade headrest.

An onlooker would have known that her thoughts were not happy ones as her forehead wrinkled and her eyes clouded over. She sat still for some time, then got back up and walked over to the chest of drawers where her son had placed her handbag. She opened it and looked for her address book. It was not there and she gritted her teeth in annoyance.

"Damn them!" she said to the empty room.

# CHAPTER 4

"Stop worrying about your mother, love. Robert said she was away."

"Yes but away where? He was really vague, saying she'd gone for a rest. Why would she need a rest?"

"Honestly, Pauline. What do you think's happened? Do you think he's murdered her?"

"No, silly, but she might be ill and he's trying not to spoil our holiday."

"Since when was Robert ever so considerate? He'd be first to tell you to come home and take the visiting off his shoulders."

"And I can't raise Matt. I keep getting his voice mail."

"Right! They've both murdered your mother. Better get on to the police then."

Pauline came out of the tiny ensuite, grinning and threw a towel at her husband who was reclining on the bed.

"OK so I'm worrying over nothing and we'll be home in about a week's time. Sorry, my love. I promise I won't let it spoil our last week here.

Now go and get washed. Peter and Barbara will be wondering what's keeping us."

Their B&B host and hostess were taking them to a local meadery that night. Pauline had first met the couple when she and a friend, Jean, had travelled for the first time to Cornwall while in their early twenties. They had taken their two dogs and had stayed first in Tintagel with a sweet old lady called Mrs Bray who loved all animals and had welcomed them with open arms and spoiled the dogs rotten while they were there. They had moved on to Land's End, been disappointed with it and had almost decided to return to Tintagel when they had decided to take a look at the Minack Theatre and had come across Porthcurno with its breath-taking view of the ocean and its lovely beach. They had searched for a B&B and found Peter and Barbara Scott who had also welcomed their dogs. Pauline had always meant to take her husband there but the years had passed when their daughters were growing up and this was their first holiday on their own. Pauline had kept in touch with the Scotts who had stopped doing B&B but said that they'd be delighted to have them stay as friends.

The meadery was crowded but they managed to find a booth in a far corner and ordered their drinks. Pauline had warned Stewart about the potency of all the wines which sounded innocuous - peach wine sounded like a fruit juice but she had found out to her cost when she was here the first time, that a few of these had the strength of about four whiskies. She ordered a mead wine, a small one, and then the menu arrived.

They arrived back at the Scott's bungalow in a mellow, contented mood and sat back in the lounge to sample some more of Peter's CD collection. He had every musical ever produced and they were singing along to "Another Suitcase in Another Hall" from 'Evita' when Pauline realised that her mobile phone was ringing. Excusing herself, she went into the hall, returning about five minutes later, looking anxious. She motioned Stewart to come out into the hall.

"What is it?" he asked.

"That was Kim and Lucy. They got back today from Majorca, late this afternoon, and went to see Mum, only to find a 'For Sale' sign in the garden with a 'Sold' sticker across it."

"What!"

"It gets worse, Stewart. They managed to contact Robert and he and Matt have had Mum put in a home.

They looked at each other, stunned by what they had found out. It was Pauline who broke the silence.

"The bastards," she hissed. "They must have had this planned to coincide with all of us being away. Poor Mum. She'll be..."

"...furious," supplied her husband.

"Well yes, angry, and helpless for the first time in her life. Can we go home, Stewart, tomorrow, please?"

"Probably nothing we can do now, especially if the house has been sold but yes, of course, we'll leave tomorrow first thing. Have the girls seen their grandma?"

"Robert wouldn't tell them where she was at first but good for Lucy; she threatened to go to the police if he wouldn't tell them, so he did. She's in Tall Trees in Netherlee."

"So, have the girls seen her?"

"Yes. They went over this evening and have been with her for a few hours then they phoned me. Apparently Kim didn't want to tell us till we came home and Lucy thought we should know right away. They've been at home arguing. Kim thought that Mum had settled in but Lucy thinks that's impossible. Thank God Lucy won. Imagine the shock of going round to Mum's and finding her gone!"

"When did all this take place?" her husband wanted to know.

"About a week after we left. No wonder I couldn't get her on the phone on Wednesday but..."

"...I know...I told you you'd have heard if she'd been taken ill. I never guessed at this."

"I'm as much to blame. I didn't want anything to spoil our first holiday away by ourselves," his wife smiled at him tremulously, tears beginning to spill down her cheeks.

They went back into the lounge. Seeing their expressions, Peter switched off the CD. Stewart explained what had happened and told the couple that they would be leaving in the morning, a week earlier than planned. They made their excuses and went to their room to pack. Pauline wanted to ring her brothers but Stewart dissuaded her, telling her that losing her temper over the phone would be fruitless.

A Cornish mist was swirling round them as they loaded the car early next morning. The mist would clear and by the time they had crossed Bodmin Moor, the sun would probably be shining. They hugged Peter and Barbara and promised to phone them when they arrived home. Pauline waved as they drove off, and then settled back into her seat.

Stewart made good time and by stopping only twice for the toilet and a quick coffee, they were turning into their street in Waterfoot just after ten o'clock in the evening. The girls were out of the door almost as soon as the car stopped. They helped their parents in with their luggage and Kim, ever the practical one, insisted that they sit down to a late supper she had prepared for them.

"We'll tell you everything while you eat," said Lucy.

The girls were identical twins. They had inherited their father's thick fair hair and both wore it in a ponytail. Over a heaped plate of macaroni and cheese, Pauline and Stewart heard that Grandma had been in Tall Trees for about ten days now. Lucy expressed her opinion that the old lady was beginning to settle in as she was full of stories about the other occupants and Kim agreed, telling them that her carer, a Sandra Keith, had told them of her determination not to stay when she first arrived.

"I don't suppose poor Mum had any other option. I'm still furious with my brothers but if Mum is settling down then maybe things aren't so bad," said Pauline.

"I told Grandma you were coming home early," said Kim. "She said you needn't bother but I told her it was too late to stop you."

"We've been again this morning and met her card friend, Fred," said Kim.

"Too late to go down to Netherlee now, love," said Stewart. "Let's sleep on it and go down fresh tomorrow."

"At least we'll be here when your exam results come in," laughed Pauline, standing up and hugging both daughters.

"Don't remind us," groaned Lucy. "They should be here the day after tomorrow. I just know I've failed English."

"You always say that," said her sister, serenely and Pauline thought for the umpteenth time how different her twin daughters were. Kim wanted to be a primary teacher. She was calm and peaceable, only stirred to anger if anyone upset her sister. She was still going out with her primary school boyfriend. Lucy on the other hand was tempestuous; shedding boyfriends like a snake sloughs its skin. She wanted to travel the world before she settled down but she wanted to do this with Kim who was just not interested.

"Come on, old woman. Bed," said Stewart who was trying hard not to yawn. They said goodnight to their daughters and went upstairs. They had long ago given over the large front bedroom to the twins, taking the second, small room at the back for themselves.

"I wish we had room for Mum to stay here," Pauline said as she had said many times in the past.

"You know your Mum didn't want to stay with us. She could have offered to help us buy a larger house but..."

"...but she knew you were too proud for that, love," said his wife.

"Yes and she was too proud too. She valued her independence."

"That's why I'm surprised at her apparently settling down in Tall Trees," said Pauline, worriedly as she got undressed.

# CHAPTER 5

Pauline was not the only one to be surprised at how well Adele Stevenson had settled down after the first few days. She had stayed in her room at first, refusing all efforts on the part of the staff and Fred Graham, to get her to mix but on the fourth day she had appeared at breakfast in the dining room, wheeled there by Julie Harrison as it was Sandra's day off. Once again, she was placed next to Fred but she looked round with interest this time and asked him who the other people were.

At the 'red' table is Mrs Mohammed..."

"...yes. I met her on my first night when she very kindly brought me the newspaper for the TV guide," said Adele, smiling across at the tiny little lady who today wore a turquoise blue salwar kamiz.

"Beside her is Claire Williams...Miss. She's eighty-seven and a bit of a battle-axe. She was the headmistress of a private school just outside Edinburgh and she still thinks she's in charge."

Once again Adele turned round to look at the table referred to and received a glare from the big-boned, steely-grey haired woman sitting across from Mrs Mohammd. It was almost as if the woman was telling her to turn round and not stare because it was bad manners. Adele stifled a laugh.

"The other woman sitting with them is Martha Cowan. It's extremely unusual to see her down here. She keeps herself to herself. I don't think she has any family or any friends either. Certainly no one ever comes to see her. In the vestibule there's a visitors' book which I've read and there's only Bob, my grandson and an ex-teacher friend of Claire's who comes weekly and occasionally Claude's nephew from London who visits, I believe, about four times a year.

"Comes to make sure he's still in the will."

Fred's imitation of Claude's reedy voice was good. Adele had heard Claude complaining a few minutes ago that his egg was underdone and again she found herself smiling.

"Maybe others come who don't sign the book," she ventured.

"Anyone coming in has to sign it, in case there's a fire. They sign themselves out too. Oh yes, there's also the church worker who comes sometimes and takes one of us out for coffee.

At the other table, the 'yellow' one," he continued, "is Donny Bryant, a sad case. He's only about fifty. He has a form of dementia, or is it Alzheimer's. I never know which is which," Fred admitted.

"Me neither though I think that dementia covers all mental states for us oldies," she said, wryly.

"Well, Donny has something called Lewy Body Disease. He told me about it in one of the lucid moments which he has quite regularly. It must be extremely hard for his wife. She told me once when I came across her crying outside, that it's as if he's kidding her on, he's not really ill. They don't have any children. He's been here the longest of us all. He loves the garden and Victor Smith, Matron's husband, lets him help with simple things there."

"How sad," commented Adele. "I've never heard of anyone as young as that having dementia. I like gardening too. I must speak to him."

If Fred was astonished at this suggestion that Adele was accepting that she was going to stay in Tall Trees, he did not say anything.

"Finally, across from Donny, is Claude Ferguson whom I mentioned before, very proud of the fact that he's the oldest resident."

"How old is he?" asked Adele, glancing round again, this time at a hunchbacked little man wearing a formal suit in dark-grey serge material. He wore instead of a tie, a silk cravat in pale pink which had acquired a splodge of egg yolk. Fred noticed that too and told Adele that the staff were always taking his clothes to the dry-cleaner's.

"But we pay for that sort of thing ourselves, along with getting a haircut ...or a manicure," he added, looking down at his companion's well-kept fingernails.

"He's a bit over-dressed for breakfast, isn't he?" Adele said, quietly.

"He's always dressed like that and I think he's ninety- three."

"Better not tell him that I'm ninety - four then," smiled Adele, the smile softening her usual severe expression.

Breakfast over, Adele suggested to Fred that they meet up later for a game of bezique. He was delighted and said that they could play in the lounge on the ground floor or in the smaller lounge, next door to her own room. She chose the latter, telling him that she intended spending the morning in the garden, getting to know Victor Smith and perhaps Donny Bryant.

"I'll have lunch in my own room, I think, and then a wee doze and I'll be ready for our game at, say, three o'clock. Is that OK?"

"Perfectly," said her new friend. "I'm expecting my grandson this morning. Bob always comes on Saturday mornings after school football and in the holidays, like now, he still keeps to the same day and time and often stays to have lunch with me."

Adele had an interesting morning in the garden which she found was quite extensive, more so than she'd expected from her bedroom window. She discovered that Victor was not really a gardener by profession. He was a retired accountant and he and his wife ran the home which they had bought a few years ago. Gardening had been his hobby while working in town and this hobby now saved them the salary of a gardener. He told Adele that in his saner moments, Donny gave him good advice. He and his wife had a large house and a big garden in Eaglesham. Their mortgage had been paid off the year before he was diagnosed with dementia and he still went home some weekends. His wife, Katy, found the large house and garden difficult to run, along with a full-time job but she knew that in order to have Donny home, the house had to be a familiar one for him.

"She'll be coming for him after lunch today, I expect," Victor informed Adele.

Adele wheeled herself over to a flowerbed where Donny was raking the earth and they were soon in deep conversation. She told him who she was and he talked to her quite rationally at first, telling her what Victor had planned for this raked-over bed. It was disconcerting when he leaned on the rake and asked her who she was, his eyes clouded over in bewilderment. She called Victor over and he took the rake gently from Donny's hand and led him over to a bench where he sat, staring into space. Adele wheeled herself round the garden, eventually out of sight of the house and manoeuvred herself into the large shed which she came across. It was obviously quite old and inside it was very messy, quite unlike the tidiness of her own shed. Back out, she moved across to a small pond in which she was sure she could see some carp. She sat there, wrapped in her thoughts until Victor came for her to say that lunch was being served. Donny had gone from the garden and Adele hoped that his wife would find him responsive when she came later.

Clutching her capacious handbag which had been in danger of falling off her lap while she wheeled herself round the garden, she made a mental note not to take it everywhere in future and held onto it tightly as Victor wheeled her into the lift and pressed the button for the first floor. The bag slipped again and he caught it for her.

"Women! They keep the kitchen sink in their handbags!" he laughed.

Inside her room, she laid the bag on her bed and wheeled herself up to the small table which was already set for her lunch.

Fred came along to her room at three o'clock and they decided just to stay there and play. Julia had cleared the table and it would suit them, bezique not needing much space. They agreed on an end score of five hundred for each game and the winner would be the one who won two out of three games. Adele won the first game, convincingly and Fred the second, by quite a narrow margin. Adele gambled all on getting double bezique in the final game and lost. Fred had the queen of spades which she needed and had had it right from the start, he told her, grinning in delight at his success.

"My son, Robert is coming tonight. He agreed that the least he could do was come in occasionally to play me at bezique but I know his real reason. He wants me to give him and Matt joint power of attorney."

Fred looked horrified. She had told him of her two sons scheming to have her put away in this home in order for them to sell the house which was in their name.

"I think Arthur was trying to save me the worry of caring for a large house," she had explained.

"You won't give them power of attorney, will you?"

She sagged in her chair, looking suddenly as old as her years for the first time since he had met her.

"What's the point of refusing? I'll give in on condition that my daughter, Pauline, is also included, a three way power of attorney. What do I need money for now? Anyway my doctor has already been convinced that I'm in the first stages of senile dementia. Sandra gave that away not long after I got here. The lass said that she was surprised that I was showing none of the usual signs when my son Robin had written confirmation from my doctor saying that I was in the first stages."

"That's criminal," Fred had protested.

"No, just human nature. Dr Anderson's a young man in the same golf club where Robert is captain and very influential."

"Why have you given in, Adele...sorry, Mrs Stevenson."

"Fred, I've realised that sometimes it's no use fighting, especially at my age. And you can call me Adele, though I'm going to insist that the staff still use my surname."

There was a brief flash of the feisty old lady who had arrived at Tall Trees and then she sighed.

"Now if you don't mind, I think I'll have another short nap before dinner. Would you mind leaving your cards until I've got new ones for myself. The boys threw my old pack out with so much that was precious to me. Although they did keep my poetry books, thank goodness."

She glanced across at the bookcase and Fred asked her who her favourite poets were, saying that his was John Keats, especially, 'Ode to Autumn' which he said he could still quote from beginning to end.

"I've got a friend, my best man, who can recite the whole of, 'Tam O'Shanter'," he said.

"My favourite poets are the Confessional ones. Robert Lowell, Sylvia Plath and Anne Sexton," she added, seeing his bewilderment.

"Why are they called "confessional?" he asked.

"Because they tell, or confess all their personal weaknesses whereas most poets write about things unconnected with themselves. For instance, both Anne Sexton and Sylvia Plath tried to commit suicide and Robert Lowell and Anne Sexton were in mental homes. They...sorry...I'm off on my hobbyhorse. I did a degree in English quite late in life and I did my dissertation on the two women."

"Don't apologise. I'd be interested in reading that sometime, if I may. You said your sons threw stuff out. That was cruel, to do that without consulting you."

Fred caught a look of something in her eyes, then they clouded over and her eyelids closed so he got up saying, "No problem, Adele. You're welcome to use my cards any time except when Bob's here. Enjoy your dinner and sleep well."

Robert was not baffled by his mother's apparent docility. He had explained to Matt that he had given the home permission to use calming medication on her and he saw tonight that this must have been done. She was playing solitaire, which she still insisted on calling patience, when he arrived and she told him that her carer had found her two old packs of cards which she would use till Pauline could buy her new ones.

"I haven't accepted being in here, Robert," she said now, as he prepared to leave.

"I'm just content to wait till I see Pauline and Stewart. They'll get me out."

"The sale of the house has gone through, Mother and as you know, it belongs to the three of us so you can't contest it."

"I think you'll find that I can. It was only left to you on the condition that I could live there till I chose to leave or until I died."

His mother's calmness was more frightening than her anger had been and Robert felt uneasy as he got into the lift. He had never known his mother so controlled when thwarted and it made him nervous. She asked him to play bezique which he did for a short time. When he got home, he refused Margaret's offer of supper and locked himself in his study to phone his brother.

"I think we should leave off trying to get her to sign the power of attorney document, Matt. It might look suspicious under the circumstances and after all we made nearly two hundred and eighty thousand on the house sale."

He went on to tell his brother what their mother had said and his brother reassured him, saying that probably their sister would buy a larger house with her share of the proceeds and take their mother to live with her.

"That'll be what she meant tonight when she said that they would get her out," he said cheerfully.

Later that night, Matt got a phone call from the home, asking that he come along as his mother wanted to see him urgently. When he arrived he was shown into the room by matron. When she left, Adele got out of her chair and started pacing the floor.

"Matt. I think that Robert is trying to have me certified. I'm sure I'm being given medication which knocks me out and I don't feel as sharp as usual."

Matt was in a quandary. He wanted his mother to trust him, naturally, but he did not want to have his brother suspected. They needed to present a united front.

"Mother, don't be silly. If the nurses are giving you extra medication, it will only be to calm you down a bit, not drug you."

Adele had stopped pacing and sat down, apparently reassured. Matt had stayed with her for a while longer and was glad to see that she appeared to be calmer when he left, even telling him to bring the lawyer as soon as possible to witness the power of attorney. Once home, he rang Robin and told him what had happened.

"All good news, bro. She even wants the lawyer to get the power of attorney done as soon as possible and, surprisingly, she doesn't want Pauline involved. Said she knew that we would include our sister in any decisions we made."

"I think the medication is taking off her rough edges," laughed Robert.

"She wants me to go in and have a game of that dratted bezique with her on Wednesday!" added Matt.

"Well, it's small price to pay for what we've gained and will gain, surely," replied Robert and rang off.

Adele wrote in her diary:

"Robert played cards with me tonight. Matt coming in on Wednesday. I do so love bezique."

# CHAPTER 6

Curiosity prompted Adele to knock on the door two along from her own. She had only seen Martha Cowan once, at breakfast and was quite surprised when the woman opened the door on Sunday afternoon.

"Miss Cowan?"

"Yes."

"I'm sorry to bother you. I wondered if you would like to have tea or coffee with me this afternoon. I don't want to have it in the lounge with all the others, yet I feel a bit alone today for some reason."

Adele gave a tremulous smile but did not receive one back. The woman opened the door slightly wider and, obviously reluctantly, invited her in.

"I have some Earl Grey tea. I don't want to leave my room but you're welcome to come in."

Her voice was anything but welcoming but Adele went in anyway.

The room, like Adele's own, was a pleasant, airy one if somewhat dark, due to heavy curtains. The window was open. It could have been anyone's room, there being few personal belongings apart from several bookcases, even though Fred had told Adele that the woman had been living here for quite some time. Adele said that she would go back and get her cardigan.

"Have you been here long?" Adele asked the woman when she was seated.

"Long enough," was the reply.

"I only arrived last week and I was determined not to stay but I think I could grow to like it here."

Adele was struggling to keep up some conversation.

Martha Cowan boiled water for the tea, saying nothing.

"That's a good idea, having your own kettle in the room and crockery. I must get my son to bring me mine," Adele said.

"I have two sons and a daughter and three grandchildren," she continued. "I don't ever see my eldest granddaughter. She went to Russia as soon as she graduated."

Suddenly, as if this had unleashed the words, Martha Cowan spoke. In a voice, husky, probably from infrequent use, she told Adele of her twin sister who had gone to work in Leningrad and had never returned.

"We were orphans and were brought up by foster parents. Kind people who died in a car crash when we were still at university. They left us enough money to see us through. I became a librarian. Never married. Never wanted to. I love reading. Books are my life."

The quiet voice was oddly staccato, short sentences from someone unused to holding a conversation, Adele thought.

She looked round the room, noticing that the bookshelves were crammed full of books and that there were piles of books on the floor.

"And your sister? Does she ever come home?"

"She'd dead."

"And her family?"

"One daughter."

Adele knew she was being inquisitive and tried to think of a different topic of conversation. Martha spoke briefly then silence came into the room and lingered there. The tea was brought in a delicate, flower- patterned cup.

"What are you reading just now?" Adele asked.

The other woman got back up and, with an effort and clearly ill at ease with this intrusion into her private life, went across to the table where she had laid her current novel.

She held it out in silence and Adele took it.

It was, 'The Outsider', by Camus and it was written in French.

"I haven't read that one. I prefer to read poetry," she volunteered.

There was no reply.

Adele finished her tea, thanked Miss Cowan and left. There was no invitation to return and she was certain that as soon as she had gone, Martha Cowan would have forgotten all about her and returned to the fiction that was her only companion.

Adele had put on her cardigan, long, blue and with pockets and had been glad as the room she had come from had been quite cold so she took it off now, emptied the pockets and hung it in her wardrobe. Robert had delivered another suitcase of clothes to her so she had everything she needed for wearing. She missed all her little knick-knacks and her games and cards but being an eclectic reader, she had found plenty to suit her in the home's library on the same floor as her bedroom and she at least had all her poetry books and some Agatha Christie's and some by her favourite new crime writer, Alex Gray, who like herself was from Glasgow.

That evening she received surprise visitors in the shape of two anxious granddaughters. When she opened her door, they almost fell in in their rush to see if she was OK. They were tanned from their holiday and wearing their usual uniform of denims and tee-shirts.

"Grandma. What on earth are you doing here?" asked Lucy. "We came home today and went to see you and there was this big 'Sold' notice in the garden of Elmtree. I phoned Uncle Robert and he told us you were in here! Does Mum know...no she couldn't or she'd have told us...What..."

"Calm down, Lucy. Poor Grandma can't get a chance to speak. Come on and sit down, Grandma and tell us all about it."

Kim was calm as always.

"Who let you in, girls?" Adele asked.

"A Mr Smith. He said your room was number seven on the top floor and he showed us to the lift and asked us to write our names in a book and to write them again on the way out. Why's that, Grandma?" asked Kim.

"I think it's in case of fire. They need to know who's here to make sure they all get out safely. Don't think your uncles bother with it. One of the residents was talking about it and he said there were only three people who used it."

"Our uncles wouldn't. Things like that are only for normal mortals," sneered Lucy.

Kim led her grandma into her chair, then she and Lucy sat on the two-seater settee that along with the bed, table, chairs, wardrobe and TV, made up the room.

"Sorry I can't offer you anything to eat or drink. I'm not that organised yet," said Adele.

"Don't worry about that," said Kim. "We've both eaten too much on holiday. I know that my jeans feel really tight."

Adele looked at her. Like her sister she was tall and slim. They both took after their father.

It did not take long to acquaint them with the treachery of their two uncles. Kim at least had guessed at their part in the transaction but they were surprised when Adele told them that she had quite settled down now.

"I knew that your Grandfather left the house to your mother and uncles but I had hoped that I would see my life out there, even though the house was, as Robert and Matt said, too large for one person, "Adele said ruefully.

"Did they give you no warning?"

Lucy was incensed at the unfairness of it all.

"None. Matt drove me and they bundled me off in the wheelchair before I could contact your mother. She'd given me the number of the B&B in Cornwall, naturally but when I got here, someone had removed my address book."

Adele smiled at the girls' looks of horror. She patted them both gently on the knee.

"I was furious at first. Told everyone who would listen that I wasn't staying. That your mother would come home and take me away."

"Of course she will," said Lucy.

"Where to Lucy?" asked Kim worriedly. "We haven't got the room and Grandma has always refused to stay with any of us, even if Uncle Robert and Uncle Matt had offered," she added, practically.

"Your Uncles got my Doctor to sign that I was in the first stages of senile dementia and I think they must have sanctioned some kind of calming medication because I don't remember much about my first two days here…"

"That's…that's..criminal!" shot Lucy.

"Probably not, Lucy," reasoned Kim. "But Grandma, why do you seem quite content now? What's happened to make you change your mind?"

"Well, I've met a nice gentleman. No nothing romantic," she added, seeing two grinning faces looking at her. "I'm well past that sort of nonsense. We play cards together and the garden is beautiful and I talk to the man who looks after it and he's promised me a flowerbed of my own to care for."

"Well, we'll phone Mum when we get home."

"Tell her not to cut short her holiday. I'm fine, really I am."

Lucy and Kim left. On the way out, they met a nurse and on finding out that she was the carer for their Grandma, they asked about her state of mind.

"Oh she was in a right temper when she arrived," laughed Sandra. "She told everyone she met that she would not be staying but over the last few days, she seems to have settled. I think meeting another resident with similar card-playing habits has helped considerably."

Kim and Lucy signed themselves out and left, arguing about whether or not they should tell their parents.

They had hardly gone when Sandra came in to ask Adele where she wanted to have her light supper.

"Here, please and just my usual, please, Sandra: two slices of toast and marmalade and a cup of tea."

Sandra laughed.

"You're a right Paddington Bear, Mrs S...sorry Mrs Stevenson. Marmalade for breakfast and supper and sometimes even after high tea. I could bet on you and Martha Cowan."

Interested, because of her brief visit next door, this afternoon, Adele asked what Martha Cowan always had.

"And you can keep calling me Mrs S. I like that. Less stiff but still formal," she added.

"Miss Cowan always has a cup of Ovaltine and two tea biscuits," Sandra told her.

She went out, closing the door and Adele heard her knocking at number five. There was a silence then another, louder, knock and Adele heard her voice calling out to Miss Cowan then muted footsteps passing her door on the thick, expensive carpet.

When her supper arrived, Adele asked if the other lady had indeed asked for her usual drink and biscuits. Sandra looked a bit worried.

"No answer from her, yet she's not a good sleeper and sits up late reading. She doesn't like anyone going in without knocking either."

"She was fine when I saw her earlier," Adele said. "What age is she?"

"She's one of the youngest, seventy-eight. Fred is the youngest apart from Donny. He's seventy-five."

"Better not tell my granddaughters. They'll call Fred my toy boy," laughed Adele.

"You said that you saw her! How come?"

"I knocked and she opened the door and very reluctantly asked me in. We had tea together, briefly."

"And she was OK then?"

"Yes. She was just anxious to get back to her book - all in French. She must be one clever lady."

"All the same, I think I'd better tell Matron, in case she's taken ill."

Sandra hurried off and Adele picked up one slice of toast.

About five minutes later, she heard two pairs of footsteps and another loud knock next door. She heard muted voices from the room next to hers, and then the door closed again.

Not expecting to hear anything till the next morning when Sandra came in to take away her dirty plates and see if she was ready for breakfast either in her room or downstairs, she finished her supper and started to prepare for bed. She showered in the morning so it was only a case of washing her face and hands and brushing her teeth in her small ensuite bathroom. She had just got under the duvet when she heard more voices, a man's one this time. She switched off the light. Some minutes passed then there was a gentle knock on her door.

"Come in." she called out.

It was matron this time. She switched on the bedside light and sat down on the bed.

"Mrs Stevenson, I'm sorry to tell you that Miss Cowan has passed away. The doctor is with her now but I wouldn't think he could do anything. I've seen too many dead people in my time to be in any doubt."

"Was it...was it peaceful?" Adele's voice trembled.

"Very. I think she must have had an upset tummy as there was a bottle of gaviscon by her side but apart from that she was just lying back in her chair, with her book on her lap."

"A heart attack then. Maybe she confused the symptoms with indigestion. I've heard that often happens."

"Well, we'll leave all that to the doctor. I thought I'd tell you as Sandra had told you she couldn't rouse her. Would you like a wee sleeping pill?"

Adele said that she would and, promising to send Sandra upstairs with it, Matron went back next door.

# CHAPTER 7

"Dad, I'm not five. I'm twelve!"

Pippa Davenport, standing in the lounge in her new Bradford High School uniform looked thunderous but her father, Charles Davenport, was adamant. As DCI in charge of one section of Glasgow's largest police station, he was not about to be dictated to by his daughter

"I want a photo for the album so just stand still and if you don't want future boyfriends to see you scowling on your first day at secondary school, try to give me a smile."

Pippa gave a weak smile, the picture was taken and she dashed off back to her bedroom where she had been spending a lot of time during the last days of the holiday. She seldom joined her father in the lounge at nights now, preferring to listen to her iPod or watch DVDs. Charles was a bit sad as they had been good companions for each other since he had divorced Pippa's mother some years ago. Pippa had just been on holiday with him and Fiona Macdonald, now his fiancée, but had had a week in Arran with her friend Hazel and her parents and then spent the last two weeks down South, with her mother.

However, he rationalised with himself now, it certainly left him free to be with Fiona and they had a lot to talk about with their forth-coming wedding at the beginning of September and a baby on the way. He grinned as he thought about what the reaction of his staff would be when they found out about the baby. They had been surprised enough about their engagement though Frank Selby, one of his PCs, had claimed, in retrospect, to have had his suspicions. Fiona was adamant that they tell no one about the baby until after the wedding, in fact until she was at least four months 'gone'.

"I've always been on the plumpish side," she reasoned. "So they'll just think I've put on weight over the holiday."

"I certainly did," grumbled Charles, as they had sat together the previous evening, he in the armchair and she on the floor between his legs with the back of her head on his lap.

"I don't want a fat man waiting for me at the church," she laughed, turning her head and poking him in the stomach.

He had promised to go on a diet for the next two weeks and, thinking of that now, he went into the kitchen and got two apples and a banana to take for lunch.

"Pippa!" he called up the stairs. "It's time to go!"

She had refused to have a school blazer which was optional but he thought she looked very grown-up in her navy skirt, white blouse and red tie. Unfortunately, although reasonably tall for her age, she would look very childlike in the midst of the older pupils, he realised, especially the senior ones with their royal blue ties. He hoped that there was no precedent of bullying the first years. Sighing, he accepted that there was nothing he could do about it, if there was.

She came clattering down the stairs now and pulled her navy jacket off the coat hook at the door. He thought she looked unusually pale.

"OK pet?"

"Yes. Fine, Dad."

They sat in unusual silence on the drive down to Newlands where they stopped off to pick up her best friend, Hazel Ewing. Ralph Ewing had left for work and Sally Ewing was standing, looking very smart and ready for her job as a history teacher at Greystone Academy which was in the West End of the city.

Charles got out of the car and they both came across. As the girls greeted each other, Pippa getting into the back seat to be with her friend, Sally said quietly that she hoped that their daughters would be in the same class which was possible, she said, with their surnames being close together alphabetically.

"Though all schools don't do things that way. I didn't like to ring them and ask if they could be together."

"Me neither," said Charles. "But I'm keeping my fingers crossed."

"I'd better dash. Don't want to be late on the first proper day of school," she laughed, and ran to her car.

Charles let her get off in front of him, then he released the brake and set off towards Shawlands. It was unusually quiet in the back seat. When Pippa and Hazel got together, it was often a duet of voices as they vied for who was to speak first but today they both looked white-faced and nervous as he pulled up outside the red sandstone building.

Wishing that he could go with them but knowing that they would hate that, he waved them off and soon they were engulfed in a wave of children, all making for the entrance. He drove off to the station, knowing that he would be later than usual but knowing also that things were quiet at the moment and had been since he had returned from his holiday.

"'Morning, Sir."

"'Morning, Bob. Has the desk been quiet overnight?"

"Yes, Sir. I'm just waiting for Derek to take over in half an hour. The gang are all in."

Charles smiled at this name for what he liked to call his 'team' and made his way up the silent corridor. He looked into the main room. Salma Din, his sergeant, was on the phone, listening intently and Frank was reading his Daily Record. He hurriedly stowed it in his desk drawer when he saw Davenport watching him from the doorway.

"'Morning, Sir," he said, flicking back the lock of errant hair that tended to flop over his forehead.

"Good morning, Selby. No work for us yet, I see."

On the other side of the room, Fraser Hewitt hastily put his newspaper, The Guardian, under his blotter. Davenport said good morning to him and smiled at Salma who smiled back, still listening.

As he walked up to his own room, passing the closed door of the room belonging to Fiona Macdonald who as well as being his fiancée, was also his detective sergeant, Charles thought back to a poem he had read once about a couple lying in bed, the man reading The Observer and his wife The Mirror. The poem had suggested that the husband was the clever one who 'observed' and she merely echoed or 'mirrored' what he said and did. Seeing his constables with their respective newspapers, he felt it summed up their differences.

Frank was the Glasgow secondary school - educated constable and Fraser the university graduate one.

Fraser had been drafted in from another department when they were busier, to replace PC Penny Price who had been badly injured in a bus crash the previous month.

As he seated himself at his desk, Charles thought that he must pay Penny another visit. She was living with her mother and stepfather at the moment, not being well enough yet to return to her own flat. There was a knock on his door and Salma came in.

"Sir, that was a call from Tall Trees nursing home. They've had a sudden death. Nothing suspicious. The doctor who attended last night said that it was a heart attack. The woman was on warfarin after an earlier attack. The doctor told matron to notify the police. There aren't any relatives."

"Succinctly put as usual, Sergeant," Davenport smiled at the beautiful, raven-haired young woman, immaculate as always in her uniform trousers and white shirt and tie.

"Do you want me to go over there, Sir?"

"Won't do any harm. We haven't had any dealings with that particular nursing home, not while I've been here anyway. A courtesy call would be a good idea. Take Fraser or Frank with you since we're so quiet."

Thus it was that Salma and Frank spent the next hour talking to Matron, Sandra Keith and Adele Stevenson who had been the last person to see Martha Cowan alive. The body had been removed to the morgue so they all congregated in the dead woman's room. Frank whistled when he saw all the books there.

"Hey, Serge! You should've brought brain-box Hewitt with you instead of me. He'd have had a field day with all these."

He swept his arm round the room, encompassing bookcases and piles of books on the floor then went across to one pile and lifted a book off the top.

"Gerard Manley Hopkins. I've never heard of him."

He opened the book and a look of disgust crossed his face.

"Poetry! 'Pied Beauty'? I thought it was called Pied Piper, that one about children and rats following some bloke with a pipe."

"That is an entirely different poem, young man. "Glory be to God for dappled things," it begins. It's a poem about the beauty of nature."

Adele Stevenson's voice was tart and Frank felt his face flush. He put the book back on its shaky pile.

"So, Mrs Stevenson, you noticed nothing unusual about Miss Cowan yesterday evening?"

Salma drew the old lady's attention back to the matter in hand, throwing Frank a sympathetic look as she did so.

"She was completely unusual," said Adele. "She only asked me in reluctantly, almost threw me a cup of tea and showed me out immediately afterwards. The only time she was remotely animated was when I mentioned Russia and she told me about her dead sister living in ...Leningrad, I think she said."

"Was Miss Cowan always like this, Mrs Smith?" asked Salma.

"Oh yes. She was practically a recluse, seldom came out of her room, even for meals. She never had any visitors, apart from the doctor occasionally, never received any letters apart from junk mail."

"How did she come to be here?" was Salma's next question.

"She put herself in, so to speak. Came to see me one day, asked if we had any vacancies. We had this room. She moved in the next week."

"And paid the fees herself?" asked Frank curiously.

"Direct debit on her bank, every month and this is a private home so we're not cheap."

"Miss...Mrs Keith?" Salma smiled at the younger woman.

"Mrs. Sandra," said the carer.

"How did you find her to care for?"

"No bother at all. She seldom asked for anything, not even a newspaper or magazine. She went out once a week and presumably bought everything she needed then. Every time I came in, which wasn't often, she was reading over by the window, in the chair she was found in. She went to bed very late. There was a light under her door sometimes as late as 2am, wasn't there Matron?"

"Yes, the night staff commented on it often," Mrs Smith replied.

"Do you know if she left a will?" asked Salma.

"Yes. I have it in my safe. She deposited it there when she arrived and it's never been moved."

"When did she come in here?" asked Frank.

"Almost five years ago now," matron answered.

"Well, I think that's all we need to know unless anything very unusual turns up in the will or the doctor has second thoughts about the cause of death," concluded Salma.

She turned to leave the room and Frank followed her, looking back over his shoulder at the bare little room with its masses of books.

They walked down the drive, having left the police car outside the grounds.

"She was right, Matron, when she said the place wasn't cheap," said Frank. "Did you see all those huge pictures everywhere? And I'm sure the furniture was good stuff too. It certainly was gleaming."

"Yes and the carpets were thick and expensive too," agreed Salma.

"Should we have a word with the doctor, Dr Ferguson, they said? His practice is in Netherlee," asked Frank.

"Might as well, just to draw a line under the death."

Once they got past the frosty receptionist who seemed to think she was guarding the crown jewels, Dr Ferguson was happy to confirm what Matron had told them. Martha Cowan had had a heart condition, had taken some stomach medicine that evening, probably confusing heart trouble with indigestion. She had died in her chair.

Salma reported back to the station and offered to write up the visit, much to Frank's relief as he never relished this chore.

# CHAPTER 8

Adele did not know who had informed Claude that she was older than him by one year. She suspected Fred who obviously did not like the little man. However he had found out, he became quite unpleasant towards her whenever he got the chance, even going so far as to spill his coffee over her the afternoon after the death, in the lounge, when they were sitting next to each other.

"So sorry, Mrs Stevenson," he grinned, showing his uneven, yellowed teeth. "I hope that wasn't your favourite blouse and skirt."

Gritting her teeth and determined not to let him think he had upset her, Adele smiled back and told him that he must not worry. This was an old outfit. Claire Williams from across the room shouted out that Claude ought to be in geriatric hospital, not a select nursing home.

"Stupid old man! Be more careful in future!" she hollered. Adele had been told by Fred that Claire needed a hearing aid but refused to wear one. This of course meant that her so-called asides to whoever she was sitting beside, could be clearly heard by all and sundry and her comments were always critical. She was knitting as usual. From the needles hung a baby's matinee jacket in white wool.

Turning to Fred on her other side, Adele asked him who Claire was knitting the baby things for.

"I have no idea. She knits nothing except baby clothes yet I don't think she has any family and her only friend is, as I told you before, an elderly spinster, ex-teacher friend."

"Why have I been given two cups of coffee?" Donny's wavering voice interrupted their musings

Tom Carew, his special carer, looked up from pouring out another coffee for Claude.

"You've only got one cup, Donny," he said.

"No I don't. I have two. I have two, I tell you."

This time Donny was really agitated. He stood up, sending his cup flying, coffee spurting over his neighbour, Mrs Mohammed who jerked her arm sending her own coffee flying. Brown stains appeared on her delicate, cream salwar kamiz.

Tom took Donny's arm and led him out of the room to the sound of Claire saying loudly, "Now his eyesight must be going, poor man."

Fred got up, saying that his grandson would be arriving soon. He went slowly out of the room, calling back to Adele to come along later to tell him what had happened when she visited Miss Cowan.

Claire immediately demanded to know what Adele knew about the woman's death.

"I don't know anything, Miss Williams. It's just that I seem to have been the last person to speak to her."

She was saved saying any more as Julia Harrison who was the special carer for both Mrs Mohammed and Claire must have been alerted by Tom and she came into the room and tried to dab the stain on the Asian lady's cream outfit.

"It's no use, Mrs Mohammed. We'll have to get that off and into some water with Vanish powder before it leaves a permanent stain. Come on. I'll get you another cup of coffee once you've changed."

Adele got up too, pointing to her stained skirt and blouse but remembering that she had told Claude that it was an old outfit, she merely told Julia that she wanted to get changed as she was sticky.

"My goodness, what a lot of accident-prone folk you are," Julia laughed.

The threesome left the room.

Adele changed into another skirt and blouse and went back downstairs, knocking on Fred's door this time. It was a young man who came to the door and realising that this must be Bob, Fred's grandson, she apologised for interrupting them.

"Is that Mrs S's voice I hear? Come away in."

Adele went in, apologising again but Fred was keen to hear about Miss Cowan. He only knew that she had died but had been unable to find out any more at breakfast.

"This is my grandson, Bob," he said proudly and Bob and Adele shook hands. "He's paying me an extra visit today. Sit down and tell me all the gory details about Martha Cowan's death."

"There aren't any details, gory or otherwise," said Adele, sitting on his bed. "She must have taken a heart attack. That's all."

"Tom told Claude that you'd seen her just before she died."

"No. I saw her in the afternoon. I was in her room, briefly."

"Gosh, you were honoured," said Fred.

"I invited her into my room for tea and she said to come in to hers instead. I was in for about fifteen minutes. No more."

"Did you find out anything about our mystery woman?"

Fred's eyes were curious.

"Gramps, you're a right old sweetie-wife," teased his grandson.

"I don't care. Did you? Find out anything?" he repeated.

"Only that she had a sister in Leningrad and they were both orphans. The sister had died. She had a niece she had disinherited for some reason.

Oh and she loved reading. Her room was packed full of books and the one she was reading was in French."

"You've found out more in your fifteen minutes than I've found out in eighteen months," he exclaimed. "I wonder who she's left her money to."

Bob looked at his watch and said that he would have to leave in about an hour, so if his grandfather wanted a game of cards they would need to get started. Adele got up to leave, saying that it had been nice to meet Bob and that she would see Fred for their usual games of bezique in the evening, after dinner.

"My son's coming this week, Matt, the younger boy, to give me a game. My daughter came this morning but I'll tell you all about that later. Enjoy your game."

Back in her room, having decided to miss out on coffee, Adele thought about Pauline's visit. Her daughter had been tearful at seeing her mother in a home and had declared her intention of taking Adele back to live with her.

"Stewart and I will sleep in the lounge on the bed settee, Mum, so you'll have your own room. I rang Robert before I came here and he informs me that I'm now a wealthy woman so we can move soon and get a bigger house with a granny-flat for you."

Adele had let her finish.

"All I want you to do for me, my darling, is bring me in some home comforts, a kettle, some crockery and cutlery and some new playing cards, ordinary ones for playing patience and bezique cards too if you can get them. I've ordered my Glasgow Herald every day and The Sunday Post for Sundays but maybe you could buy me a book of codewords and a crossword book. The boys threw out my old ones."

Pauline looked at her with a puzzled expression.

"The girls said that you'd settled in Mum but I couldn't believe that. Yet you seem to be accepting the fact that you're in a nursing home. What's happened to you? Are they drugging you?"

"At first they gave me a sedative but no, my dear, it's just that I've found a friend here and I can still do a little bit of gardening without having the responsibility of organising a gardener. My room's very pleasant and the food is good. I can still have a little tipple in the evenings. Not that I'll ever admit it to them, but Robert and Matt seem to have done me a favour."

"So they've got away with their devious plan?"

Pauline sounded disappointed.

"We're not going to let them know that, just yet. I've already told them that I can fight them and assured them that I won't be staying here. I've got them coming up to play cards with me, like little lambs, trying to keep me sweet. I'm going to milk that for a while and you can help me. I've told both of them that I'm willing to have them given power of attorney but when they bring a lawyer up here, I'm going to look baffled and deny having ever said that. They want me be to be demented, I'll give them demented!"

Adele grinned and Pauline was relieved to see a flash of her 'old' mother.

"And Pauline, if they ask you, you tell them that I didn't want anyone having that power over me. OK?"

"We can tell them that they're being left out of your will, Mum," she suggested.

"Oh and they will be, my dear. They will be," said Adele softly. "I've phoned my lawyer and he's coming up on Friday. I told the boys he was coming then and why. No doubt they'll have decided to drain my bank accounts before I depart this mortal coil."

Pauline grinned at her.

"I'm off now, Mum. Is there anything else I can get you?"

Adele mentioned a couple of other things she wanted.

Later that evening, Adele told Fred about her daughter's visit as she had promised to do. She told him that his grandson was charming and said that in the days of matchmaking, she would have tried to throw Bob and Lucy together.

"Kim's set to marry her childhood sweetheart but Lucy, the wild one, needs a nice young man like your Bob," she said.

"Well, we can't arrange things but we can contrive to get them coming here at the same time," he suggested, smiling.

They settled down to their game of bezique, Fred bemoaning the fact that there were not another two to make up a four for whist.

"Or bridge even," countered Adele.

"Claire plays bridge but even if we could find someone else, there's no way I would play with her," said Fred and Adele agreed.

They would have been envious of Charles Davenport and Fiona Macdonald who were in the middle of their first game of bridge since their holiday. They had decided to leave their news till supper time and after handing out the holiday presents, a pashmina for Jean and fake Rolex for John, they got down to business.

Jean had lost her nervousness and even bid four no trump, asking her partner for aces and going on to five no trump, asking for kings. She made a bid of a small slam in hearts and won it, much to her delight.

Charles had been having terrible hands until about eight hands had been played when he got eight diamonds and made a pre-emptive bid which Fiona supported. John doubled Charles but

Charles was successful so North - South recouped some points.

Supper time arrived. Jean whose turn it was to host the game, went into the kitchen, Fiona following her to help as usual. Jean had made egg sandwiches and her famous coffee cake which they all loved. They drank tea at this time of night, declaring that coffee would keep them awake.

Once they were seated again, Charles took Fiona's hand in his.

"You're not very observant, you two," he laughed, holding up her left hand.

"I asked Fiona to marry me and she agreed."

The other two were delighted and joked about concentrating too much on the cards to notice the diamond ring.

"The wedding's the first Saturday in September and..."

"September? This September?" gasped Jean.

"No point in waiting months at our age," said Charles.

"How did Pippa react?" Jean wanted to know, having met that young lady.

"She's delighted. Anyway, I think she's too wrapped up with her new school to get too bothered about anything else right now though she was thrilled about being a bridesmaid when we first told her," said Charles.

John asked how school had gone that day and Charles told him that unfortunately Pippa and her best friend Hazel were not in the same class, Pippa being in 1C and Hazel in 1D, narrowly missing being in the same class as they had been called out alphabetically and one boy whose surname was Everet, had been last to get into 1C.

"They met at the interval and at lunchtime but Hazel brought another girl from their primary class, someone called Vicky so my daughter told me that she was going to take a girl called Kerry, tomorrow."

"I never kept up with my primary chums after we went into secondary," said Jean. "You get a set of new ones usually, I think," she added and Fiona agreed.

The men looked puzzled, saying that they had all met up to play football in the intervals and at lunchtime and didn't really have special friends till later on when the special friend was female.

Charles ran John and Fiona home and went home to relieve his sister Linda who had been at his house. They had not dared mention the word 'babysit' but had just reminded Pippa that it was the law that she had someone with her, at her age. Pippa was in bed but she had left instructions for her father to cover her textbooks.

"She had some homework already, Charles," said Linda. "A few maths sums to do and some French vocabulary to learn."

"Did she talk much about it? She was quite quiet over dinner."

"No, she didn't say much at all. Just did her homework at the kitchen table, then went to her bedroom to listen to her music."

"Any problem getting her to go to bed?"

"None. She seemed quite tired."

Linda went off home. Charles covered the three textbooks with brown paper and put a label on each, leaving them blank for Pippa to fill in herself. He too was tired and the house was in darkness by eleven o'clock.

# CHAPTER 9

A dele had hardly got back to her room after visiting Fred, when there was a knock on her door and her eldest son came into the room with a middle-aged man.

"Hello, Mother, I don't think you know Mr Knowles. He's one of the associates at Browne, James and Knowles."

Adele proffered her hand but remained seated.

"Good afternoon, Mr Knowles. I've had dealings with Mr Browne and Mr James but not had the pleasure of meeting you."

She looked inquiringly at her son.

"You seemed quite keen to get this power of attorney thing seen to, Mother, and Mr Knowles was good enough to fit us into his busy schedule today."

"Power of attorney, Robert? What do you mean?"

Robert looked bewildered and rather annoyed.

"Mother it was only the other day that you agreed...or rather asked about this. It means that you're letting Matthew and I take over handling your affairs now that you're here in Tall Trees."

"Why on earth would I want to do that Robert? I've always managed my own affairs quite well since your Father died."

Her voice rose as she continued.

"As for managing my affairs, have you not caused enough damage, manoeuvring me in here without my consent? Selling my house from under me so that you could get your hands on money, you and your brother?"

"Calm down, Mother."

Robert was sweating. He ran his forefinger round the inside of his collar as if his tie was too tight.

"Calm down! Mr Fraser perhaps you would oblige me, since you are here, by telling me how I can go about charging my sons for selling the house that was left to me for my life time. My husband would turn in his grave if he could see me in here!"

"The house was left to Matthew and me...and Pauline. We did what we thought best for you, Mother. That house was too big for you..."

"...yes and I was spending your inheritance tending to it and myself, wasn't I?"

The lawyer coughed, embarrassed.

"And now you want me to sign my life away, completely. No doubt you'll get Matron to give me more drugs till I get confused and then you'll no doubt move me to somewhere cheap and nasty."

Robert turned to the lawyer.

"Mr Knowles, I am so sorry. As you will probably realise, my Mother is in the first stages of dementia and has obviously totally forgotten that she asked me to bring a lawyer here so that she could sign a power of attorney document."

The lawyer sent him a sympathetic look, and then he spoke gently to Adele.

"Mrs Stevenson, I'm leaving now but should you reconsider, I'll be delighted to come up and see you again. Your son...sons have only your best interests at heart, I'm sure. If you think rationally you will forget the idea of contesting what they have done by settling you in here."

"I'm not an vindictive old woman, Mr Fraser. My three children and my three grandchildren are all well catered for in my will but right now I want to run my own affairs. I will think carefully about whether or not I want to have them charged with forcing me out of my home. Good afternoon."

The lawyer turned to the door and Robert went with him. The look he sent back to his mother was not a kindly one.

As the door to her room closed, Adele lay back in her chair and closed her eyes. She had enjoyed the skirmish while it lasted but now she felt drained and exhausted. She half expected Robert to return but he did not reappear.

She was woken from an unpleasant dream, in which Robert and Matthew were chasing her down a long corridor with axes in their hands with Pauline running behind them, trying to catch them with a fishing net, by a knock at her door. It was Sandra, coming to see if she wanted to go downstairs for her evening meal. Although tired, Adele did not want to be alone and felt that the company of other people might take the bitterness from her brain.

Fred was full of chat about his grandson and their card games. He had beaten Bob twice and was delighted with himself, informing Adele that he was razor-sharp tonight and would beat her hands down later. Donny was missing from his table. This was unusual. Adele hoped that he had gone home with his wife but was anxious that he was still unsettled as he had been earlier in the lounge. When Tom, Donny's carer came to see Claude, she called him over and asked for his younger charge.

"He's not well tonight, Mrs S. When his wife came, later this afternoon, he didn't seem to recognise her. That hasn't happened before. She was terribly upset, poor soul. I gave him an extra dose of his medication and he's sound asleep now."

Dinner over, Adele asked Fred if they could have their game right away as she was expecting her son, Matthew, later. He was only too happy to agree, having he said, seen the news twice already that day.

"And it's all doom and gloom these days," he grimaced.

They went to Fred's room this time, on the ground floor. They opened the door and went in quietly, hoping not to disturb Donny who was next door. Adele looked round Fred's room with interest. It was the room of a military man, tidy and masculine, with photographs of his army life on a number of surfaces. The only photo which was different was one of Fred with a sweet-faced, woman much smaller than himself. Adele wheeled herself over to the table it was on and picked it up.

"My dear wife, Ethel," Fred informed her.

Adele put down the photo. She had tried hard not to become interested in any of the residents, convinced that she would leave as soon as possible, yet here she was getting to know Fred and she already cared about Donny. She shook herself mentally and wheeled herself over to the table where Fred was already seated, shuffling the bezique cards.

Either she was tired from her tussle with Robert or Fred was indeed razor-sharp as he had boasted he was earlier. Whatever the reason, he beat her twice. She declined another game, saying that she was going to have a stiff brandy before meeting up with Matthew soon. She told Fred that she had had an argument with her elder son before dinner which had tired her.

"You should have seen the look on his face when he left with the lawyer. I decided not to give him and Matthew power of attorney," she explained. "He looked as though he'd have liked to murder me. I'm sure they both would if they thought they could get away with it," she added ruefully. "I'll be making them both play bezique with me tonight," she told him, smiling.

Thanking him for the game and promising to be more competition tomorrow, she went into the downstairs lounge where Tom Carew poured her a brandy. She let him wheel her to the lift and accompany her to the room where she drank gratefully and felt the drink warming and relaxing her.

Pauline had come that afternoon with everything she had asked for, with one exception. She picked up the two new packs of playing cards, tore off the cellophane wrapper and shuffled both packs. She glanced at her watch. An hour till Matthew arrived.

# CHAPTER 10

"What have you got on your timetable today?" Charles asked over breakfast, that same morning.

"English and maths again, PE and science and I forget the other thing," Pippa answered.

"What were your teachers like yesterday? Sorry I didn't get much of a chance to talk to you. I'd forgotten that you started school on my bridge night."

"They were OK but my English teacher's really old and fussy. He didn't let us sit where we wanted and the book he gave us is an old thing, called "A Midsummer Night's Dream". We started it yesterday and the words are all spelled funny."

"I expect you'll get a few of those books on your way through, pet. Shakespeare's a famous playwright and he wrote a long time ago so his English is a bit different. Have you got a home reader?"

"He's giving us that today. Hazel has a young man for English. She said he's really funny. I wish we were in the same class."

"At least you got a chance to meet up at the interval and lunchtime."

"What did she want to bring Vicky Fullarton with her for, both times?" grumbled Pippa.

"Well, it makes sense to get friendly with someone in your own class. Did you not speak to anyone in yours?"

"We never liked Vicky in primary."

Pippa was not letting her feathers be smoothed. Her father tried again.

"Was there no one nice in your class?"

"The only people from primary were John Caldwell, Maria Davis and Anne Carter and those two are really close friends. I did sit beside quite a nice girl in English when Mr Snedden moved us. Her first name's Kerry."

"Snedden? He's the PT of English. He's not that old, probably about the same age as your old Dad. Is it Mr Fraser Hazel has?"

"Yes. How do you know them?"

"I met them through work some time ago."

Charles had met quite a few of the school staff when he had been responsible for solving two murders there, not long after he arrived at his new station but he thought it prudent not to tell his daughter about that. He was glad that she had Alex Snedden who was a conscientious teacher and not Peter Fraser who was a bit of a chancer.

"Why don't you do what you said last night and take Kerry to meet Hazel today?"

Charles and Fiona left work early that afternoon to visit Penny Price at her mother's house. They were delighted when it was she who came to the door to let them in. She was moving slowly but the bandage had gone from her head.

"Do you like the new hairstyle?" she asked them, grinning and she certainly did look odd, with one side of her head covered in dark curls and the other side tufty and bare in parts where it had had to be shaved after her accident.

"I don't think you'll start a trend," said Charles, wondering how many young women would react like Penny to her altered appearance. "Does Gordon like it?"

"He said he'd buy me a wig, cheeky thing," Penny looked indignant. "Said I'd scare his animals away if they saw me."

Gordon, her boyfriend, was a vet and had two dogs and a cat at home in his King's Park flat. He was lucky to have a good neighbour who took the dogs out during the day and he had a cat flap for the cat. He and Penny had been going together for some months now and apart from a setback when Penny had involved him in some nefarious police work, they seemed to be getting along well again.

"Oh. Funny story about Gordon's pets. Seems that Rory, the wee spaniel, managed to get out through the cat flap the other day and Fred the collie tried to follow him and got stuck. Luckily Gordon's neighbour heard Rory barking the place down and went out to investigate and managed to manoeuvre Fred out and keep them both till Gordon got home."

The threesome laughed, then Penny offered to get them coffee and Fiona went with her to help carry the mugs. In the kitchen, Fiona asked Penny what the doctor had said at her last visit and was told that she had a sick line for another week at least.

"I'm getting really bored, Ma'am. What's happening at work?"

"Nothing doing except for the usual spate of robberies. We'll have to send Fraser back if we don't get busier. You'd probably be bored at work too so just take it easy and do what you're told," Fiona told her.

When they went back into the lounge, Penny's mother's cat, Pickle was lying on his tummy being stroked by Charles.

"An unusual cat, this one," he said. "Usually when you try to rub cats' tummies, they try to claw you to bits."

"Pickles thinks he's a dog. He even sits up and begs," Penny told him.

They drank their coffee and then Charles and Fiona left, telling Penny that she should come into the station when she felt stronger, to see her chums and meet up with Fraser whom she had met the last time he had worked for them when Salma's mother died.

Charles drove Fiona to her flat and went to collect Pippa and Hazel whom he had promised to drive home that day, Ralph Ewing having taken them both to his house the day before so that Charles could pick up his daughter from there. He sat outside the school and was amazed at the speed with which the building emptied itself of both staff and pupils. He recognised some of the staff, Fiona Donaldson the HE principal and her colleague Laura whose surname slipped his memory. They were so different, Fiona fiery and assertive and Laura calm and biddable. He wondered which woman Pippa would get for HE and wished that she could have known Irene Campbell, who had taught PE before she was murdered. Pippa was not sporty, like her friend Hazel and he would have liked her to get some encouragement in that field, encouragement he was sure Irene would have given her.

The rush for the gates had slowed slightly and he saw Pippa, Hazel and a girl he did not know coming through them. As they approached the car, he could see that Hazel looked a bit glum and it did not take his policeman powers to guess that the other girl was someone Pippa knew as the other two were smiling and talking to each other as the threesome approached the car.

"Dad, this is Kerry. Can we give her a lift? She lives near Fiona, in Tassie Street."

"Of course. Jump in all of you."

Pippa and Kerry got into the back seat, leaving Hazel to get in the front beside Charles. Luckily, Pippa included her in the school chat so she had cheered up by the time they dropped Kerry off. She got out and joined Pippa in the back for the short drive to Newlands.

"What happened to Hazel's new friend?" Charles asked, as they made their way up to Mearns.

"She lives in the other direction, opposite Queen's Park. She's quite nice, I suppose. The four of us met up at lunchtime and sat together in the dining room."

Charles prepared their evening meal of sausages, mashed potato and baked beans while Pippa got changed out of her uniform. She brought her schoolbag into the kitchen, informing her Dad that she had quite a lot of homework, including two chapters of her new book to read.

"It's called, 'The Demon Headmaster'," she told him.

"That sounds good."

"At least it's in ordinary English. We started that play today. I'm Titania, queen of the fairies but she hasn't come into it yet. Mr Snedden told us to be careful reading it as we don't stop at the end of each line, unless there's a full stop of course. One of the boys was awful, Dad. He could hardly say any of the words. Mr Snedden had to help him a lot."

"What was science like?"

"We drew a Bunsen burner and the teacher showed us how it worked. We sit round big, wooden tables and there's only half the class. The others were next door with another teacher."

"Yes. That's normal. The practical subjects usually have smaller numbers. What about PE?"

"Just the girls. We went outside and played hockey. There should be eleven on each side but we only had eight each."

"What position did you play?"

"At the back. I had to try to stop the other side from scoring goals. It was really hard to stop the ball with that wee bit at the end of the stick."

"When I played, that wee bit was bigger, rather it was longer. I think your stick had an Indian club head. What was the other subject you couldn't remember this morning?"

"History. PE and Science were double periods."

"So what homework have you got tonight?"

"More maths, those two chapters of the book and I've to read about Scara Brae for history and write four important sentences about it."

Dinner over, Pippa settled herself at the kitchen table and Charles sat down in the lounge and put on the TV.

Over at Tall Trees, Adele Stevenson was phoning her son Robert. She asked him if he would call in that evening as there was something she wanted to ask him to do for her. He had been furious with her, telling her that she had made him look a fool in front of the lawyer and enquired why Matt could not help her as he was coming over that evening to play cards. Adele had reminded him, rather caustically, that he should be trying to keep on her good side after the stunt he and his brother had pulled in moving her into the home against her will and he had reluctantly agreed to come over at 7pm. Matt was expected at 8.

Pauline arrived in the afternoon with some things that Adele had asked for. She did not stay long. Robert duly arrived at 7.10.

"Did you remember to sign the visitors' book this time?" she asked him. "It's a fire precaution and matron told me she had noticed that neither you nor Matt had signed it."

Robert had not signed it and was not pleased to be asked to return downstairs to do so.

Adele spent a short time with him, telling him that she wanted her old gardener given money and also her daily help. Both had been with her for many years and she had promised them an annuity when the time came for her to sell the house.

"I'll pay of course. I just want you to set it up."

Adele named the amount and Robert became angry, as she had known he would.

"That's ridiculous, Mother!" he shouted, going quite florid in the face.

"It's my affair and my money," she shouted back, sweeping her right hand, angrily and knocking the playing cards from her table onto the floor.

"Pick those up for me, please," she demanded. "They're new cards Pauline bought me and they're very slippery."

Then her face had changed, softening completely.

"Robert dear, would you ask my lawyer, Mr Browne or Mr James to come up. We'll need to get that power thing sorted out."

Robert was speechless. He picked up the cards, slowly.

"But Mother, you said this afternoon that you didn't want to give us power of attorney."

"When dear?"

"This afternoon when I brought Mr Knowles to see you."

"Oh you must be mistaken, dear. I played cards this afternoon with that nice Mr Graham. Now bring me one of my new cups and put the kettle on. I feel like a nice cup of tea."

Robert complied then left, looking stunned.

As he went through the hallway, he bumped into his brother. Matt looked surprised to see him so Robert explained the reason for the visit.

"Though why she couldn't just have told you to tell me, goodness knows," he grumbled.

He told his brother how much their mother was intending to give to the two old family retainers but Matt was unruffled.

"I think, brother dear that she intends to make us both jump through some hoops after what we did to her. At least you're not having to spend an hour or so playing damned bezique."

"She's playing solitaire right now. She's got twenty games written down and is scoring them off as she gets them to come out. She's still calling it patience of course. Matt, I think she really is getting dementia."

He told his brother what had transpired that afternoon and how his mother seemed to have forgotten all about the visit.

"Well, keep trying Robert. We need that thing signed before she does go off her chump."

Robert left, hurrying down the drive to where he had left his car. There was not much parking space in front of the home and if other visitors were there, his beloved BMW might get scratched or dented. He noticed that Matt's Mercedes was outside the door, parked carelessly as usual.

Matt climbed the stairs, rather than take the lift. He knew that he needed the exercise and had no intention of getting flabby like Robert. Unlike Robert, he was unmarried so had no wife to cook him the large meals that Margaret made for his brother. He was happy to be single and preferred a steady line of casual girlfriends.

He knocked briskly on the door to number seven and without waiting to be invited in, opened the door and walked in.

"Did you sign the visitors' book, Matthew?" his mother enquired sharply.

"No"

"Well just go back down and sign it now, please."

Her voice was quite loud and she seemed agitated.

Taking off his jacket, Matt sat down across from her at the small table where cards were set out in a clock formation.

"I'll do it on the way out."

"You'll do it now. They need to know who's in in case there's a fire. Go down and sign it now!"

Her voice had risen further, the 'now' being shouted out.

Muttering under his breath, Matt got back up and went downstairs. When he arrived back the solitaire hand had gone and two packs of cards sat expectantly on the table.

When Sandra Keith came to call Adele for breakfast the next morning, she got no answer. With a feeling of deja vu, she went for matron once again and Mrs Smith found Adele dead in her chair at the table.

"Was she well enough last night when you took her supper, Sandra?" asked Matron Smith.

"She rang down about 8.45 to the kitchen to say not to bring any supper as her two sons were still with her and they'd have something together," said Sandra.

They looked round the room. Cards lay strewn over the table and the floor and her diary sat in front of her, open at the following week where she had written in for Thursday:

'Matt for cards. 7.30'

# CHAPTER 11

When Davenport arrived at the station on Thursday morning, having dropped Pippa off at school, there was an excited buzz in the air. Fiona was in the main room with the others and they all seemed to be talking at once.

"Good morning, folk," he said loudly but no one noticed him.

"I said, 'Good morning, everyone!'" he shouted.

Four faces turned towards him, startled.

"Sorry, Sir," said his DS. "Never heard you arrive. There's been another death at that nursing home."

"Tall Trees. Another old lady found dead of a suspected heart attack," said Salma.

"Seems a bit unlikely, two heart attacks within a few days, Sir," added Frank.

Fraser Hewitt said nothing, probably realising that it had all been said by his colleagues.

"Who was it this time?" asked Davenport.

"An Adele Stevenson. She was found dead in her chair this morning," said Frank. "She was the one who was last to talk to Miss Cowan who died a few nights ago."

"Has the doctor been called?" queried Davenport.

"The matron who called us this morning, called the doctor first. She wants us to go round, as one of the other residents is creating a fuss about two deaths. She wants to be taken away from Tall Trees and has called her friend to come and get her."

"Right. Salma, you and Frank went the last time. Get off there again. Anything suspicious, contact me here."

Davenport walked up the corridor to his own room, followed by DS Macdonald who was in turn followed by a faint tune, suspiciously like, 'The Wedding March'. Davenport decided to ignore it but he grinned at Fiona as she came into his room and shut the door.

"I suppose I should pull him up on that but at least it's a change from Scottish tunes. Come to think of it I've not heard any of them since we got back from our holiday."

"Me neither. Don't worry, love, we've only got two weeks of pre-wedding days to put up with Mendelsohn."

She gave him a hug which he returned with interest, turning her face up to kiss it gently.

Salma was telling Frank off as they walked to their car.

"Frank, 'Speed Bonny Boat' was bad enough when they wouldn't understand that it was aimed at them but whistling the wedding tune isn't too subtle, is it?"

"They'll be so happy they won't mind," he said imperturbably. "Oh, I've just remembered something. Wait for me."

He dashed off and came back in a couple of minutes.

"I forgot to tell the boss that matron had called yesterday to say that Miss Cowan had left nearly everything to the home and a couple of thousand to her niece. I imagine we'll have to look into the financial state Tall Trees is in."

"I imagine this second lady will have left everything to her children," said Salma.

It only took about fifteen minutes to reach Tall Trees and soon they were in Matron's room, sitting in comfortable chairs in front of her beautiful rosewood desk. It transpired that once again Sandra Keith had gone upstairs to see where Mrs Mohammed and Mrs Stevenson wanted to have breakfast. This time she had told Mrs Mohammed that she had knocked on Mrs Stevenson's door and got no reply. With a feeling of having done all this before, she had gone downstairs for Matron and they had come upstairs. Matron had knocked and gone in. Mrs Mohammed had joined Sandra outside and told her that Mrs Stevenson had had two visitors the night before and that there had been loud voices a couple of times. Matron had come out to tell them that Adele Stevenson was dead. The doctor had been called again and once again, he had diagnosed a heart attack, though this time, with Adele being new, he had known of no previous heart condition. The elders son, contacted by matron, had provided them with the name of his mother's doctor.

"I told Mr Stevenson that there was no point in him coming up to the Home right away as there was nothing that could be done for his mother."

"Did her doctor come straight over?"

"Yes. He did. He was a young man who knew little about his patient but he had her records and he said that there was no history of heart trouble. He examined Mrs Stevenson, and then agreed with Dr Ferguson that she must have taken a heart attack, there being no signs of another cause of death."

Salma asked Mrs Smith why she had contacted them and she said that one of the residents, a Miss Claire Williams, had become hysterical when she heard, saying that they were all going to be murdered in their beds and insisting that her friend be contacted to take her away.

"Obviously she's overreacting as neither woman was actually in bed but another resident, Frederick Graham, said that Mrs Stevenson had been very well when he had last seen her and it was a bit suspicious that two people had died in the same circumstances within a few days of each other. I felt it prudent to call you back to set minds at rest."

Salma and Frank were taken upstairs to Adele Stevenson's room. Cards were strewn across the table and carpet. Frank read the diary that sat on the table.

"Did her son come regularly to see her? It says here that Matt was going to come for cards on Thursday."

"Well she only came in about two weeks ago but yes, both sons came both weeks. I looked at the visitors' book last week and they hadn't signed out or in so I asked Mrs Stevenson to remind them to do both every time they came. It's necessary for fire precautions," she added.

"I looked at the book just before you arrived and both sons had signed in but not out, last night."

Adele must have been sitting facing the door as the diary was on that side of the table. Frank was looking at the bookcases. He went across the room, picked out a book and opened it.

"Oh God, another poetry freak!" he exclaimed.

"Who knew Mrs Stevenson best?" Salma asked Matron.

"I'll ask Sandra. She'll know," Mrs Smith replied and left the room. Frank showed Salma the book he was holding. Called, "Ariel", it contained poems by a poet called Sylvia Plath.

"Do all old dears love poems?" Frank asked.

Salma had gone over to the bedside cabinet. She opened the drawer and withdrew a large diary.

"A five year diary," she said, opening it up at last night's page.

"Listen to this. 'Robert came up this afternoon with a lawyer. He came up later and we argued. Matt came up.. We all argued. I played bezique with them both as usual. Made Matt wait till after my game with Robert. They hate playing it. Had supper all together. Will keep them coming here. Hopefully will annoy them. Must contact my lawyer."

"There was a lot of arguing going on last night, Frank. I wonder what about. And this mention of seeing her lawyer. I wonder if she told them that."

"I think I can tell you that," came a voice from the door and, turning, they saw an elderly man standing on the threshold with Matron supporting him. Salma invited him in and he sat down on the chair across the table from the one Adele had been found dead in.

"What were they arguing about, Sir?" asked Salma.

"They wanted their mother to give them power of attorney. She told me she'd only agree to that if her daughter was included. I think she'd changed her mind. It wouldn't surprise me after the way they had her put in here. I was very surprised when she said she'd agreed."

"Oh, Fred, don't be giving the police the wrong idea. They reluctantly put their mother into care because of her dementia," said Matron.

"Dementia! I saw more of Adele than you did and she had no dementia. She was as sharp as a tack," said Fred. "She told me that her husband had put the house into the names of his three children and they wanted to sell the house. Have already sold it, I think she said. She told me that she was sure that both her sons would murder her if they could get away with it. I imagine she meant so that they would get all her money"

Matron protested once again that Fred was being unfair to the two men whom he had never met.

"I don't suppose that you have Mrs Stevenson's will, Matron?" asked Salma.

"No I don't. I imagine her eldest son will have that, or her lawyer."

On the point of leaving, Salma suddenly wondered about the person in the next room. She asked Matron if she could speak to this person and Matron took her next door and introduced her to Mrs Mohammed, dressed in a brilliant shade of blue.

"Mrs Mohammed, what a beautiful salwar kamiz!" Salma exclaimed. The tiny woman smiled in pleasure and invited Salma in. Matron returned to room seven.

"Mrs Mohammed. Did you hear anything from next door last night?"

"Yes. I told my carer, Sandra Keith, that I heard shouting...twice but I couldn't hear what was being said."

"Have you any idea who was in there with Mrs Stevenson?"

"Sorry, no. I am not a nosy person but I think that there were two people. I fell asleep. I didn't hear anyone leave. Sorry."

Salma thanked her, complimented her on her lovely wall hangings and fire screen and joined Frank next door.

"I suppose both sons really were here? Is there any way we can prove that, Matron?"

"I saw their names in the book. I can show you that."

Mrs Smith took them downstairs and handed Salma the visitors' book. Both Robert and Matthew Stevenson had signed themselves in but neither had signed himself out, as she had told them

Matron made a tutting noise of vexation.

"It is so important that visitors sign in and out in case of fire."

Salma thanked her and she and Frank once more left Tall Trees. In the doorway, they passed a couple coming in. The woman was leading the man who looked bewildered and walked very slowly.

"He looks a bit young to be an inmate," said Frank.

"Not an inmate, Frank. He's not a prisoner. A resident and you're right. He does look too young to be in a nursing home."

When they arrived back at the station, Salma went along to the DCI's room and reported that the second death was possibly more dubious than the first but that two doctors had summed both deaths up as heart attacks.

"Anything make you suspicious, Sergeant?"

"Just that there'd been an argument that evening between Mrs Stevenson and her sons. Both arguments were recorded in the old lady's diary."

"Any idea what the arguments were about?"

"One elderly man said that it was probably about them wanting to have power of attorney and in her five year diary she wrote that she must get her lawyer to come and see her. Matron seemed to think that the dead woman had dementia but the old man said she hadn't. It seems that the two boys had their mother put into the home against her will."

"Anything linking the two dead women, Sergeant?"

Salma thought for a minute.

"Well both were found dead in their chairs..."

"...and both were poetry nuts," said Frank's voice from behind Salma.

"Thanks, Selby," said Davenport, drily. "Anything else?"

"Maybe the home was in financial difficulties, Sir and Miss Cowan's money stopped them going under. Matron didn't say how much she left them," added Frank, impervious to his boss's caustic tone.

"Well I think on the grounds that two deaths in a row is a bit suspicious though it's probably an acceptable coincidence given that both were elderly...how old were they, by the way?"

"Miss Cowan was 78 and Mrs Stevenson 94," said Salma, looking at her notebook.

"Given that it's possibly suspicious, get on to the home, Selby, and tell them to lock both rooms and leave everything untouched. I'll get on to Ben Goodwin and get him and his SOC team to give both rooms the once-over. Anything else Salma?"

"No Sir."

"Selby?"

"Well, if there are any more deaths at that place Sir, send Fraser along. Maybe the clue's in the poetry books and he can solve it for us."

Davenport could not help the smile that crossed his face. As he told Fiona later, Frank was often impudent but he could not help liking the young constable.

"Do you think I should get Martin to take a look at both bodies, love?"

"Maybe that would be a bit of a waste of tax-payers' money, Charles. I mean old ladies do die of heart attacks. What are you thinking? That the sons heard of one death and it gave them the idea of killing off their mother?"

"Well, at least one of them was heard arguing with her that evening."

"But where's the link with the first murder."

Davenport laughed.

"OK. I give in. No Martin Jamieson unless Ben finds something suspicious.

# CHAPTER 12

Davenport was standing, looking out of his window and drinking coffee when he saw Ben Goodwin's silver Mercedes coming into the forecourt. Ben seldom used this lovely car for work, preferring an old Fiesta which he also used for his fishing trips. He got out of the gleaming car and looking up, saw Charles watching him and waved cheerily. Minutes later Goodwin had joined him in his room.

"Coffee, Ben?"

"No thanks. Trying to wean myself off my caffeine fix and my chocolate one too," he laughed.

Charles noticed that the head of SOC was looking more trim and said so. They both sat down, round a small coffee table.

"Funny case this one, Charles. Mind if I smoke?"

"Not given up all the vices then?" said Charles.

"Give me some pleasures."

"No, go ahead. I'll open the window though if you don't mind."

Charles suited the action to the word. He came back and sat down again.

"What's funny and do you think we have a case here? I thought it was just two elderly ladies, by coincidence, taking heart attacks in quick succession in the same nursing home. Not beyond the bounds of possibility, especially given that the most recent was, what? Ninety-five?"

"Ninety-four. I said funny, not suspicious, by the way."

"Right, what was odd?"

"Well, both were reading the same book and not a lightweight thing either. 'The Outsider' by Albert Camus...and in French. I asked Matron and she said that the first woman, Miss Cowan had it on her lap. In the other room it was on the bedside table. Mrs Stevenson must have been playing cards. Some of the cards were still on the table. Two brand new decks of cards."

"And was the book the only thing that makes these two deaths odd?" Charles asked.

"Probably another coincidence but both ladies had a bottle of Gaviscon in their rooms. I asked the matron and she said that the bottle had been on the table beside Miss Cowan when she found the body. There was also a bottle on the table beside the cards in Mrs Stevenson's room."

"So you mean that both ladies suffered from indigestion before their heart attacks. Is this so unusual? I thought that heart trouble and indigestion were often confused."

"Yes they are," agreed Ben Goodwin. "But there are countless indigestion remedies. Why did both women have the same one?"

"Maybe the first lady recommended it to the second?"

"Were they friends?" asked Ben.

Davenport went to the door and shouted down the corridor for Salma who came hurrying up to his room. She said hello to Ben Goodwin and he smiled back at her.

"Salma, the two old ladies who died, do you know if they were friendly?"

"I'm sure they weren't, Sir. Mrs Stevenson said that Miss Cowan had asked her in... reluctantly... I think was the word she used, and the matron said Miss Cowan seldom came out of her room and never had visitors."

"Thanks, Salma," said Davenport. "That's all."

Salma left, shutting the door behind her.

"I think you should find out where both ladies got their Gaviscon, Charles," advised Goodwin.

"I've taken both bottles away to have them checked."

"You mean it could have been poisoned?

"It's possible."

"But why? "

"Who have they left their money to?"

"Selby said that the first woman left nearly all her money to the nursing home which is quite natural given that she had only a niece she never saw. She left her a few thousand. Seemingly she had no friends. We weren't treating these deaths as murder, till you came along with your hare-brained ideas! Do you seriously suggest that I get Martin Jamieson onto this?"

"Wouldn't do any harm and if you wait too long, the first woman might be buried or worse, cremated."

"Knox will *not* be pleased if I set forensics off on a wild goose chase!" Charles said in exasperation.

"Would he be thrilled if you found out later that the second wifey had been murdered and you had to shell out to get the first one exhumed?"

"Ben Goodwin! Give me back Vince Parker. He would have been too busy reading up for his next interview to spot *odd* things! Did you get any fingerprints?"

"Yes in the case of Mrs Stevenson. Three cups were sitting on the window ledge, presumably waiting for the staff to take away and wash. There were no facilities for washing dishes in the room but I think she must have given them a cursory rinse in her wash-hand basin. I've taken them away. I asked about the other woman. There were two cups found in her room but they had been rinsed out and left on the side of her wash-hand basin in the ensuite bathroom, the carer told me, so I looked and got them too. I brushed the table in Mrs Stevenson's room and got some fingerprints there, her's and her sons', I imagine. I heard that they had both visited her that evening and with the playing cards being new, they might have some prints too, so I've taken them."

Goodwin stood up, brushing cigarette ash off one trouser leg. He went over to the open window and flicked the butt out.

"Well, you never offered me an ashtray," he complained, seeing the look on Davenport's face. "Now can I get off, please? I was on my way to Edinburgh."

"Special function? I noticed you had the Merc instead of the clapped-out Fiesta."

"Got rid of the old girl a few weeks ago and the function is the theatre."

"Theatre? Is this Ben Goodwin talking? I thought the nearest you got to culture was page three of the Record! Theatre, old car gone, on a diet, off coffee. Are you in love?"

Ben's wife of twenty-four years had died some time ago and he had moved to Glasgow to get away from the memories of her last months dying from cancer. Davenport wondered if he had been thoughtless with this remark but he need not have worried. Ben blushed, ran his fingers through his greying, dark hair and replied that he had been seeing a woman from Edinburgh for a few weeks.

"I met her on a course through there. A widow with two grown-up kids," he added.

"Serious?"

"Give me a chance. It's only been two weeks but..."

"...but serious enough to make you take pride in your appearance and get rid of the old jalopy," finished Davenport.

"You can talk, Charles Davenport! I heard on the grapevine that you got yourself engaged while on holiday and to your own DS Macdonald no less!"

It was Charles's turn to blush.

"Your invitation to the wedding will be arriving soon. Will we send it to you and a partner?"

"Maybe a bit soon for that," replied Goodwin. "But I'll be delighted to come. What can I get you both for a wedding present?"

"Fiona doesn't want to give suggestions but I would say glasses if you're stuck."

"Wine? Whisky?"

"Wine, I think. Neither of us has been doing much entertaining over the last years so we don't have many of them. Thanks."

"Now I really must dash. Let me know if you do rope in Jamieson."

"And you let me know if you find out anything about the fingerprints. Did you take prints from the home staff to eliminate theirs'?"

"I did. If I find any unmatched ones, I may have to try the residents and the relations but hopefully that won't be necessary."

Goodwin left and Davenport went down the corridor to tell Salma and Frank what had taken place.

"I hope he doesn't have to take the prints from the old battle-axe who's threatening to leave," commented Frank who had taken the phone call from Matron telling them of the second death.

"I hope he doesn't have to take any at all," said Davenport dryly.

"Are we treating either of these deaths as suspicious, Sir?" asked Fraser Hewitt.

"Ben Goodwin found out two odd things that make him think we should involve Martin Jamieson but I think I'll wait till I've had time to interview the family of Mrs Stevenson and find out who benefits from both deaths. DS Macdonald and I will go this evening to see the two sons and the daughter. Fraser, get on to Tall Trees and ask the matron to let us know how much the home was left. If she's reluctant to tell you, get the name and address of the woman's lawyer if she had one."

Davenport left to tell Fiona their plans for the evening and to ring his sister to ask if she would take Pippa to her house for the evening and feed her. Linda was used to doing this at short notice and Pippa kept spare clothes there so would not have to stay in her uniform.

"I should be able to collect her before nine o'clock. Sorry for the short notice, Lin."

Fiona told him that she had been going to write the invitation cards that night but there was still time to do it the next night and get them posted in time. He suggested that they get a takeaway meal and eat it in her flat. Lastly, he rang the home and asked Matron for the address of Robert Stevenson. He would get the other two addresses from him and hopefully all three would be at home.

Frank came to see him before they left, to tell him that all the will stated was that Martha Cowan's estate, apart from £10,000, was to be left to Tall Trees.

"So Matron thinks £10,000 is a couple of thousand? That must mean that Tall Trees' share must be considerable. Thanks Frank."

# CHAPTER 13

Robert Stevenson's house in Giffnock was a detached villa. His BMW and another, smaller car were in the driveway so Davenport parked his Audi on the road outside and he and Fiona walked up the drive. The garden was very well maintained but rather too manicured for Fiona's taste.

"It looks as if a gardener comes to do this. It's too weed-free. Unless someone who lives here has just spent a day working in it. Look at the serried ranks of roses," she commented, as they stood outside waiting for someone to answer the doorbell.

It was a woman in her thirties who came to the door. She was dowdily dressed, in an old-fashioned beige, pleated skirt with a brown shirt blouse. Her mousey-fair hair was severely cut, almost like a short back and sides, Davenport commented to Fiona later.

"Yes?" she asked, without smiling.

"DCI Davenport and DS Macdonald to see Mr Robert Stevenson," Davenport said.

The woman went into the house, closing the door behind her. Charles and Fiona looked at each other, Charles grimacing and Fiona shrugging her shoulders.

"Should I ring again?" he asked.

Just then the door was opened again and the woman, still unsmiling, invited them in and showed them into a front room which looked unused and formal with a piano in one corner and a three-piece suite the only other piece of furniture. It was in leather, black leather and there were no cushions to relieve the starkness of the material.

"My father will be along shortly," the woman said, turning on her heels and leaving them alone.

They remained standing but did not have to wait for long. A man entered. He was wearing a dark suit with a white shirt and a black tie.

"Robert Stevenson," he said, brusquely.

He shook hands with Davenport but ignored Fiona. Charles felt himself bristling at this sleight to his fiancée and work-colleague but he kept the smile on his face.

"DCI Davenport, Mr Stevenson and this is my DS, Fiona Macdonald. I'm here because of your mother's sudden death..."

"...Sudden but not unexpected, Inspector. She was after all ninety -four."

"True, Sir but there was another death yesterday in the same nursing home so we are having to look into both deaths. Understandably, some of the residents are upset and one or two are frightened."

"What of? Do they think there's a mad poisoner working in the home?" sneered Stevenson.

"What makes you mention poison, Mr Stevenson?" Davenport asked.

"What else could cause a death that appears to be a heart attack, man? Could hardly be a mad axe-murderer. It would be a bit of a give-away if both old ladies had their heads chopped up which they haven't."

Knowing Charles well by now, Fiona could sense his dislike of this supercilious man and she intervened quickly.

"Sir, all we need to know from you is to whom your mother has left her estate. I'm sure you appreciate that in a sudden death, so matter how old the deceased, we need to look into these things."

"This is ridiculous. You'll be saying next that I killed my mother for her money!"

Stevenson's face was puce, the veins in his temples, bulging.

"Nobody's saying anything of the sort Sir," said Davenport. "We merely have to know your mother's heirs as a formality.

At this moment the door opened again and a slightly-built, dowdily dressed, middle-aged woman appeared. She took one look at her husband and gripped his arm.

"Robert. What's the matter? Calm down. Remember your high blood pressure, dear."

Robert Stevenson took some deep breaths. He smiled thinly at the woman.

"This is my wife, Margaret, Inspector. As far as I know, my mother left her estate among myself, my brother Matthew and my sister Pauline. She may have included her grandchildren, my daughter Avril who let you in and my twin nieces, Kim and Lucy, my sister's daughters. They still live at home. My daughter is on holiday here from Russia."

"Would you let me have the name and address of your mother's lawyer, Sir?" asked Davenport..

"It's 'Browne, James and Knowles', Hope Street," supplied Stevenson.

"Thank you, Sir. Now, if you don't mind, will you tell me how you found your mother when you saw her yesterday evening?"

"What's the problem, Inspector?" asked Margaret Stevenson.

"Just that in the case of two deaths at the same place we have to look into things," said Davenport. "I'm sure you understand."

"Of course."

"My mother was in good form, Inspector. She had rung for me to come up to tell me that she wanted to give large annuities to two of her previous staff. I argued with her about the amount, then I left."

"I was told by the head of SOC that you and your brother had both visited last night. Is this true?"

"Yes. I passed Matt, my brother in the hallway as I left. He was going up, by request, to play cards with mother. I phoned him to tell him that mother had died and he said that she had been tired and had decided not to play bezique after all. Matt was a bit annoyed as he had given up a prior engagement to humour mother."

"Thank you, Sir. Now would you give me the addresses of Mr Matthew Stevenson and your sister."

Margaret supplied these and Davenport and Fiona left, saying nothing till they were seated in the car.

"Not a very nice person, Mr Robert Stevenson," commented Fiona.

"No. I didn't like the sound of 'humouring mother'," agreed Charles. "And the diary said that they'd both played bezique."

It only took them about half an hour to reach Matt Stevenson's West End house which was the ground floor of a renovated Georgian building.

Matt came to the door with a wine glass in his hand. He invited them into his study, a masculine room with a huge desk and bookcases. He sat behind his desk and Davenport and Fiona sat in two similar chairs across from him.

"My brother rang me, Inspector, so I was expecting you."

He smiled.

Disarming and charming, he offered them a drink which they refused.

"Mr Stevenson, I believe that, like your elder brother, you paid a visit to your mother last night," said Davenport.

"I did, Inspector. I met Robert coming out. I went upstairs and had to come back down to sign the visitor's book at my mother's insistence. She is...she was...a very determined woman. She'd asked me to come and play cards with her but by the time I got back up she had changed her mind. I wasn't too pleased, I can tell you."

"Did she appear well?" asked Fiona.

"She seemed perfectly well though she did say she was tired. The heart attack must have been sudden."

"And you, as well as your brother and sister and perhaps your nieces, are the beneficiaries in her will?" questioned Davenport.

"I imagine so. Why are the police involved, Inspector?"

"We usually are in case of sudden death, Sir, and in this case there were two sudden deaths at Tall Trees."

"Hardly suspicious deaths though. Two elderly ladies might be expected to die suddenly, surely."

"Yes, Sir, probably but we have to go down the usual channels," explained Davenport.

Thanking Matthew Stevenson for his help, Davenport and Fiona once more made their exit. This time, in the car, they exchanged comments about the younger brother.

"Curious, naturally but not belligerent," were Fiona's words.

"Nicer than his brother," were Davenport's. He continued, "Yet he denies playing cards with her too. Odd. Why would Adele Stevenson lie about that?"

"Maybe they want us to think that they weren't there very long," suggested Fiona.

Finally they drew up in Waterfoot, outside a small terraced house. The name on the door read, 'Macartney'. The door was opened by a large man who invited them in when Davenport said who they were.

"Sorry. We only have one public room. This was our first house and we've never moved. There are two bedrooms upstairs. We use one and the twins have the other. Sorry, I'm prattling. Sit down. How can I help you?"

It was obvious that Robert Stevenson had not thought to warn his sister or brother-in-law about a possible police visit. Davenport and Fiona sat down on the red velour settee and the man switched off the TV.

"Is it me or my wife you want, Inspector or one of the girls? I hope no one's in trouble."

He smiled, obviously confident that this was not the case.

"It's about the sudden death of Mrs Adele Stevenson. Your mother-in-law, I'm assuming, Sir," said Davenport.

"Yes. Mum-in-law. A feisty old soul. Pauline will miss her. She's in the kitchen...Pauline I mean...I'll get her for you."

He went to the room door and called out to his wife who came into the room, wiping her hands on a tea towel.

"Pauline, love, this is DCI Davenport and DS Mac...sorry, I've forgotten your name," he said to Fiona.

"Macdonald," she supplied.

"It's about your mother's death, Mrs Macartney."

The husband and wife sat down on the armchairs which matched the settee.

"Is something wrong, Inspector?" asked Pauline.

"Probably not. It's just that in a case of sudden death, we make various checks. How was your mother when you last saw her and when was that?" asked Davenport.

"I saw her yesterday afternoon. She'd asked me to get her some new cards, a novel and some tummy medicine and to bring in a few bits of crockery and a teapot, milk jug and sugar bowl. I was pleased as I thought that meant that she was settling in and planning to entertain visitors."

Pauline sounded tearful.

"You hadn't expected her to settle in then?" asked Fiona.

"Well no. My bothers had her moved against her will, into Tall Trees, while I was on holiday in Cornwall and I was sure that she would insist on me getting her out when I came home."

"How did you find out about the move?" asked Fiona.

"My daughters came home before us, went to see their grandma, and found a 'Sold' sign in the garden of her house. They contacted their Uncle Robert then went to see Mum in Tall Trees. Stewart and I cut short our holiday but by the time I saw Mum, she seemed to have settled down. Now this!"

She sniffed and wiped her eyes with the corner of the tea towel. Her husband got up and went to sit on the arm of her chair, putting his arm round her.

"Did she seem well to you, on Wednesday afternoon?" asked Davenport.

"Perfectly well. She was taking great pleasure in the fact that she had both of my brothers coming up to see her that night. She said she was going to keep them on their toes after what they'd done."

"And the stomach medicine?"

"That surprised me. She had the constitution of an ox!"

"Did you choose the medicine then?"

"No, she specifically asked for Gaviscon. Maybe Matron, Mrs Smith, had recommended it."

Pauline gave a tremulous smile.

"What was the book?" asked Fiona.

"It was another surprise, "The Outsider", by Albert Camus. Oh, not the book: Mum was an avid reader, but I didn't know that she was conversant in French. I did ask her and she said that one of the other residents was reading it. Probably she decided to test herself. She was always setting herself goals, academic ones. I had to go into town for the book."

"Academic goals, at ninety-four?" exclaimed Fiona.

"Well if I tell you that in her seventies, she did an Open University degree in English Literature, that might give you an idea of what she was like," said Stewart, looking proud.

"Do you have any idea how your mother left her estate, Mrs Macartney?" Davenport enquired, expecting the stock response.

Pauline looked embarrassed.

"The day before she died, Mum told me that she was going to change her will. She was going to leave Robert and Matt out of it because of what they'd just done to her. She said that she'd told them the lawyer was coming on Friday. She told them that she was willing for them to have power of attorney over her but she told me she wouldn't let them have it. I don't know what she was trying to do and now we'll never know and the boys will get their share after all. Poor Mum!"

"Do you think she had accepted being in the home?" asked Fiona.

"She seemed to have. She told my daughters that she'd met a nice man and the food was good. We offered to have her here. Stewart and I would have slept here. The settee is also a bed. We'd have got a bigger house soon with the money I got from the sale of her house but she refused to come."

"I gave up my job as a surgeon to concentrate on my writing," said Stewart Macartney. "Otherwise we'd have had a larger house already and maybe had her staying here by this time."

"Don't blame yourself, darling," said Pauline. "You know that Mum was independent. She wouldn't have come even if we'd had the room."

There was the noise of footsteps clattering downstairs. The door burst open.

"Mum, we're away out...oh... sorry, didn't know there was anyone else here," said a teenage girl. "We'll be back about eleven."

She whirled back out before anyone could reply.

"That was Lucy, our whirlwind daughter. The one you can hear coming quietly downstairs is Kim, her sister," laughed Pauline, ruefully.

"'Bye Mum, 'bye Dad," came a voice and the front door closed.

"Well thanks both of you. There's probably nothing at all wrong about your mother's death but with it coming so soon after that of Miss Cowan and with it being in the same place, we have to check. Could I ask you to let us know the contents of the will when it's read?"

Davenport and Fiona left the third house and Charles ran Fiona home, stopping only to kiss her goodnight before driving over to collect Pippa at her aunt's.

# CHAPTER 14

"I see father's in a vile mood," Avril commented drily to her mother.

The police had left the house some minutes earlier and Robert had stormed into the kitchen where Margaret was busy preparing the evening meal. He sat down at the breakfast bar and demanded a cup of coffee.

"On second thoughts. I need a stiff drink. Get me one!"

"Is that a whisky or a brandy, dear?" asked his wife.

"Whisky and don't drown it with water as you usually do."

"Last slave die then father?" asked his daughter, coming into the room as her mother scuttled out. With the right clothes, Margaret would have looked like the tweeny maid from years gone by, head down trying to make herself as small as possible.

Robert growled but years of trying in vain to dominate his daughter, had taught him not to lambast her the way he did her mother and he contented himself with replying that his wife enjoyed doing things for him.

"In your dreams," Avril shot back.

He remembered only too clearly the one time he had hit Avril. She had been about ten at the time. He had slapped her face and she had stood and looked at him coolly while his handprint gradually appeared on her cheek. The next day she told her school teacher and Robert had been visited by a police officer. He had blustered about it being a mistake and it would not happen again.

It had not happened again.

Avril had left home as soon as she had her degree in medicine under her belt. She had gone first to Botswana and then to Leningrad. In both places she had dispensed medical help to needy people, pouring out her love on the unfortunate poor, love which she had never felt for her bullying father or her mouse-like mother whom she could only pity and despise. She was home now for a few weeks only, prior to moving once again, this time to The Philippines.

Robert hastily changed the subject.

"The police were here to ask about your grandmother. Apparently with sudden deaths, they feel they have the right to barge around, asking about the contents of the person's will. They almost accused me of murdering her!"

"I'm sure they didn't do that, Father. Bit of an hyperbole, surely!"

Robert looked perplexed and she surmised, rightly, that he did not know what hyperbole meant.

"Hyperbole is exaggeration for affect, Father," she informed him with a cool smile. "I forgot: self-made men don't need education, do they?"

At this inauspicious moment, Margaret returned with the glass of whisky. She handed it to Robert who grabbed it from her, almost spilling the amber liquid.

"Be careful, woman," he snarled.

"Manners maketh the man. Now where did I read that? Not in the Daily Record anyway. Interesting to see that you still read that rubbish," remarked his daughter.

Margaret threw her a pleading look as Robert stalked out of the kitchen

"Yes, he's in a vile mood, dear and you've only gone and made it worse."

"Why on earth don't you leave him, Mother?"

"You keep forgetting that I've never worked. I met your Father at school and we were married when I was eighteen. He was handsome then and other girls envied me."

"Was he always so domineering?"

"No. He was always opinionated but it wasn't until I failed to get pregnant that he turned against me. You know the rest. I had fertility drugs and had you..."

"... and I wasn't the son he wanted. I know."

"He wanted a son to carry on the business, dear. It wasn't your fault."

"Nor your's."

"Father said that the police came to find out about Grandmother's will. Does he know what's in it?" asked Avril.

"He's never discussed it with me but I imagine that she'll have left the bulk of her estate to him and Matt and Pauline, with probably a sum of money for you and your cousins but..."

"...but what?"

"He had a real argument with her over the house sale and having her put into the nursing home so she might have altered her will, Avril."

Avril's eyes gleamed.

"I do hope so! I couldn't believe it when you told me that they almost frogmarched her out of her house."

"Not frogmarched, dear!"

"I know. She would be in her wheelchair no doubt but it amounts to the same thing. Uncle Matt and Father forced her out of her home and then expected her to knuckle under. She's not like you Mother : she has...sorry had... gumption, good old Scottish smeddum. Oh how I hope she managed to change her will and disinherit the two of them!"

"They were even trying to get her to sign a power of attorney document. I overheard them talking one evening," Margaret confided and added, bravely, that she too would like to see Robert and Matt get their come- uppance.

Margaret was not so brave that evening when Robert, as he had always done when Avril had got the better of him in an argument, decided to take his revenge out on his timid wife. He came into their bedroom as she was undressing, went into a drawer and took out sexy red underwear and stocking

"Here, put this on and get dressed again," he told her, sharply.

Always biddable and knowing what was to come, Margaret did as she was told. Robert got undressed and got into bed.

"Now, undress slowly and seductively, the way you know I like and remember you'll go through it all again if I'm not satisfied. It's a long time since we did this, my dear."

Margaret shivered and undid her blouse slowly and slid it slowly down her back. She unzipped her tweed skirt and let it drop to the floor. She put on the red underwear. She caught a glimpse of herself in the mirror, wearing only a red satin bra and panties with suspender belt and black stockings.

She stopped.

"What are you waiting for, woman? Music?"

He started humming The Stripper music loudly. Margaret peeled off the stockings and as she knew he wanted, threw them onto the bed. She felt behind her for the belt fastener.

"Stop and put the stockings back on."

Her hands shaking, Margaret did so.

She undid the flimsy bra and threw it onto the bed, then peeled off the scanty briefs and threw them too.

"Now just stand there while I look at you," he ordered.

This was for her the worst part, the humiliation of being scanned from head to toe. He took his time, as he always did.

"Hm! You've lost more weight. Start eating more, Margaret. I like my women with some meat on their bones and some boobs to look at. My current floozy is size 38. Did I tell you her name? It's Jennifer. She's only 25. I pay her well. Will I pay you too? You could buy some decent, pretty clothes for our next...assignation. I see that our daughter has taken to wearing dowdy clothes too."

"I don't want to be paid," she said, in a strangled voice, "and Avril is wearing my clothes. Remember her suitcase didn't arrive with her plane."

"Probably right, you wouldn't be worth paying for, unless you've had some practice since last time, I don't imagine fucking you will be much fun. Get onto the bed."

There was nothing romantic or gentle about his lovemaking and feeling bruised and cheap, Margaret crawled under the covers.

"I've decided not to punish you this time, my dear, for the way our daughter speaks to me. I wouldn't want her to hear you cry out or see bruises tomorrow but she'll be gone soon with any luck, so keep on my good side if you know what's best for you."

"Yes, Robert," came the tearful response.

"And keep Avril out of my sight," he said, as he turned over and fell asleep.

# CHAPTER 15

Davenport took a call from Ben Goodwin just after eleven o'clock the next morning. Ben told him that as he had been quiet at work, he had got straight down to analysing the tea cups, three from Adele Stevenson's room and six from a cupboard in Miss Cowan's room. As the cups used by Adele and herself had been put away, he did not know which had been recently used so had had to check the set of six. He had done Adele's cups first and found remnants of milky tea in all three cups and quite a large trace of arsenic in one cup.

"Whoever rinsed the cups, didn't make much of a job of it," he remarked. "It was different with the cups from the other woman's cupboard. They were all clean, dishwasher-washed, I would imagine. It was lucky I got to the most recent set before housekeeping collected them."

"Any luck with fingerprints?"

"Well the person who rinsed the insides badly, didn't make a much better job of the outsides. I found two fingerprints on each cup. They don't belong to any of the staff, not the day staff anyway. I haven't managed to see the night staff yet."

"Maybe you won't need to trek over for them, if the sons' prints turn out to be the ones on the cups. What about the playing cards?"

"With the cards being two brand new packs, there were good prints over both sets, three on each. None can be the sales' assistant's or whoever gave them to Mrs Stevenson because they would come in packets wrapped in cellophane. I'm just on my way over to the morgue to get dabs from the deceased than I'll go over to the home and test out the residents. Oh, the Gaviscon bottles contained only harmless tummy medicine, by the way."

Davenport asked Ben to put off taking the prints of the other elderly people living in the home until he had ruled out the family.

"One of the old ladies is already threatening to leave, Ben. Better not get her even more unsettled," he said. "I want to see Adele Stevenson's children today so I'll get their fingerprints taken while they're here. That might eliminate some of the unknown prints. The sons were both in her room yesterday, not long before she died. Have you got anything else for me?"

Ben said that there was nothing else. He was going back to the nursing home that morning after he had visited the morgue. There were some more detailed checks to be made by SOC, now that poison had been found and the death was definitely suspicious. If he found out anything else, he would contact the station immediately.

Davenport rang off and tried to get Martin Jamieson, the police forensic surgeon at the morgue. Having no success, he left a message, then tried Martin's mobile and had to leave a message on that as well. This was frustrating and he went into Fiona's room to share his disappointment with her.

"I want to get Martin to check the contents of the stomachs of both women," he told her.

"I wish now that I'd alerted Martin to this death sooner," he grumbled, taking a seat across from her at her desk.

"You can blame me, Charles. I advised you to wait," she said.

"But I agreed with you and the decision was mine alone," he said, smiling at her.

"What's changed your mind anyway?"

"Ben's now found traces of arsenic in Adele Stevenson's teacup, so we'll have to treat the death as murder. I don't think there could be any chance of arsenic getting there by accident!"

"Do you know anything about arsenic poisoning, love?" she asked. "I certainly don't."

"Me neither. I've never come across a poisoning case in my career. I think I'll go across to the library in the other wing and get out a book on poisons."

Davenport left his part of the large station and went across the quadrangle to the building which housed the large library. It was easy to find a large tome entitled, "Poisons". He carried the book to a nearby table and opened it at the index page. Under, 'Arsenic', he read that it was commonly used as a pesticide and that it was colourless and flavourless. Death followed about twenty minutes after swallowing and it left a metallic taste in the mouth.

"Wonder how they found that out," he murmured to himself.

"100 milligrams is a lethal dose," he told Fiona when he had returned to his own domain.

"Who would want Adele Stevenson dead enough to poison her?" mused Fiona.

"Her sons for a start," answered Charles. "She'd told them, according to her daughter, that she was seeing her lawyer and she'd had arguments with both sons just before she died. About giving them power of attorney, an elderly man at the home thinks. Let's go along and tell the others."

Fiona got to her feet. She staggered a bit and Charles put out a hand to steady her.

"Are you OK, love?" he asked anxiously.

"Yes, just a bit seedy and light-headed. It's nothing to worry about. I felt like that in Penang occasionally and it soon went away. It'll be the little 'un causing it, I'm sure."

She grinned at him.

"Did Anita not have any symptoms during her pregnancy?" she asked quietly, as they were both now in the corridor and she did not want anyone to hear her.

"No, none, except going off fried food, I think."

Davenport called out to the others to come to the Incident Room and soon they were all seated there with Davenport taking his usual stance at the front. He took a felt-tip marker and wrote ADELE STEVENSON on the white board.

"Oh, so the old lady was murdered," said Frank.

"It looks like it, Selby. Ben found arsenic in one of the used teacups in her room."

"What about the other old dear? Has she been killed off too?" Frank was curious.

"Nothing in the cups in her room but they'd been washed thoroughly, it seems."

"Sir, why would the same person want to kill two old ladies?" asked Salma, sounding puzzled.

"No idea, Sergeant. I'm as baffled as you are. It's possible that Adele Stevenson's sons, one or other or both, killed her off to get their hands on her money but they'd have no reason to kill Martha Cowan. She wasn't even known to them, I'm sure. I've had no luck getting in touch with Martin Jamieson but when I do reach him, I'll ask him to test both bodies for arsenic. Just as well that the home is still searching for someone to arrange

Miss Cowan's funeral or she'd possibly have been buried, or worse, cremated, by now. Salma, perhaps you would phone Matron now and advise that the funeral can't take place yet. She doesn't need to know why just yet."

Salma left the room.

There was the sound of distant ringing and Bob came up to the Incident Room to say that Martin Jamieson wanted to speak to the DCI. Davenport went to the front desk.

"Martin, thanks for getting back to me so quickly. There are two bodies in the morgue...yes, the two elderly ladies from Tall Trees Nursing Home. At least one of them turns out to be a suspicious death...the second one, Adele Stevenson."

He listened.

"I wondered if you'd read their details and knew that they'd come from the same place. I'm afraid it's a priority case now...you will? Thanks Martin, you're a star. Yes, phone me at home if you need to."

Davenport returned to the Incident Room and informed his staff that Martin Jamieson was now on the case and would get back to him as soon as possible. He was well-known for being a workaholic and would probably work on into the evening. Luckily his wife, Kath, was very understanding.

Davenport and his team went up to Tall Trees, leaving only Fraser to man the empty fort. It was

Sandra who came to the door and she went for Matron when Davenport told her it was urgent. Mrs Smith came bustling into the hall, looking anxious.

"Your sergeant wouldn't tell me anything, Mr Davenport. Another visit and with the heavy squad this time."

She smiled rather nervously.

"What is it?"

"I'm afraid, Matron, that Mrs Stevenson appears to have been poisoned. There was arsenic in one of the teacups found in her room. Is there any arsenic on the premises, by any chance?"

"Wait a minute, Inspector. I'll get my husband."

Mrs Smith hurried out of the room and came back some minutes later, followed by Victor Smith. She introduced the two men.

"I thought that there might be some sort of poison in the garden shed and Victor says there is. He uses it for..."

"...I used it for a wasps' nest last year, Inspector. Donny, one of our residents, told me about it being the best thing and he had his wife bring some over from his house for me. I'm afraid I forgot it was still in our shed but I did put it away in an old cupboard there. Donny was with me. He told me to put it out of easy reach because it was lethal. We don't have kids here, Inspector and I didn't think anyone would take it by mistake. Do you want me to see if it's still there? My wife told me that Mrs S... sorry...Mrs Stevenson, has been poisoned."

"Yes please, Mr Smith. Selby, go with Mr Smith please."

The two men left.

"How would anyone know the poison was there, Inspector? My Victor wouldn't poison anyone and Donny is hardly likely to kill off a resident, even if he does have dementia. I've never known anyone with dementia to turn murderous."

"Who is Donny, Matron? I'd like to speak to him, please," said Davenport. "Fiona would you and Salma have a scout around in Adele Stevenson's room. Don't touch anything without your gloves on...sorry, I know I don't have to tell you that."

Fiona had sent him a wry look and he knew she would pick him up on that later. The women left the room.

"Obviously Ben Goodwin hasn't arrived yet, has he, Matron?"

"Who's that?"

"The scene of crime man who was here yesterday."

"No, he was here yesterday, as you said and took some cups away but he's not been back. Donny Bryant, to answer your last question, Inspector, is our youngest resident. He's only fifty-four and he has pretty bad dementia but can be lucid at times. He helps Victor in the garden when he's well. Maybe it would be better if you came up to his room. He wasn't good yesterday and we had to sedate him so he's been late in bed and was having his breakfast in his room this morning."

Davenport and Matron left the hallway.

"Any special reason why this Donny was bad yesterday, Matron?" asked Davenport as they went along.

"He insisted that he had two cups of coffee when naturally he had only one and when his carer told him that there was only one, he spilled it over one of the other residents who has a sharp tongue and shouted at him which of course made him worse."

They reached the room, Room 1, and matron knocked gently. The door was opened by a young man. He stepped outside and closed the door.

"He seems a bit calmer this morning, Matron," he said, in answer to her questioning look. "He's eating his breakfast now but I think that he should stay in his room today and Katy can visit him there instead of taking him home again."

"This is Inspector Davenport," said Matron. "Inspector this is Tom Carew, Donny's special carer."

Davenport and Tom shook hands.

"The Inspector would like to ask Donny some questions. It seems that Mrs Stevenson was poisoned, somehow, and Victor said that Donny's wife brought him some arsenic last year."

"Poisoned! Who on earth would want to kill Mrs Stevenson? Does that mean that Miss Cowan was poisoned too?"

Davenport did not reply. He merely asked if Tom's patient was well enough for some questions.

"We...ll. Come in and try. Can I come in too, or Matron, if you'd rather?"

"It's OK for you to come in with me, Tom. I'll try not to upset him."

Matron left them, saying that she would see Davenport before he left.

Tom and Charles stepped inside the room. Donny was sitting at a table by the window. He had a slice of toast in his hand but his attention was fixed on something outside.

Tom approached him quietly, Charles behind him.

"Donny," said Tom. "There's a man here who would like to ask you a few questions."

Donny turned to face them.

"There's a new gardener down there with Victor. I think they've gone into the shed as they're out of sight now. Will Victor still want me to help him in the garden?"

"Of course he will. He values your help. You know that," said Tom.

Charles stepped up to the table and sat down across from Donny.

"Hello, Donny," he said, holding out his hand. Donny took it and shook it firmly. Tom looked relieved. He stepped back.

"It's because you help Victor in the garden that I need you to answer a few questions."

"Fine, fire away," said Donny.

"Do you remember getting him some poison for a wasps' nest last year?"

"Yes. Katy brought it from home for him."

"What was the poison? Do you know?"

"Yes, it was arsenic. It's a very effective pesticide, arsenic."

"Did you see Victor put it away in his shed after he used it?"

"Yes. Last September it was. I advised him to put it high up out of reach but he said he'd put it at the back of his cupboard."

"I don't suppose you ever took it away from there, Donny? Or saw Victor with the bottle again?"

"Gosh no, I would get Katy to buy us some if we needed it at home and I haven't heard Victor saying that the wasps are back."

Donny's eyes wandered back to the window and Davenport got up, thanked him and Tom and left the room.

"He doesn't seem at all wandered or confused," said Davenport.

"That's the cruellest thing about this particular form of dementia. Donny can be as right as rain one moment and bewildered and confused the next. It's called Lewy Body Disease and it's quite rare. It's very hard on his wife. They've got no children to support her either. You could go back in and he could forget he's just seen you. You were lucky."

Salma and Fiona were in the hallway with Matron. Fiona shook her head.

"We didn't find anything interesting. Adele Stevenson must have been one healthy old lady. She had no medicines in her bathroom cabinet and I've just asked Matron if medicines were kept by her, for Mrs Stevenson and she says no."

"I only keep medication for any residents who are forgetful and Mrs Stevenson was a sharp old lady," Matron confirmed.

Fiona seemed keen to leave and as Frank appeared at that moment, they made their way out to Davenport's car.

"Well, Miss Macdonald. What did you find?" Davenport asked her, grinning.

She smiled back. They got into the car before she answered his question.

"Was I that obvious?" Well we found a handwritten will under her pillow. Dated yesterday morning and signed by a Frederick Graham and a Julie Harrison. It leaves everything to Pauline Macartney, except for annuities of ten thousand each to a Mr Gray and a Mrs Hobbs, thirty thousand each to Kim and Lucy Macartney,

Stewart Macartney and Avril Stevenson, Robert Stevenson's daughter, and fifty thousand to her daughter-in-law, Margaret Stevenson."

"How much does Pauline Macartney get? Does it say?"

"It doesn't say, it just says, 'my entire estate'. The envelope was addressed to, ' Browne, James and Knowles'.. No address. I held both the will and the envelope at the corner, Sir."

Fiona's eyes twinkled. He smiled back.

"The law firm should be in the phone book. When we get back to the station, you look into that please, Frank. Salma, go back into the home. Speak to Frederick Graham and Julie Harrison. Ask them about signing something for Adele Stevenson yesterday. Find out, if you can, Frank, how much Pauline inherits. If they say it's confidential, tell them that Mrs Stevenson's been murdered and they have to cooperate with the police."

Salma got out of the car.

"Frank, what about the shed? Was the arsenic still there?"

"Well the bottle was still there, Sir, but Mr Smith thinks, though he can't be certain, that the bottle isn't as full as it was. I've got the bottle here. I lifted it off the shelf. I remembered to put on my gloves, Sir. Don't worry."

Frank held up a large bottle which appeared to be about three quarters full.

"It's got no dust on it, Sir."

Davenport switched on the car's engine and was about to move off when a car came up the short driveway. It was Ben Goodwin's silver Mercedes. He manoeuvred it carefully past Davenport's Audi and stopped. Davenport switched the engine off and got back out.

"Ben, we've found a bottle of arsenic. Frank will give it to you. Get prints off it, will you? Fiona found a will under Mrs Stevenson's pillow. Don't imagine it will have any other prints except hers and the two who signed it but check anyway."

Davenport reached into the car and took the document from his DS. Holding it by a corner, he held it out to Ben..

"OK Charles, will do."

Ben took latex gloves from his pocket, put them on and took the will. He went to the back of the car and opened the door. Frank handed out the bottle. Davenport got back into his car and drove off.

Once in the station, Frank got straight on to the lawyers and when he had finished, he went up the corridor to the DCI's room. Davenport and Fiona Macdonald were sitting across the desk from each other, drinking from two mugs. Both were smiling.

"Sir, I got on to a Mr James. He said that his partner, Albert Knowles, was in charge of Adele Stevenson's affairs. Mr James was sure that he would cooperate fully with the police but he was out seeing another client and would contact you later."

Thanks, Frank. Is Salma back yet?" asked Davenport.

"No Sir, she'll be a while, I imagine. We left her without transport."

Frank grinned when he saw from his superiors' faces that they had forgotten that small point.

"Phone her mobile, Frank and tell her to get a taxi back if she hasn't already left."

Salma returned shortly. Frank had caught her leaving Tall Trees and she had been glad to call a taxi as she knew that she would have looked conspicuous on the bus.

Davenport summoned his team to the Incident Room and asked Salma to fill them in on what had happened with the will.

"Well, Sir, Julie Harrison wasn't at work today but Matron gave me her home 'phone number and I called her there. She confirmed that she had witnessed Adele signing a sheet of paper and had signed it herself. She said she had guessed that it was a will as she had done this many times at the home. Mr Graham apologised for not mentioning earlier that he had signed something for Adele Stevenson. He called her his new friend, Sir. It was quite sad. He said that he had suspected that it was her will and imagined that she was writing her two sons out of it as she had hinted to him that she might do that."

Later in the afternoon, Ben Goodwin came to Shawbank to return the last will and testament of Adele Stevenson. He left it at the desk, telling Bob to explain to the DCI that he was in a hurry now but would come in later. There was no mention of the bottle of arsenic. He also handed over a short note which confirmed that there were three sets of fingerprints on it, at the bottom where the three signers had leant and Adele's prints over the whole 'document'.

Later that afternoon, Albert Knowles rang. It was agreed that DS Macdonald would go to the offices on her way home as they were in Shawlands. Here, Fiona found out that in her penultimate will, Adele had left her estate, valued at £670,000 to her three children with annuities to her gardener and to her former housekeeper. Her three grandchildren had been left £20,000 each as had her son-in-law, Stewart McCartney and her daughter-in-law, Margaret Stevenson. She handed over the hand-written will. Knowles read it and whistled between his teeth.

"Phew. That's going to put the cat among the pigeons. The Stevenson brothers will be furious, though of course they already have the money from the house sale, about three hundred thousand."

"But will it hold up as a genuine will?" asked Fiona.

"Oh yes but they'll probably claim that she was of unsound mind and try to overturn it."

"So, Charles," Fiona told him when she rang him later at home, " her sons, now disinherited, had every reason to kill their mother before she summoned her lawyer and changed her will as she had apparently threatened to do."

"Though we only have Pauline McCartney's word for that, Fiona," replied Charles. "Another thing that's odd is that Robin told us his mother had called him up that afternoon to ask him to give £10,000 to the gardener and housekeeper, yet she left that in her will. Why try to do it before she wrote the new will?"

A silence at the other end of the line showed that his fiancée was perplexed too.

"Well, if she didn't want the sons to know she was changing the will, she would do that to throw them off the scent, perhaps," she said at last.

"Yes, but Pauline Macartney said her mother was going to tell the sons that she was sending for her lawyer to change the will."

Well, the old lady outsmarted them in the long run by writing a new will and having it signed there and then," Fiona said.

"Wonder why she left Margaret Stevenson much more in the new will," commented Charles..

"Maybe wanted to give her the wherewithal to have a down payment for a house," surmised

Fiona. "I imagine she would know that Margaret was browbeaten. You've met Robert Stevenson, Charles. A domineering husband is my guess."

"Stewart Macartney and his niece and two daughters come off better in the last will, too, by an extra £10,000," added Charles.

"But they wouldn't know that was going to happen, wouldn't know, I mean, that she was going to write a new will that gave them more. And anyway, why kill her…"

"…Give up, love. You'll get yourself tied in knots," advised Charles.

"Yes, oh wise one."

"I'm glad that you've recognised that I'm the brains of our outfit," he replied and rang off hurriedly.

# CHAPTER 16

Davenport rang Robert Stevenson the next day. His wife said he was at work but was expected shortly.

"Tell him I want to see him at the station as soon as he comes in, please," said Davenport.

Sounding flustered, Margaret Stevenson said that her husband expected his lunch as soon as he came home. Knowing that this timid woman would bear the brunt of her husband's temper, Charles nevertheless insisted that he come to the station, immediately.

Matthew Stevenson was at home and agreed, very pleasantly, to come to the station right away. He sounded curious but not worried. Pauline asked if she could bring her husband. She sounded anxious and rather frightened and Davenport reassured her, telling her that she could indeed bring Stewart and that it was only a formality. When Fiona had left for her appointment with Adele Stevenson's lawyers, the previous day, he had sent the others home early, telling them to be in sharp the next day. That was said with a warning look at Frank who was not noted for his punctuality.

"And Selby, time for another haircut, son," he added. "Look at how tidy Fraser's is."

Frank looked at Fraser's 'short back and sides' haircut, the epitome of neatness and scowled at Davenport's retreating back. He swept back his recalcitrant lock of fair hair and, taking his cap from its peg, walked off, leaving Fraser looking rueful.

Salma who had witnessed the incident, smiled at him.

"It's not your fault, Fraser. Frank has always got into trouble for his uniform, his hair, his timekeeping and...his racism, long before you joined us."

"Racist, Salma! I've not seen any signs of that. In fact he's been protective of you..."

"...of me, yes but he sees me as a person now, not a black person. I think, given the chance, he would still be racist, and bigoted too, I'm afraid, though he has a Protestant girlfriend."

Fraser laughed.

"Poor Frank. I didn't know that Sue wasn't a Catholic. That kind of thing doesn't interest me. Suppose I'm a humanist if anything. I've only met her once. She seemed very nice."

"Have you got what they call a 'significant other', Fraser?" asked Salma as they left the station together.

He blushed.

"Yes. I've been going out with Erin since secondary school. What about you?"

"My religion puts a stop to that, I'm afraid, though if I meet someone I get to feel strongly about, I'll fight for him against my family, if I need to," said Salma, looking so fierce that Fraser saw another side to his gentle Sergeant.

Charles summoned them all to the Incident Room and told them that he had sent for all Adele Stevenson's children.

"Neat haircut, Frank. Try to keep it like that."

Frank looked down at the ground.

"Martin Jamieson rang first thing. He said he was sorry not to get back to us last night. He found arsenic in Adele Stevenson's stomach along with an antacid and tea, milk and sugar. Apart from that Martin said she was a very healthy old lady. The other woman, Martha Cowan had arthritis in her spine and her hands. She had had at least one heart attack as scarring on the heart showed. There were traces of arsenic in her stomach also and also an antacid.

I asked if the antacid was surprising and Martin said that it wasn't in the least surprising."

"Why's that, Sir? " asked Fraser.

"Apparently, arsenic causes a metallic taste in the mouth, easily confused with what the medical profession calls, 'sour mouthfuls', caused by heartburn or indigestion. Martha Cowan had a thin stomach lining and would be accustomed to taking antacids I imagine, so she would automatically reach for the indigestion remedy."

"And the other woman?" asked Salma.

"Her stomach showed no signs of wear and tear."

"Odd. She asked her daughter to buy her... Gaviscon...I think it was, the day before she died," said Fiona.

"Maybe she ate something that day that disagreed with her. The food at the home might be different from what she was used to," chipped in Frank, his embarrassment forgotten.

"True. Oh, Martha Cowan had had an abortion in her youth. It seems that she was almost a recluse in the nursing home. Only went out once a week for necessities...a bitter old woman perhaps."

"What now, Sir?" asked Fiona.

"Well, I'll see the family when they get in. Salma would you ring Matron Smith. See if they've got anywhere with finding someone to arrange the funeral. I'll meet with you all this afternoon to tell you what transpires with Adele Stevenson's children."

Davenport left, Salma close behind him. Fiona stopped to ask Fraser how he was liking being back with them.

"I really like it, Ma'am. It's not right to say that I enjoy a murder case because some innocent person has to die but it's more interesting than robberies and family feuds and if this double murder hadn't happened, I think I'd have been sent back to my own department, wouldn't I?"

Fiona agreed with him. Frank who had been standing with them, asked his DS how Penny had been when they saw her. He laughed when he heard that she was bored and promised to go along and tell her about their new case.

"If that's OK, Ma'am," he added

Assuring him that it was alright as long as Penny didn't spread the information, Fiona went off to her own room.

Alone in his room, Charles went into his jacket which was round his chair and took out his diary. There were just over two weeks till the wedding. Fiona had bought her dress and Pippa's. He had a speech to write and the final touches to put to the few days' away that he had planned as a surprise for his new wife but nothing else was demanding his attention

He reached for the telephone directory and finding the number for his local florist in Newton Mearns, he dialled and ordered twelve yellow roses to be sent to Fiona in Grantley Street. He knew these were her favourites but had never sent her flowers before so hoped that she would be pleased. He liked yellow flowers too, but preferred the daffodil, thinking it such a cheerful flower.

Shortly after this, Ben Goodwin called.

"Charles. I hope you got the will I handed in earlier. Sorry I didn't have time to stop. Adele Stevenson's prints were on the two cups. Her prints were also on the new playing cards, so only one set to identify on one cup and two sets on the cards. Both books had the fingerprints of both women. Miss Cowan obviously looked after her books as there were no other prints on hers. Mrs Stevenson's book had more: hers, whoever brought it to her, I would guess, and obviously the shop assistant's. The fingerprints on the cups don't belong to the day staff at the home. We already knew that. Do you want me to go up there, tonight and take the prints of the residents and night staff?"

"No. As I said earlier, I want to get the prints of the family first. I've got the two sons and the daughter and son-in-law coming in any time now. I'll get their prints first. Should rule them out...or in."

"OK. As I said to Bob, the fingerprints on the will were what you would expect from someone writing it and two signing it."

"I've asked at the Home and I know who the two signers were but you'd better check. You have Julie Harrison's prints as she works there and you could get Frederick Graham's discretely, without alarming the other old dears. Anything else?"

"There were no prints on the bottle of arsenic, which shows, I would think, that that's where the poison came from, as I would have expected to find some on it. The murderer obviously wiped the bottle clean before replacing it."

"Thanks again, Ben. Oh, Martin confirmed the arsenic. It was in the stomachs of both women."

"Right -oh. I'll be in tomorrow some time."

"Before you go, how was the concert?"

"It was pretty boring, I have to admit. I'm not a music buff...or art or drama come to that."

"Does your new friend like fishing?" laughed Charles.

He heard footsteps coming up the corridor and, apologising to Ben, rang off, getting to his feet as Bob came in, bringing with him an irate Robert Stevenson.

"Thank you, Bob. Wait till a Matthew Stevenson and a Mr and Mrs Macartney arrive, then get off home. I'll wait till Ken arrives to take over the desk, if he hasn't arrived by the time I've finished."

Bob thanked him and left.

Robert Stevenson refused to sit down.

"What was so important that I couldn't have my lunch?" he demanded.

"Your mother's death, Sir," said Davenport, quietly.

"I know Mother died but that wasn't unexpected at ninety-four.."

"No but the arsenic found in her cup was unexpected, Sir."

"Arsenic?"

Robert sat down suddenly. His face which had been florid had drained of colour.

"I'd like you to come downstairs with me to give me your fingerprints, Sir."

"Fingerprints? What for? You surely don't imagine that I put poison in my mother's tea, Inspector."

"Did I say it was tea, Sir? Did you have tea with her that evening?"

"No I didn't have tea. I didn't stay long enough for refreshments. My mother drank tea more often than coffee. That's why I said tea."

Davenport escorted the man, complaining loudly, downstairs where he watched him having his fingers pressed into the pad then onto paper. He led him back upstairs and they met Bob talking to Matthew Stevenson.

"Hello, bro. What's this all about?" Matthew asked jovially.

"Mother was poisoned, Matt."

Poisoned? Mother? I don't believe it," said Matthew, his grin fading.

"It's true, Sir and I need the fingerprints of all the family. Did you have anything to drink when you were with your mother the day she died?"

"No I didn't. I wasn't there long enough, Inspector. I met Robert as he was coming out and I left shortly after him. Mother didn't want to play cards after all. I was a bit aggrieved. But not enough to kill her," he added, quickly..

Like his brother, he had his fingerprints taken and they left together, Robert Stevenson threatening to call his lawyer about the way he had been treated.

The two brothers must have met their sister and brother-in-law in the forecourt as she was pale and shaking when they came into the station.

"Mr ...I'm sorry, I've forgotten your name."

"Davenport, Mrs Macartney."

"Sorry, Mr Davenport. My brothers have told me that Mum was poisoned. Would she have suffered?"

Charles noted mentally that she was the first of Adele's children to be concerned about how her mother had died.

"It would have been quite quick. She would perhaps have felt a bit unwell before losing consciousness, a bit sick perhaps. I'm sorry but I have to have your fingerprints and yours, Mr Macartney."

"Of course, Inspector," said Stewart Macartney, standing with his arm round his wife.

Davenport took them both downstairs.

"That's all for just now," he told them. "I'll come to see you again once the will's been seen. That might throw some light on the murder."

"Oh Stewart, Mum told me that she was going to tell Robert and Matt that she was going to disinherit them. She told me that her lawyer was coming up on Friday...today."

"Are you sure, Mrs Macartney?" asked Davenport.

Pauline looked distressed.

"I thought she was just pretending. She said she wanted to worry them, wanted to have them dance attendance on her... to pay them back for forcing her into Tall Trees."

Davenport thanked them and, looking thoughtful, showed them out before going back to his room, putting on his jacket and waiting another fifteen minutes till Bob's replacement arrived to man the desk. It was not his place to tell Mrs Macartney about the new will. He knocked on Fiona's door and, going in, told her to get her jacket as he was taking the whole team out for lunch.

Lunch over, they met in the Incident Room once again and he told them what had happened when the Stevenson family had come in.

"Their reaction to being asked to give their fingerprints summed up their characters," he said.

"Robert was blustering and threatening to get his lawyer, Matthew was cordial and Pauline was worried about how her Mum had died. I didn't tell them about the new will. I'll leave that to their lawyer, poor man!"

Later that day, Charles went to the school to pick up Pippa. She was on her own and sat deep in thought as he drove home, coming out of her reverie as he stopped outside the house. He asked her what she been thinking about and she told him that she thought that her friendship with Hazel might be ending.

"We're never in the same part of the school at the same time, Dad so she's in a different playground a lot of the time and she's joined the hockey club on Tuesdays after school and I've joined the Book Club on Thursdays after school. Oh, I don't need picked up till 5 o'clock on Thursdays."

"Does not seeing Hazel upset you, pet?" he asked.

"A bit, Dad but I really like Kerry and she's joined the Book Club too. She's not sporty either but she has a bike so we can meet up for bike rides like I did with Hazel."

He supervised her homework and listened to her excited chatter about that day's school. She had stopped being morose and was back to her cheerful self, obviously settling down in her new school and from her previous conversation, clearly accepting that her friendship with Hazel could not be as close as it had been.

When she went to bed, he rang Fiona and told her what Pauline Macartney had said about her mother deciding to alter her will.

"And it seems that she did do just that," he added.

"It was interesting how they all reacted to the news that their mother was poisoned."

"Yes. As you would have expected having met them all. Robert blustered, Matthew was charming and Pauline was worried about whether or not her mother had suffered at the end. What I didn't point out to the others was that none of them seemed curious about who could have done it."

"At least someone cared about the old lady," commented Fiona, "but I agree, that it's funny that none of them said, 'Who on earth would kill Mother?' or 'Why would anyone kill Mother?' Oh, Charles, on another subject altogether, I have another admirer. A beautiful bunch of yellow tea roses arrived minutes ago."

"Wicked woman! I asked them to put, 'From Charles, with love'" Charles informed her.

"Well, all it said was, 'With love'", laughed Fiona.

Telling her he loved her and reminding her that there were only seventeen days till their wedding, he rang off and going into the lounge, poured himself a whisky and lemonade.

# CHAPTER 17

" **R**obert Stevenson, said he hadn't poisoned his mother's tea and I hadn't mentioned tea but he covered up by saying that she nearly always drank tea. Salma, check that up with Matron and Pauline McCartney, will you, please."

The team were once again in the Incident Room. It was Saturday, three days after the murder and Davenport had driven Pippa down to Newlands to play with Hazel Ewing as had been arranged the previous weekend, noting as he did so that she was not as enthusiastic about his plans for her as she would once had been.

"What if Hazel's got Vicky there?"

Even though she had explained last night about not being as friendly with Hazel as she had been, for once Charles was short with his daughter.

"Surely you can manage to be a threesome if she is! I'm not asking you to stay with a three-headed monster."

The journey down to Newlands had taken place in silence. It was unlike Pippa to sulk but she made a good attempt at it and got out of the car as soon as it stopped. Charles had rung Ralph Ewing, so Pippa was expected and the door opened as the car drew up and he was pleased to see Hazel run towards the car, looking delighted to see her friend.

"Sorry, love, to be so grumpy. I'll pick you up around four o'clock," he said, through the open window. "Fiona's coming home with us tonight and we'll have takeaway of some sort. OK?"

"OK Dad," she replied, sounding happier.

Now he had his team to organise. He continued.

"Fiona. I want both sons brought in again. Interview them both, official:, tape recorder, the lot and get their version of what happened when they visited their mother on the evening of the murder. I want that book that was found in both ladies' rooms read. It's a long shot but as they were both reading it, maybe it can shed some light on the case."

Frank's face showed panic. Salma, watching him, could only guess that he had never read an intellectual novel all the way through. Davenport must have shared her thoughts.

"Frank, will you...no, only joking. I imagine you would be the sort who would buy the comic version of any home-reader you were set at school... Fraser, will you read the book please, if you haven't already read it."

"Sorry, Sir I haven't read anything by Camus."

"Well, skip-read this one. If you don't know French, buy the English version."

"I do read French, Sir," replied Fraser, earning a glower from Frank who had often proudly declared that his second language was Glaswegian. "It was my other subject in joint honours' year."

"What about me, Sir?" Frank asked.

His usual insouciant nature returned and he added, "You were right, Sir. Dell comics were a great help with "Kidnapped" and "The Tale of Two Cities". I'm more of a doer than a reader, Sir."

Davenport grinned.

"OK, Action Man. You get off back to Tall Trees. I want Frederick Graham questioned but not here on account of his age and I think he has some kind of disease that makes him unsteady on his feet. He seems to have been closest to Adele Stevenson in the short time she was there. Salma, go with Frank to the nursing home and see if you can have a friendly chat with the other residents. Find out if they know anything at all about Martha Cowan and bring back a copy of that book."

Fraser was hovering. Charles smiled at him.

"Something troubling you, young man?"

"Sir, I thought about what you said about the family's reaction to their mother's murder, once I got home last night and do you not think it was odd that none of them asked who could have killed their mother or why anyone would want to kill her?"

"Well spotted, Hewitt."

Fraser blushed. Frank, who had heard the conversation, looked torn between wanting to stay and listen to his boss's reply and wanting to leave in case he had to listen to Fraser being praised again.

"Well Sir, it was similar in, 'Macbeth'. He and his wife murdered their king and when they were told about the murder, she said, "What? In our house!" and someone was suspicious and said, "Too cruel anywhere."

"What did that mean?" asked Frank, interested in spite of himself.

"The person was pointing out that it didn't matter where it had happened. I felt it was as if one or all of them knew that their mother had been murdered, especially the men. I mean Mrs Macartney's reaction was caring rather than curious and that was natural, I suppose, but the other two weren't upset so should have been inquisitive, shouldn't they, Sir?"

Davenport laughed.

"That's what the DCI said to me last night, Fraser," explained Fiona. "Good for you spotting it."

"I'm going to bear it in mind when I question them today," added Davenport.

"What are you going to do, Sir?" asked Fiona.

She was now finding it awkward calling Charles, "Sir" and knew that Frank would have a field day with this behind their backs. She could hardly call him Charles, however. He smiled at her, seeming to realise what she was feeling and addressed her as DS Macdonald when he replied that he would be interviewing the other Mrs Stevenson while her husband was at the station.

Fiona rang Robert Stevenson. She got his wife first. Margaret Stevenson sounded anxious as she informed Fiona that he was just about to set off for his weekly golf match and even more nervous when she was asked to tell her husband that golf was not to be on his agenda that morning.

"Oh dear, I can hardly tell him that. He plays every Saturday."

"Mrs Stevenson, his mother's been murdered! Surely he can understand that that takes priority over his golf game."

Then, taking pity on the woman and feeling glad that she would never feel like this with Charles, she asked Margaret to call Robert to the phone.

"What is it now?" he demanded in a blustering voice.

Angry at his tone and sure that he would not have taken that tone with Davenport, Fiona told him that he was needed at the station as soon as possible and the imp in her added, "and that doesn't mean after golf, Sir."

"Don't be impertinent, Sergeant..."

"...*Detective Sergeant* Macdonald, Sir. You must understand that for the foreseeable future your first priority is helping us solve this murder."

There was silence at the other end of the phone.

"OK. I'll be right over," he grunted.

"Ask your wife to remain at home Sir. My DCI wishes to speak to her too."

"What on earth for?"

"I can't speak for my superior, Sir. I'll see you shortly."

Robert was almost puce with rage and as usual he took it out on his wife. He stormed into the kitchen. Remembering all too well the night before, she looked down submissively, saying quietly, "Robert dear. I'm sure George won't mind rescheduling your game in the light of what's happened."

She added as she usually did when he lost his temper, "Remember your blood pressure."

"I don't want the whole world knowing my business, you idiot."

Margaret glanced down at the work surface on which The Herald lay. The murder of Robert's mother was splashed over the front page under the headline TWO DEATHS AT LOCAL NURSING HOME: RESIDENT FEARS FOR HER LIFE. He had not seen it yet but his eyes followed hers and he snatched the paper up, almost snarling.

"Stupid bitch! Does she think there's a short-sighted Jack the Ripper killing off old bags?"

"Lovely way to describe Grandma, Father," came the laconic voice of his daughter from the doorway.

Robert spun round but whatever he had thought to reply died on his lips when he saw his daughter's cold look. He muttered something under his breath and brushed past Avril.

"Oh dear, now he's even more furious," bleated Margaret.

"Tough shit."

"But it's not you he takes it out on Avril. It's me."

"You must stand up to him, Mother. I've told you that time and time again."

"But he doesn't..."

"...doesn't what? Hit me like he hits you? Oh yes, I know he hits you. I'm not deaf or blind. I left because I couldn't stand knowing what went on behind the closed bedroom door and guessing the rest."

Margaret looked so distressed that Avril put her arm round her.

"Maybe he'll be arrested for killing grandma and you'll get some peace."

"Oh dear, do you think it's possible?"

"Yes. I do."

Avril walked out of the kitchen and just after she left, Robert put his head round the door.

"I'm off. The chief wallah's coming round to see you this morning, Margaret. Remember to tell him that I wasn't long at the home, that day."

"But I was asleep when you came in, dear."

"I know that. But you won't mention that. If you're a good girl and say what I told you to say, I'll maybe let you sleep alone tonight."

She shivered.

Matthew Stevenson had been asleep when Fiona Macdonald had rung him. Unlike his brother, he was charming and obliging, saying that he had had nothing planned for the rest of the morning and even if he had, he knew that this was more important. When he hung up, however, he looked worried. He knew that he had only his brother's word for it that they had passed each other in the hallway at Tall Trees and no one's word for it that he had not stayed long at the home. If only he had signed that dratted book on the way out but then the police might suspect that he had simply written in the wrong time. Living alone, he had no one to support him about the time that he had arrived home.

The two brothers converged on the police station, Robert seeing Matthew's back as he went through the outside swing doors. It did not improve Robert's temper that Matthew, arriving first, would be interviewed first.

"I'm the elder brother," he said pompously. "I should take priority," he informed Fiona who had been summoned to the desk.

"I'm speaking to Matthew first," she told him briskly. "Bob, please show Mr Robert Stevenson into the waiting room and give him tea or coffee if he wants a drink."

Downstairs, she ushered Matthew into Interview Room 1 where she had already placed a tape recorder. Fraser, with nothing to do until the book arrived, had been allocated the job of sitting in on the interview and he was already in place.

"DS Macdonald and PC Hewitt in attendance. Interview with Matthew Stevenson, August 23rd, 10.22am. Mr Stevenson, you went to visit your mother on Wednesday 20th August?"

Matthew nodded.

"Please speak for the recording machine," Fiona told him.

"Sorry. Yes, I visited my mother on that date, in the evening about 8pm. I ran into Robert, my brother, in the hallway. I didn't know he was going up to see Mother that evening. He told me about their argument about the annuities for two old servants."

"And what did you say to that?" asked Fiona.

"It didn't bother me," replied Matthew. "I think I moaned about having to play bezique but in the end mother didn't want to play..."

"...she said in her diary that she had played it with you, Mr Stevenson." Fiona interrupted him.

Matthew looked puzzled.

"She must indeed be...sorry...she must indeed have been becoming senile."

"Sorry, I interrupted. Carry on."

"Well she made me go back down and sign the visitors' book. I did that then came back and sat down across the table from her but she said she didn't want to play bezique after all. I was rather annoyed at having been called up for nothing."

"What did you do? Did you have a drink with her?"

"No. She wanted a drink of water. I brought her that."

"She wrote in her diary that you all had supper together."

"We didn't. I wasn't in her room at the same time as Robert and I had nothing, I can assure you."

"Did you touch the cards?"

"No...yes..."

"Which?"

"No, I didn't. At least I don't think I did. There were two packs lying on the table."

"She wrote in her slim line diary that you would be coming up the following Thursday to play again."

"Well she never mentioned that either," Matthew said.

"Did she complain about having an upset stomach?"

"Mother? She had the constitution of an ox. She didn't have an upset stomach in her life, as far as I know."

"So you left when?"

"I didn't look at my watch but I couldn't have been there for longer than twenty minutes."

"Did you go straight home?"

Fiona was not sure but there might have been a second's hesitation.

"Yes I did but there was no one there to prove that I'm afraid. I live alone except for a woman who comes in to clean for me every morning and no one phoned or came to see me."

Fiona finished the interview.

"Thank you, Mr Stevenson. You can go now. We'll be in touch again, no doubt."

Matthew said goodbye and shook their hands. Fraser went with him back upstairs. Robert was sitting, rigidly, in the waiting room, an untouched cup of coffee in his hand. As the door was open, he saw them coming. He rose as they approached.

"This is a piece of nonsense. I don't know why you want to see both of us. You should be busy trying to find our mother's killer. I'm going to write to..."

"...Robert, the police are just doing their duty," said Matthew.

He patted his brother on the shoulder and telling him he would no doubt see him soon, he walked out of the station.

Fraser motioned to Robert Stevenson to follow him and the two went downstairs and into the Interview Room.

"Sit down please, Mr Stevenson," Fiona said politely. She made the customary speech for the tape recorder and then sat back, looking relaxed. Fraser, beside her, followed her lead. Robert, across from them, was once again rigid, his hands clenched together on the table.

"Mr Stevenson did you visit your mother at Tall Trees Nursing Home on Wednesday 20th of August?"

"Yes, I did."

"Please tell me what happened," said Fiona pleasantly.

"I got there at about 7.10pm. She made a big fuss about me not signing the visitors' book so I had to go all the way back downstairs to sign it. She told me that she wanted her old gardener and her daily help given £10,000 each. Seemingly she had promised them this if she ever sold the house. I pointed out that it was us, Matt and I, who had sold the house. That put her in an angry mood. I was angry too. I thought the amount ridiculously high."

"What happened then?"

"It was really odd," he said, unclenching his hands.

"What was?"

"She asked me to bring up her lawyer to get the power of attorney sorted out."

"Why was that odd, Mr Stevenson?"

"I'd brought Mr Knowles up that very afternoon to do just that and she refused to do it."

His face became suffused with an angry red.

"She had asked me to bring the lawyer up yet she denied it and..."

He stopped suddenly. His hands were clenched again.

"And what, Sir?"

"Nothing. She refused to sign the power of attorney, that's all. I was so embarrassed."

"Going back to the evening of that day, Mr Stevenson, did you stay for a drink with your mother?"

"She didn't offer me anything. She just asked me to bring her a cup and put the kettle on as she felt like a cup of tea. I wouldn't have stayed for anything anyway," he added petulantly.

"Yet she wrote in her diary that the three of you had supper together."

"She really had lost her marbles," he said, cruelly.

"So when did you leave her?"

"I wasn't there long. I met Matt in the hall on my way out. My wife will tell you that I arrived home about 8.20."

"Your mother wrote in her diary that you played bezique with her, Sir. She wrote that she played the game with both you and Matthew, separately, and that she made Matthew wait till your game with her was finished."

Robert looked astonished.

"She was playing solitaire, what she persists in calling patience. She said she didn't want to play bezique. Said she'd already played that afternoon with one of the other residents."

"Which one?"

"Fred Somebody. I can't remember his surname."

"Another thing, Mr Stevenson, did your mother mention having indigestion or heartburn?"

"No she didn't and if she had it would have been a first. My father suffered from an ulcer and he had indigestion but not mother."

"One last thing, did you touch the playing cards at all?"

"No I did not...wait...I did. She knocked some onto the floor and I picked them up."

Fiona concluded the interview.

The three of them rose and Fraser ushered Robert out of the room and upstairs. He seemed eager to go and hurried away to the door.

"Odd. No history of tummy trouble, Ma'am, no game of cards either, according to both sons and neither had supper. Do you think the old lady *was* going senile?"

"Either that or they're both lying for some reason, trying to make us believe that they only stayed for a short time."

"Robert has his wife to back up the time of his arrival home," added Fraser.

"Yes, it will be interesting to hear what the DCI gets from her. I imagine that he'll be back soon. He had only one interview to do to our two."

As if on cue, the outside door opened and Davenport came in.

# CHAPTER 18

Charles had taken the fingerprints to Ben Goodwin at his laboratory in the police college, in Glasgow, on the banks of the Clyde and Ben had promised to check them against those he had taken from the cup and playing cards and let his friend and colleague know the results later that day. It was a short drive to the Stevenson house in Giffnock. Charles hardly recognised the young woman who answered the door. She was wearing black trousers with a white shirt blouse and looked very business-like.

"DCI Davenport, isn't it?" she smiled. "Please come in. I hope you don't want my father."

"Who is it, dear?" called a voice from the kitchen.

"Excuse me. I'll fetch my mother."

The woman slipped from the room and came back with Margaret Stevenson who was wiping her hands on her pink apron.

"This is DCI Davenport, Mother. He was here the other day, remember?"

"Margaret held out her hand and Davenport shook it. It felt tiny and brittle, an old woman's hand. He was careful not to squeeze it too hard.

"My husband's not here, Mr Davenport...but then you must know that. Is it me you want to speak to?

"Yes, it's you I want to see, Mrs Stevenson."

The tiny woman looked frightened. She glanced round at her daughter who took her hand.

"Can my daughter stay, please?"

"As long as she doesn't interfere. Is it Miss Stevenson?"

"Yes, Inspector, Avril Stevenson, their only child. Come into the sitting room. It's cosier than the front room."

They walked in single file through to the back of the house and went into a room which housed the TV and some comfortable chairs. They sat down.

"Mrs Stevenson. Would you tell me when your husband arrived home on Wednesday evening?"

It was a simple question but she hesitated slightly before replying that Robert had come in about eight o'clock. Asked if she was sure about the time, she said that she remembered because Coronation Street had just finished. She had made him some supper, she told Davenport.

"What did you make him?" he asked her.

"Oh...a bacon sandwich. His favourite," she replied.

"Miss Stevenson, were you in the house on Wednesday evening?" Davenport asked Avril.

"No, Inspector. I was out visiting a friend. It's a pity. I'd have enjoyed a cosy bacon sandwich."

She glanced at her Mother who looked back at her steadily.

"Did you know what was in your mother-in-law's will, Mrs Stevenson?"

"Oh no. She never discussed it with me."

"But father must have known, surely," put in Avril.

"If he did, he never told me, dear," Margaret was looking distressed.

Thanking them for their time, Davenport left the house. He was almost at the station when his phone rang. He pulled over and switched off the car engine. It would have been embarrassing to be caught answering his mobile phone while driving, he told Fiona later.

It was Ben Goodwin.

"Robert Stevenson's prints on one cup, Matthew's on another, Charles. Neither on the cup with the poison but on the other ones which had been used."

"So at least one of them, probably both, must have drunk tea with her and dropped the arsenic

185

into her cup when she wasn't looking," Charles said.

"You'd have thought he'd have cleaned the cups thoroughly, in that case." argued Ben.

"I don't think Mr Robert Stevenson has ever done any housework in his life. He has a very, as we Scots would say, shelpit wife. No doubt if it was him, he thought he had rinsed the cups well. Matthew lives alone so would probably wash up more thoroughly. What about the cards?"

"Both Robert's and Matthew's prints were on the cards. There were a couple of prints belonging to Pauline Macartney on the book but hers were not on the cups or cards."

Thanking him for his speedy work, Charles rang off and, restarting his car, set off for the station once again.

After a quick cup of coffee which he shared with Fiona, Charles summoned the others to the Incident Room. There, he added the name of Martha Cowan under Adele Stevenson's

"Right team," he said as they settled in their chairs. "We apparently have two murders. Arsenic was found in both bodies. The cups from Miss Cowan's room were washed free of prints but one cup from Mrs Stevenson's room had a fingerprint belonging to her elder son Robert Stevenson and another had Matt's prints on it. Neither was the cup which contained the poison."

"So one of them killed his mother!" said Frank eagerly.

Yes, Selby, either could have dropped the poison in and possibly wiped the poisoned cup."

"To incriminate the other brother, do you mean?" asked Fiona.

"Again, not necessarily. The guilty man wouldn't know for sure that his brother had touched a cup. Remember that whoever washed the cups did not make a good job of it but obviously didn't realise that."

"What about the playing cards and the book, Sir?" asked Salma.

"There were prints of both sons on the cards and only the daughter's on the book. Now what about all of you? Frank first. What did Frederick Graham have to say?"

"He said that she left him that day, saying that she was going to make both sons play bezique with her as they hated it. She had told him about refusing to discuss power of attorney with the lawyer and... wait for it, Sir...she said Robert looked as if he'd like to murder her."

"So, she wasn't being demented when she refused to sign the deed; she did it on purpose. Anything else, Selby?"

"The old man has a good memory, in spite of his disease. It's called Parkinson's disease, Sir. He remembered that Adele Stevenson told him she'd found out that Martha Cowan's sister had died and that she had disinherited her niece. The sister had lived in Leningrad."

Davenport wrote under Martha Cowan name -

"Disinherited niece
Sister lived in Leningrad"

He wrote under Adele Stevenson's name:

"New will disinherits sons but not daughter or grandchildren
She says they played bezique - they deny this."

He wrote a new heading: "Both" and under this wrote -

"Both had Gaviscon and had drunk some, though AS had no history of indigestion.
Both reading, 'The Outsider', in French."

Davenport stopped writing.
"Did you bring the book for Fraser, Selby?"
"Yes, Sir."
"I've started it, Sir. It shouldn't take long. It's a short novel."

Davenport sat on the table in front of the others and looked at Salma.

"Sergeant, who did you manage to speak to?"

"Well Sir, in spite of being scared of being murdered in her bed, Miss Williams seemed anything but timid. She said she thought the murderer was a man called Donny Bryant. She said he was peculiar and saw things. She had never spoken to Martha Cowan and the only other thing she said was that Claude Ferguson was a disgusting old man, Sir, whose nose was put out of joint when he found out that Adele Stevenson was older than him."

"Right. Who else?"

"Claude Ferguson seemed delighted that Adele Stevenson was dead. He didn't venture any opinion about the murderer except to say that Adele was annoyed with her sons for putting her into the home but that there was nothing she could do about it. The only other person I saw was a Mrs Mohammed, Shahida Mohammed. Like Martha Cowan, she seemed to keep herself to herself but had gone into Mrs Stevenson's room on the first evening to give her the newspaper page for the TV. Mrs Stevenson had told her she wouldn't be staying. Mrs Mohammed said that Adele Stevenson had sounded quite bitter. Although they had lived together for some months, she had never spoken to Martha Cowan and was surprised to learn that

Adele had actually got into Miss Cowan's room. That's all, Sir."

You didn't see Donny Bryant then, Salma?"

"No, Sir. He had gone home with his wife just before I arrived. Matron seemed to think he would be better off the premises while the investigation was taking place and Katy, his wife was going to get a nurse in and keep Donny at home till we'd gone."

"Thanks. Now, DS Macdonald, what transpired at the interviews?"

"Excuse me, Sir," said Salma "Before Ds Macdonald makes her report, you asked me to find out about Mrs Stevenson's drinking preference and Mrs Smith at the home said to ask her carer, Sandra Keith so I did that. She said that she usually drank tea, especially in the evening when she took her supper up to her and she went on to say, Sir, that on the night before she was found dead, Adele Stevenson rang the kitchen to say that she didn't want supper brought up because her sons were with her and they were having supper together. Do you want me to check with Mrs Macartney, Sir, about whether tea was always her preference?"

"No. If tea was her usual choice in the home, it was probably what she usually drank so we can't pick up Robert Stevenson on that comment he made about tea. Thanks, Sergeant"

He looked at his fiancée and nodded.

"From what Salma has said, it appears that both sons are lying about the card playing, being together in their mother's room and having supper," she said, then went on, "I saw Matthew Stevenson first, Sir."

"He was very cooperative. He denied playing bezique with his mother and pointed out that she had dementia, or senility he called it," Fiona said, looking at the notes that Fraser had taken at the interview. "He said he was a bit annoyed at being called up for nothing, especially as he'd climbed the stairs twice when she insisted that he sign the visitors' book. I asked if he'd had a drink with her and he said, no. He didn't think he'd touched the cards but wasn't sure. He had noticed them lying on the table. He brought his mother a cup of water which she asked for just before he left."

Fiona stopped.

"Anything else?"

"When I asked about his mother ever having stomach trouble, he laughed and said she had the constitution of an ox and when I asked if he went straight home, I think he hesitated...Fraser, what do you think?"

"Yes, Ma'am, I thought he hesitated but only for a second. I could be wrong."

"Was that all?"

"Yes, Sir. Robert Stevenson was completely different. He was obviously uncomfortable in the

Interview Room, sat quite rigidly and kept his hands clenched most of the time, except when he was talking about the lawyers' visit."

"What happened then?"

"He said that his mother had asked to see her lawyer then when Robert took him up, that afternoon, she denied it and refused to sign the power of attorney over to her children."

"But he was uptight at the rest of the interview, you said?"

"Definitely. He had an argument with his mother about the amount she wanted given to her gardener and daily help. Then she seemed to have forgotten seeing the lawyer in the afternoon and asked Robert to get him up to get the power of attorney seen to."

"Anything else?"

He didn't have a drink with his mother. He said he brought her a cup and put the kettle on at her request. He denied playing that game..."

"...bezique, Ma'am," offered Fraser.

"Yes, bezique. He said she told him she'd already played with Mr Graham that afternoon."

"Yet according to Mr Graham, she said she was going to make them both play," Davenport said.

"He had never known her to have indigestion or heartburn and he did touch the playing cards as she knocked them off the table and he picked them up and left. That's all, Sir."

Davenport added to Adele Stevenson's list :

Indigestion??
Going senile??
Supper??

"All I got from Margaret Stevenson," said Davenport," was that Robert came in around 8pm. She made him a supper of bacon sandwiches, she said. The only jarring note was that her daughter sounded a bit ironic when she said she wished she had been in… for a "cosy bacon sandwich"… were her words. Mrs Stevenson claimed not to know anything about the will and the daughter put her oar in and said surely her father must have known what it contained.

Ben Goodwin rang me. Robert and Matthew's fingerprints are on cups and cards. A few of Pauline's are on the book."

Davenport added to his list for Adele:

Sons' fingerprints on cups and cards
Daughter's fingerprints on book.

He looked at his team.

"Sir," said Salma. "Why would her sons be so careless about cleaning their cups?"

"Ben asked that too and I said that Robert Stevenson had probably never washed a cup in his life…"

"…and Matthew Stevenson told me that he had a woman who came in every morning to clean for him," added Fiona

"Lucky beggar! Every day? I'd live on my own if I could have that," said Frank.

"So neither of them was used to cup-cleaning," said Fraser.

"Right," concluded Davenport, "it's late, folks. Get off home. I think things can wait till Monday. Enjoy a day off."

Chattering like a troupe of monkeys, Salma, Fraser and Frank made for the door and Davenport held out a hand to Fiona. She rose from her chair, looking a bit weary.

"Come on old thing. I promised Pippa I'd pick her up at the Ewings' and we'd get a takeaway. Do you mind letting her choose what kind? She'll be feeling neglected."

"Not at all. I don't feel like decision-making and less of the 'old thing'. I'm only just older than you are!"

Laughing, they went to their respective rooms to collect their jackets.

# CHAPTER 19

Charles and Fiona picked Pippa up in Newlands, having dropped Fiona's car off in her street. Pippa seemed happy and chattered away from the back seat. She and Hazel had gone out for lunch in Shawlands with Hazel's Mum and Dad. Charles was not very fond of pizzas so they seldom went to Di Maggio's on the corner of Pollokshaws Road and Minard Road which was where the quartet had gone.

"Hazel and I shared a huge pizza with bacon, cheese and pineapple and her Mum and Dad shared a smaller one – pepperoni I think it was called," she informed them. "We spent all day talking about school. How sad is that!" she laughed and Charles thought how grown-up she sounded. Fiona,, looking at his face, noticed a sad expression come across it. She wanted to remind him that he had another child coming along to fill the space of the child Pippa but as it was still a secret from everyone, she made do with squeezing his hand as he changed gear at the first set of traffic lights.

"So you'll not be ready for another meal then?" Charles suggested.

"Dad, it was hours ago and I'm hungry again," she told him.

"Well, what's it to be, Chinese, Indian or good old fish and chips?"

"No prizes for guessing what your dad wants, Pippa, eh?" said Fiona.

"I think he wants Indian, Fiona," giggled Pippa.

They both knew that Charles had little stomach for spicy food as he had kept away from it during their holiday recently in the Far East.

"OK you two, stop ganging up on me and tell me where to stop for our meal," Charles said, mock severely.

"You win, Dad. Fish and chip shop it is."

Charles drove up to Sheddens' roundabout, to his favourite shop and he and Pippa got out after finding out that Fiona wanted a mini fish supper. There was a long queue and they had to stand outside for a few minutes. As they moved into the shop, the Italian owner, called out to ask what they wanted.

"A mini fish supper, fish supper and a child's sausage supper," Charles told him.

"A special fish please," called out the man behind them.

Slowly the queue snaked round until Charles and Pippa were at the front. Two teenage boys had come in behind them. They were talking loudly and rather rudely, the F word taking pride of place in every second sentence.

"Fucking hell, mate. This queue's like going for ever, like," said one, the taller of the two. Both were wearing denims and hooded jackets. Inevitably the hoods of their jackets were up, even though they were inside and the evening was warm.

Pippa looked round and the smaller boy nudged his pal.

"Hey Spud, you've got a wee lassie looking at you. Maybe she fancies you."

He roared with laughter, his spotty face peering out from under his hood.

"In your dreams, Spotty," retorted Pippa.

"Who're you calling Spotty?" demanded the boy.

The two boys moved forward, menacingly.

Pippa stood her ground and just stared them down. They backed away and stood muttering. Charles was given his meals and, without interfering, he made his way out of the shop, Pippa following him.

"Pippa, I know you felt that you were in the right there but please be careful, especially if you're on your own or with one of your pals. Sometimes these neds can turn violent. I was there this time and they backed off but please, not all bullies can be tamed the way you tamed Ronald when you were in primary school."

Ronald had become her friend until he left for secondary school after she had stood up to him as a new girl at primary school. He had carried her schoolbag home on many occasions.

"OK, Dad. No problem," Pippa said now.

They got back into the car along with the tempting aroma of chips and vinegar and it took only minutes to reach home in Newton Mearns. Charles gave Pippa the front door key and she leaped out and opened the door. Fiona got out wearily, reaching back in for her briefcase and handbag. Charles came round and took her arm, steering her round the car to the door. Jackets off, they all congregated in the kitchen. Pippa wanted baked beans with her sausage and chips so she got a large plate from one of the cupboards and a small saucepan. Soon the beans were sizzling away and she spooned them onto the plate and added the contents of her wrapped meal. Charles and Fiona made do with just opening their parcels and eating their fish with their fingers.

Seated round the breakfast bar, they were silent for a time and then Pippa demanded to know what they had been doing all day. Charles told her that two old ladies had been poisoned and that they now had a double murder case on their hands. As usual, he gave his daughter no details and she did not ask. She and Hazel had once tried to do some sleuthing on their own, during one of her father's cases and he had been annoyed with them so she had taken little interest from then on.

"Are you back at the station tomorrow then?" was all she asked now.

"No. I've given the team Sunday off," he replied. "Maybe we can all go to the pictures together."

"Let me off, Charles," said Fiona. "I've got a lot of wee things to do for the wedding, people to phone and I want to visit Caroline too because I haven't seen her for ages and I don't want to see her at the wedding, without having had a chat first. I know we've got two weeks but this case might take up more of our time than we think right now."

"Fine, love. Well, Daughter, what about you? Are you deserting me too or will you come with me to the pictures?"

He could see on Pippa's face, the struggle going on in her mind and knew that she was probably weighing up the desire to see a certain film against not wanting to go out with her father in case she was spotted by schoolmates.

"Only last year she wouldn't have worried about that," thought Fiona, feeling sorry for him.

"OK, Dad. If I can choose the film," she decided.

"Why don't you ask Kathy if she wants to come? You didn't see much of her this holiday," he suggested.

Kathy was quite a recent friend, from the same neighbourhood and Pippa had been away most of the summer holiday so they would have a lot to talk about and as Kathy went to Mearns Castle they would probably not meet up much during term time.

"Oh, yes please, Dad. I'll go and phone her now," said Pippa, putting her dirty plate under the tap and running the water over it before putting it into the dishwasher. She went upstairs. Like most youngsters these days, she preferred using her mobile phone to the landline in the hall.

"Less embarrassing than to be with Dad on his own," said Charles, ruefully. He and Fiona finished their meal in companionable silence.

Pippa came hurtling downstairs and erupted into the kitchen.

"Kathy says yes and we both want to see, 'Toy Story 2'," she informed her father who looked less than delighted.

"You'll enjoy it, Dad," Pippa told him. "Kerry's Mum went with her last Saturday and she enjoyed it."

"How are you getting on with Kerry?" asked Fiona.

"Great. We sometimes meet up with Hazel and Vicky at lunchtime but not at playtime 'cos we're often in different parts of the school the period before. I was telling Dad that yesterday."

"What about Ronald? Have you bumped into him at all?" asked Fiona.

Pippa blushed.

"He came over on Friday afternoon and said, hello. He was with another boy called Scott."

Sensing that the youngster did not want to continue the conversation, Fiona tactfully changed the subject, asking if Pippa had put her bridesmaid's dress away somewhere safe. The talk went on to the wedding. Pippa was thrilled to be playing an important part in the wedding, especially as Hazel would be there with her mum and dad. Hazel had already been a bridesmaid and had told Pippa all about it ad nauseam.

It was quite early when Fiona said she would have to go home. Charles helped her on with her jacket and saw her into a taxi.

"Enjoy your day tomorrow, my love," he said. "See you on Monday."

# CHAPTER 20

O n Sunday, Salma took the chance to visit her Aunt Zenib and Uncle Fariz with her young brother, Rafiq and sister, Farah. Her aunt was a godsend when Salma was on a case and she babysat often, especially when Salma's older sister, Shazia, could not help out, having moved from the family home shortly after the sudden death of their mother. Shazia was a primary schoolteacher and Salma suspected that she was getting friendly with an Asian colleague who was deputy head at the same school, as she was seldom available for child-sitting duties at the weekends.

"Any word from Shahid?" asked her aunt when they were seated at the table for lunch. Shahid was what Salma referred to as a 'trolley-dolly', with British Airways and lived in London, although at present he was on leave after his wedding to Bushra in Pakistan in early August. When he came back, he was going to wind up his affairs in London and move back home to Glasgow where he was to be stationed. Salma was relieved that he would be there to take some of the responsibilities off her shoulders but was also anxious that he would try to curtail her freedom. They had had some rows after her mother's funeral and she thought that she had brought him round to her way of thinking but now that he had reverted to being what he called, a 'good' Muslim and with a very young schoolgirl wife to protect, he had become more conservative in his religious views. He would no doubt want Salma to be a role model for Bushra, and Salma was none too keen to be cast in this role.

Now she answered her aunt.

"The wedding went well. He has lots of photographs for us to see. They should arrive in London next Wednesday. Shahid has two weeks to work out, then they'll move here."

Zenib looked pleased. Shahid had always been her favourite, Salma knew. She was grateful to her aunt who had taken her side in her argument recently with her uncle and brother but wondered if with Shahid living at hand, she might not be persuaded to change her allegiance.

Lunch over, Salma took Farah and Rafiq back home to Glasgow's West End. Here she supervised some homework that they had omitted to do, as usual, and then the trio settled down to watch Sunday evening TV. Penny rang after the youngsters were in bed and demanded all the details when Salma told her that they were, once again, involved in a murder case.

"Frank came up this afternoon and told me you had a double murder case on but, you know men, hopeless with detail," she complained.

Salma, warning her friend not to tell anyone about the case, filled her in on the details.

"There's a bit of tension between Frank and Fraser, Pen. Frank's got an inferiority complex because Fraser's got a degree. Fraser never tries to lord it over him but Frank's still prickly with him. It doesn't help that the boss obviously thinks highly of Fraser."

Across the city, Frank was trying to explain this to his girlfriend, Sue Wilson.

"Fraser's a know-it-all, Sue. He can speak French and knows all about poetry and stuff like that."

"Well, silly, I know all about Maths but you don't think I'm a know-it-all, do you?" she laughed and tossed back her long, auburn hair which had as usual fallen across her cheeks.

"Well, Maths isn't involved in this case," he grumbled.

"And is poetry and French?" she enquired.

"Not really but there's a book come into it and the boss wanted one of us to read it and it's in French."

"So?" she asked.

"So… I couldn't read it, could I, so Brainbox Hewitt got to do it."

"So he's having to spend his Sunday reading a clever-clever book! Would you rather be doing that right now?" she asked, pushing back his errant lock of hair gently and kissing him on the nose.

"If you put it like that," he grinned and kissed her back. Fraser was forgotten and the rest of the evening was spent listening to their favourite music. They were in the flat Sue shared with her brother Pete who was in his bedroom with his girlfriend, leaving them the lounge and the CD player. Frank had not yet introduced Sue to his parents although he had met hers a few times. Frank came from a very devout, Catholic family and Sue was a Protestant. Frank was sure that his father, especially, would disapprove strongly.

Fraser Hewitt lived in Newlands, not far from the Ewing family, Ralph, Sally and Hazel, in a large sandstone house. His parents approved wholeheartedly of his girlfriend, Erin, whom he had known since fourth year at secondary school. They had gone through university together, Fraser studying English and French, doing double honours in these subjects, Erin doing English too but going on to Jordanhill

College instead of doing honours. She had been very lucky to do teaching practice in a secondary school with a good reputation, then be given a permanent post in the same school. Fraser had always wanted to join the police force. They both knew that they were two of the lucky few who enjoyed their jobs.

Tonight she had come over to Fraser's house after her evening meal, with a carrier bag full of jotters. They had gone to the cinema on Saturday night and had agreed that they would both work on Sunday evening. She was at a table, correcting S4 essays on Macbeth's ambition and he was sitting on the floor with his back against the settee, reading, 'The Outsider', in French.

"This is boring," he said now. "Not much of a story! I think I must have got out of the habit of reading intellectual novels."

"Me too, after reading books suitable for first and second years. Even the older kids' novels aren't very intellectual. The only one with any meat to it is, 'To Kill a Mockingbird' which I'm doing with my Higher class this year."

"Fancy a break? I'll get us a tea or coffee. I've only got about twenty pages to go."

At that moment, his mother came into the room, a small lounge on the ground floor, armed with a tea tray on which resided two mugs and a plate of biscuits.

"Ready for an intermission?" she asked with a smile.

"Mum, you're an angel," laughed Fraser.

They had their supper, sitting on the floor on two cushions, then Fraser picked up, 'The Outsider' and Erin returned to her dwindling pile of jotters. Fraser finished first. Not wanting to disturb Erin, he walked over to the table and picked up one of her discarded jotters.

" 'Macbeth was a wimp who did what his wife told him to'. Are they allowed to use colloquial speech like that?"

"As long as they sound genuine, they'll get away with it. It's their opinions the markers want. I've only got two left to do. Give me peace for a few more minutes, Fraser."

Erin put the last jotter on top of her finished pile and got back down on the floor beside Fraser.

"Did you get anything relevant to your case from the novel?"

"Nothing at all!"

"I wonder why both old ladies were reading it then?" mused Erin, to whom Fraser had told that part. "Was there anything else strange?"

Fraser looked worried. He was fiddling with the book.

"I don't suppose I should be telling you anything about this case, Erin."

"You know I won't tell anyone anything!"

"Well, both old ladies had been taking Gaviscon, though the second lady didn't have tummy trouble."

"That's weird. Unless she asked the first woman to recommend something as she had an upset tummy because of something she ate at the nursing home."

"I suppose so. Have you any logical suggestion about why they would both be reading an obscure book – in French?"

Fraser threw the book onto one of the chairs, grabbed Erin, pulled her up from the floor and sat himself and her on the settee.

"Let's relax now, forget about our jobs and watch TV."

He picked up the remote control and switched on the TV. They were soon engrossed in, "Taggart" which, surprisingly, Fraser enjoyed.

"Though the police always swear in it. I can't see our DCI approving of that," he said now.

Fiona had spent a relaxing evening with Caroline whom she had met when Caroline's husband had been murdered. The woman had been vulnerable and lacking in friends and Fiona had befriended her, especially after the case had been solved and Caroline cleared of blame. Caroline had quite recently rmarried a Paul Whittaker who was a teacher as Caroline's dead husband had been, though in a primary school in Paisley where they now both lived.

"Fiona, I've got some special news for you. I'm pregnant," said Caroline when they were seated.

"Oh Caroline, I'm so pleased."

Caroline looked a bit misty-eyed.

"What's wrong? Is there a problem?" Fiona asked anxiously.

"No. The baby's fine. I've had the amniocentesis test and no…I don't know if it's a boy or girl," she added seeing, from her friend's expression, that that was the question to be asked next.

"It's just that David always wanted children and I let him think that I'd come off the pill. I really was a cow to him, Fiona."

Fiona had tried to console her, reminding her that David had loved her very much and would be the first to excuse her. At that, Caroline had burst into tears, then apologised, saying that her hormones were all over the place. Fiona looked thoughtful.

"I haven't told anyone else this, Caroline and won't till after the wedding but…I'm expecting a baby too."

As she had hoped, this news cheered Caroline up. She promised to tell no one, except Paul.

The evening ended as Fiona returned from Caroline's, Charles, Pippa and Kerry returned from the cinema where Charles had indeed enjoyed, 'Toy Story 2' and Fraser arrived home after walking Erin home, carrying her bag of jotters for her. Salma went to bed early and Frank stayed the night with Sue, planning to rise early the next day to be on time for work.

# CHAPTER 21

The last few mornings had been tense in the Macartney house. Added to the upset caused by Adele's death and the ensuing discovery that this death had been murder, Kim and Lucy were expecting their exam results. Surprisingly, now that the advent of these results had arrived, it was Kim, not Lucy who was most anxious.

"Oh, Mum. I wish now that we'd arranged to have the results sent by email," wailed Kim. "When's the postman due again?"

"Darling, keep calm. You worked hard for your exams and whatever you get I'll be proud of you," said Pauline, patiently. "The postman doesn't arrive at the same time every day and if he has lots of exam results to deliver that could hold him up. Where's Lucy?"

"She's still asleep! How can she sleep in at a time like this?"

"Did someone mention my name?" a sleepy voice enquired.

Lucy was standing in the kitchen doorway, in her pyjamas, yawning and holding two buff-coloured envelopes.

"Did no one hear the letterbox? I guess this is what we've been waiting for, Sis."

She held out one envelope to her sister who shrieked, grabbed it and ran out of the room. They heard her footsteps pounding up the stairs and then the bathroom door closing. Stewart, who had been in what they called their den where he wrote and his wife painted, came out and asked what all the noise was about. On hearing that the exam results had arrived, he put his arm round Lucy as she opened her envelope.

"Mum, Dad, I've passed everything! I've got…. three As and 2 Bs."

"Oh darling, I'm so glad for you," said Pauline.

Lucy looked suddenly sombre.

"Kim hasn't come out of the bathroom. Oh gosh, I hope she hasn't done badly."

She ran out of the kitchen and up the stairs. Her mother and father listened anxiously as Lucy knocked quietly on the bathroom door. They heard the door being opened, then closed again.

Silence.

Pauline switched on the kettle and put some bread in the toaster then she took a tea towel and started to dry two cups on the draining board while Stewart set their tiny kitchen table for breakfast, a meal they always tried to have together. Neither of them spoke. It seemed ages but was probably only a few minutes before they heard the upstairs door open again and footsteps coming downstairs. Lucy had her arm round her sister who had been crying.

"Oh, pet. Don't cry and you're shaking. Come on sit down and tell us what happened."

Pauline sat Kim down on one of the chairs. The others sat down. Lucy, always impatient, said, "She's done fine. Tell them Kim. They think you're upset because you've failed everything."

Kim looked up through her wet lashes.

"I'm so sorry, Mum. I got so nervous, then when I saw these, I just burst into tears."

She handed her certificate to Pauline who read it out.

"English A
History A
French A
Biology A
Art B"

Stewart laughed in relief. He had always told his daughters that as long as they had studied hard, paid attention in school and tried their best, he did not care what results they got but he had known that Kim, in particular, would be disappointed if she, in her words, "let them down".

"My two brilliant girls! Must take their brains from their old Dad."

Pauline swiped at him with the tea towel.

"I did quite well at school, too, thank you," she said. "And Kim takes her artistic flair from me. You couldn't even draw a straight line!"

"I wish we could tell Grandma," said Kim, wistfully.

"Pet, I'm sure she knows," said Pauline, gently.

"Talking of Grandma, we'd better have breakfast and get ready. We're meeting Robert and Matt at Robert's house in….about an hour," said Stewart looking at his watch.

"What's a will-reading like, Dad?" asked Lucy, helping herself to the cereal.

"I've no idea, Lucy. I was an only child, remember, so everything came to me when your Grandpa Macartney died, with my mother dying some years before him," said her father. "I imagine that we'll all sit around your Uncle Robert's lounge and the lawyer will simply read out what your Grandma has left everyone."

"It should be quite straightforward. My mother always intended to leave her estate among the three of us, Robert, Matt and me and I imagine that she's left you two and Avril something as well."

They tucked into breakfast which was a calmer affair than it was when the twins had to get to school and were invariably late. With their favourable results, Kim would start at teacher training college at the end of September and Lucy would start at either Glasgow or Strathclyde University in October. She had said nothing more about travelling the world recently, probably because, for once, her easily-led twin had been adamant about not wanting to see the world before settling down.

Breakfast over, they departed for bedroom and bathroom and were getting into the car at 9.50. The drive to Robert's house took only ten minutes and they met Matt getting out of his car. Stewart threw an envious look at Matt's new Mercedes, one of the dearest of the range. His own eight-year old Passat looked very shabby in comparison. They all walked up the drive, Matt and Stewart in the lead.

Margaret had seen them coming and held the door open. She was sombrely dressed, in a black wool dress with a string of pearls at her throat.

"I knew I should have worn a skirt," muttered Pauline.

"Don't be silly, Mum. You look fine in your black trousers," said Lucy.

"Aunt Margaret never wears trousers at any time, Mum. Uncle Robert wouldn't let her," added Kim.

They all trooped into the hall. Robert came out of the lounge, looking stern as always.

"Mr Knowles is here already. He's a busy man. We mustn't keep him waiting."

"Ten o'clock you said, Robert, and ten o'clock it is," smiled Stewart who was not afraid or in awe of his pompous brother-in-law. He led his family into the lounge, smiled at his niece and the lawyer and sat down on the settee with Pauline and Kim, Lucy choosing to sit on the arm of the settee, apparently not noticing her uncle's frown at her choice of seat. Matt sat in the chair matching the one Avril sat in and Robert and Margaret settled themselves on two chairs brought in from the hall.

"Everyone's here. Let's get started," said Robert.

"No, Sir. Everybody's not here. We're waiting for a Mr Gray and a Mrs Hobbs," said the lawyer.

"What, her old housekeeper and the gardener! Why should they be here? Mother promised them annuities, that's what she called me up to discuss then other day…"

"… and have you seen to that Father?" enquired Avril, sweetly.

"No, I haven't had time."

"Well, just as well Grandma has them in the will then or they might not have received anything at all," Avril commented.

Robert scowled at her but at that moment the bell rang and he got up to open the door for two elderly folk who looked embarrassed as Avril fetched two more chairs from the hall and settled Mrs Hobbs into the comfortable seat she had been sitting in.

"Now everyone *is* here so I'll make a start," said Mr Knowles.

He picked up a page of notepaper.

"That's not my mother's will, Knowles!" said Robert.

"I have to disagree with you Mr Stevenson," said the lawyer, politely. "This document is headed, 'the last will and testament of Adele Stevenson' and is signed and dated Tuesday nineteenth of August of this year."

"The day before my mother died," whispered Pauline to Stewart. "She *did* change it."

The lawyer coughed.

"I will continue. 'I, Adele Stevenson being in my right mind, do hereby bequeath my estate to my daughter, Pauline Anne Macartney with bequests of fifty thousand pounds to my ...'"

The lawyer coughed again.

'...long-suffering daughter-in-law, Margaret Stevenson.'

Margaret gasped, caught her husband's eye and sank back on her chair. The lawyer was continuing.

'Thirty thousand pounds to my three granddaughters, Avril, Kim and Lucy and to my son-in-law Stewart Macartney and ten thousand pound each to my faithful Mrs Hobbs and Mr Gray. My two sons, Robert and Matthew Stevenson got the proceeds from the house they sold over my head this month and are to receive nothing more.'

This will is signed by Adele Stevenson and witnessed by two people who have signed and dated the will."

"But that's p..preposterous!" stuttered Robert. "She must have been going senile to write that."

"I thought you knew that she was in the first stages of dementia, Father," said Avril. "Didn't you tell mother and me that the doctor had…"

"Shut up!"

Robert had risen from his chair.

"Matt and I will contest this…this…will," he said, menacingly.

"If you like," said the lawyer. "But I can assure you that it will hold water and all you will gain is a costly legal bill."

"I won't be contesting anything, Robert," said Matt. "I would say, 'Game, set and match to Mother," he added, in a tone of admiration.

Pauline, sounding embarrassed, asked what her mother's estate came to. The lawyer informed her that it was around six hundred thousand pounds, once all the bequests had been deducted, adding that the funeral expenses would also come off that amount.

Margaret, looking anxious, left the room, hurriedly. Avril followed her and returned with a trolley holding crockery and two plates of scones and pancakes.

"Mother is bringing in tea and coffee," she informed them.

Mr Knowles thanked her but said that he had other commitments. It was Stewart who showed him out. He returned to a room bristling with unvoiced comments. Margaret brought the tea and coffee and poured out with a shaking hand though not even her critical husband reprimanded her for spilling tea into the first saucer. Avril poured the remainder of the hot drinks, then pulled a chair across to the settee and started talking to her two cousins whom she had not seen for some years. Matt drank quickly, refused anything to eat and left, saying nothing to his elder brother who was staring out of the window. Pauline had engaged Mrs Hobbs in conversation and Stewart was speaking to Mr Gray.

Half an hour later, Avril summoned a taxi for the two elderly retainers. She showed them out, thanking them for their hard work and loyalty to her grandmother. When she went back into the lounge, the Macartney family had risen and she went with them to the door.

"It was nice to see you all again. I'm leaving for The Philippines but not until the New Year, thank goodness. Mother will need me now, more than ever and if necessary I can put off taking up my new appointment until things are settled here."

Without anything being said, Pauline realised that her niece was telling them that she would protect her timid mother from her father. On the way home, she voiced this opinion to her family.

"I rather think that Avril will encourage Margaret to leave Robert," she said.

"I agree Mum," said Lucy. "I hope she does... Aunt Margaret...leave Uncle Robert."

"Yes, Grandma left her money so that she could be independent," voiced Stewart.

"Will you leave me, now that you've got thirty thousand pounds," teased Pauline.

"What? No way! I want to help you squander your inheritance," laughed her husband.

Kim had been silent.

"Kim. We can go on that round the world trip now before we settle down at college and Uni," said Lucy, excitedly.

"No, Lucy. I said I didn't want to go travelling and I meant it even though we're now well-off," Kim said quietly. "I have other plans for Grandma's money."

"What, love?" asked Pauline.

She was astonished at this first sign of a disagreement between her twin daughters. Kim had certainly been against the travel plan but she had thought, on hearing about their inheritance, that Kim would change her mind.

"I'll tell you later. I have a visit to make first. Dad would you drop me off at the next bus stop, please?"

That evening, over dinner, Kim dropped her bombshell.

"I went to see Brian," she said. "I proposed to him."

There were three gasps at this news.

"You what? *You* proposed to *him,*" Pauline said, amazed.

"I knew you were serious about Brian but I wasn't expecting that, love," was Stewart's response.

Lucy was silent.

"You know we've always loved each other. We planned to get married after college. Brian has decided to go in for teaching too, but secondary teaching: History. His results were really good. He got six A passes so will go to Glasgow Uni for four years, hopefully, then a year teacher training. Getting Grandma's money made it all seem less of a dream, so I proposed to him today. We'll get engaged sooner than we'd planned and the rest of the money will be a wonderful start to our savings towards a home of our own."

She turned round to face her sister.

"Lucy, please be happy for me."

Lucy gave her a quick kiss then got up and left the room. Pauline and Stewart told Kim that they were glad for her and would be delighted to have Brian as a son-in-law in five years' time, then Pauline got up and went upstairs to find her other daughter. Lucy was lying on her bed staring up at the ceiling.

"Lucy. What's the matter? You knew that Kim wasn't keen on globe-trotting and you knew that she was serious about Brian."

"I know, Mum. I like Brian but I kept hoping that it would fizzle out and Kim and I could share a flat when we left home. We've been together all our lives. It'll be awful without her."

Lucy burst out crying and Pauline sat on the bed and hugged her.

"Love, they're not getting married for five years. You'll still have her until then. Maybe by that time, you'll have found some young man to fall in love with and you could have a double wedding."

Lucy gave a tiny giggle through her tears.

"A joint wedding! Kim in her meringue outfit, with three bridesmaid and two page boys in kilts and me in denims and a tee shirt!"

Pauline laughed too at this reminder of her twins: so close, yet so different in many ways.

"Sorry, Mum. I was being selfish."

Lucy got off the bed and went to the dressing table to wipe her eyes. She went downstairs with her mother and the rest of the evening was spent in discussing Grandma's murder, Uncle Robert's fury, what Pauline and Stewart were going to do with their windfall and whether or not Aunt Margaret would set up house on her own and divorce Uncle Robert.

# CHAPTER 22

Davenport stopped on his way to his office on Monday morning, to ask Salma what she had found out about the funeral arrangements for Martha Cowan. He had forgotten all about it on Saturday and so obviously had his sergeant, as she apologised for not telling him what Matron had told her. The nursing home had been left about one and a quarter million pounds much to Mrs Smith's amazement and delight and the unknown niece was to receive ten thousand pounds if she ever turned up.

"Did that old man in the home not tell us that Miss Cowan had disinherited her niece?" Salma said now.

"Mr Graham, Frederick Graham, it was who told me that," piped up Frank who had been listening to their conversation. "It seems that Mrs Stevenson found that out the day she visited Miss Cowan."

"Well, it must have been a very old will…no that can't be it as Miss Cowan wouldn't have left money to Tall Trees until she had stayed there, would she?" mused Davenport.

"No, Sir so she must have changed her mind about leaving her niece something. I wonder what caused her change of heart," mused Salma, adding that Matron had promised to 'phone them if anything came to light about the niece. The lawyer had an address for the niece as next of kin but he had tried to contact her there and she had long since left.

"Matron said that she had asked Miss Cowan about her next of kin but the old lady had been quite brusque with her and refused to discuss it, saying only that her lawyer was her executor and he had a copy of the will and the niece's address. Martha Cowan asked that her copy of the will be kept in the Home's safe and made no secret of the fact that it was Tall Trees that would inherit when she died."

"So what about the funeral which was my original question?" asked Davenport.

"Well, Sir, Matron Smith is putting off making any arrangements, to see if the niece can be contacted. The lawyer suggested that she wait a few more days then she can decide what to do."

At that moment, Bob appeared in the doorway with the news that a Mrs & Mrs Macartney were at the desk wanting to speak to the DCI. Davenport left and the others saw the three walk past,

Davenport talking to Pauline Macartney and Stewart Macartney bringing up the rear on their way to Davenport's room.

Davenport pulled two chairs across in front of his desk and sat down behind it, motioning to them to sit down.

"Now, Mrs Macartney you say it's about your mother's will. Is there a problem?" asked Davenport.

"Yes, Sir, there's a big problem, " said Pauline Macartney. "My mother left nothing to my two brothers. She said that they had got enough with selling her house over her head. She …"

"..She left her entire estate to my wife, Inspector with bequests to myself, our daughters, our niece and Margaret her daughter-in-law. Oh and something to two old family workers," added Stewart.

Davenport whistled. Pauline looked upset.

"Phew. Leaving something to Mrs Stevenson and nothing to Robert would have fairly put the cat among the pigeons!"

"It did, Inspector," said Pauline, shakily. "Robert threatened to have the will challenged, on the grounds that my mother was not in her right mind but Mr Knowles said that he doubted if it could be changed."

"What about your other brother? How did he react?"

"Matt took it really well. He sounded as if he admired Mother for what she had done. He told Robert to accept it. I thought you ought to know, Mr Davenport."

"Thanks, Mrs Macartney and you too, Sir, " said Davenport, looking from one face to the other. "Who is going to make the funeral arrangements?"

"That's another thing we wanted to ask you, can we go ahead and arrange Mum-in-law's funeral or do we have to wait until the murder is solved?" asked Stewart.

"No. You go ahead. Is it you who are doing it?"

"Well, Matt left Robert's house right after the will was read and I doubt if he would even think about arrangements having to be made and Robert was so angry that I doubt he will have anything to do with it," said Pauline.

"Except criticise everything on the day, I expect," said Stewart, wryly.

"Well, please let me know when things have been decided. One of my team will attend," said Davenport.

Pauline and Stewart Macartney left and Davenport summoned all his team to the Incident Room.

When they were all seated in front of him, he sat on a desk, swinging his legs. His hand strayed up towards his left ear and he pulled on the ear lobe.

"Well team, the family now knows about the most recent will of their mother and have taken it the way we would have expected. Robert is furious about being disinherited and says he will contest the will, Matt has accepted it and Pauline, I imagine, feels guilty at being the one to inherit the estate. I wouldn't like to be in Margaret Stevenson's shoes."

Seeing a look of puzzlement on Fraser's face, he explained to his PC who had not been present when they had discussed the finding of the handwritten will, that Robert Stevenson's timid wife had been left a large sum of money.

"I believe, if I remember what I read correctly, that Adele referred to her daughter-in-law as 'longsuffering' or words to that effect."

"Maybe she'll have the guts to leave him now," said Salma.

"Why should she leave him? He's worked all his life and given her a big house. Bet she's never done a day's work in her life," said Frank.

"Selby, your sexist views are showing again," said Fiona, acerbically. "You never saw them together. The woman is afraid of him. I think he expected a lot for the 'big house' and her not having to work."

"Right, Salma, I want you to go up to see the lawyer, Mr Knowles. He saw Adele Stevenson not long before she died. Ask him if she hinted at making changes to her existing will and find out what relations were like between Adele Stevenson and her eldest son. Fraser, you go over to Tall Trees and speak again with Mr Graham who seems to have become quite a close friend, in spite of the short time she was in the home," ordered Davenport.

Salma and Fraser left the room quickly, to get their jackets and hats.

"What about me, Sir?" asked Frank, sounding like Penny did when she thought she was going to be left out of any action.

"Nothing for you at the moment, Selby. You'll have to man the fort. No reports to write up?"

Frank grimaced. He had not, as his boss had guessed, written up any of his reports on the case. He had seen Fraser printing off his no doubt beautifully written account of the interviews he had attended and knew that his own finished article would not stand comparison, especially without his friend Penny to put his scribbles into some semblance of order. He had visited her recently and wondered if she would have done them for him if he had taken them with him. Too late now. He sighed and left the room slowly, failing to see the amused smiles on the faces of his DS and DCI.

"Poor Frank. He isn't the sharpest knife in the cutlery drawer, is he?" said Fiona.

"Not when it comes to paper work but he's improving in other areas," replied Davenport. "I think he misses Penny's help."

"What about us? If Frank is to defend the castle, I guess you have something in mind for us," laughed Fiona.

"I want you to pay a visit to Matt Stevenson. I think he wasn't quite truthful about what he did after seeing his mother. See if you can get him to be more forthcoming in the light of the fact that, being disinherited, he might have had a reason for wanting his mother dead, quickly, before she could do this."

"What are you doing, then, Charles?"

"Like Frank, I'm not very happy with my chore. I'll have to go up and see Knox. He was away last week so I could put it off but no doubt he will have expected me to have solved the case in the week he wasn't here!"

"Poor you!"

"Never mind. We'll have a lunch, just the two of us, when we get back," said her fiancé, giving her a peck on the cheek before they left the room.

# CHAPTER 23

Charles was humming cheerfully as he went up in the lift. He was getting married in a few weeks and even the thought of his forthcoming meeting with the man he described alternately as God or a lion in his den at the top of the building, didn't deflate his spirits.

The lift doors opened on the second floor and a man got in. Charles recognised him as Roger Dickson, the inspector who had twice lent him Fraser Hewitt when he was understaffed. He had only met the man on a couple of occasions and found him difficult to talk to.

"Roger, how's it going?" he asked now, smiling broadly.

"OK, though I prefer to be busier than we are right now. You seem to get all the good murders."

Charles laughed but Roger remained impassive. He obviously had not been joking.

"*Good* murders, Roger. Bit of an oxymoron, surely," he retaliated.

"An oxy...what? You sound like Fraser Hewitt. He's always coming out with stuff like that. I'm a bread and butter sort of policeman. None of your fancy university stuff for me."

He looked huffy, as if suspecting that Charles had been making fun of him in some way.

"Probably thinks I called him a moron," thought Charles.

"Oxymoron is just using a contrasting adjective to describe something. You know, saying, the darkness was bright, that sort of thing.

"Why would you say that, man?"

"For effect, I suppose," said Charles, lamely, wishing that he had not attempted to explain.

"So why was saying a good murder an example of it?" Roger asked now as the lift came to a halt at the top floor.

"Just that murder can hardly be described as good, can it? Where are you off to, Roger? It can't be to see God as that's where I'm going." The words were hardly out of his mouth when he knew he shouldn't have used them.

"God? What do you mean now, Charles?" said Roger in bewilderment.

"It's my metaphor...my nickname... for Knox as he's so high up here and he's in charge."

"More of your fancy language, Charles. I think you'd better keep Fraser and let me have your least clever constable in his place."

As they were now almost at the suite of rooms occupied by the chief constable, Charles was saved from replying to this stupid comment. They could not exchange constables as if they were football cards in a school playground!

He knocked on Knox's door, just as Roger stopped at another door, obviously on his way to see Solomon Fairchild, the assistant chief constable. Hearing Knox's secretary say, "Come in," Charles entered the outer office. The boss's secretary, maybe through constant association with Knox, was almost as stern as he was. She looked up, unsmiling. He thought fondly of the last secretary who had been almost timid in comparison and certainly friendlier.

"Do you have an appointment, Inspector Davenport?"

"You're much too efficient not to know that I haven't, Miss Leonard. I just came up on the off chance that Mr Knox would see me."

"He's a very busy man, Inspector. He has a meeting with the local MP in half an hour."

"Is he doing something right now, then? I'm quite busy too, with two murders to solve."

The irony of his words was lost on her. She seemed almost disappointed when she told him that, at the moment, the chief constable was having his midmorning coffee and she would buzz through and see if he would speak to Davenport.

This she did and informed him that Mr Knox would see him.

"Go in," she instructed him.

"Davenport, what is it man? I haven't got long. Got the local MP coming up shortly. He wants me to talk at a public meeting on policing in the Govanhill area."

He did not invite Charles to sit down but then he never did and he was going to sit drinking his coffee while offering Charles nothing. He sat down behind his desk, making Charles feel like an errant schoolboy called to see his headteacher. Had he been visiting the assistant chief constable, they would both be sitting at his coffee table, with a coffee each.

"While you were away, Sir, two murders were committed at a nursing home in Netherlee: two elderly ladies, both poisoned by arsenic within a day of each other."

"When did this happen, Davenport?"

"One happened about a week ago and the other one, last Wednesday. I…"

"…have solved the case, I hope, as the scent will have gone cold by now if you haven't," said Knox. "Not that you're noted for your speed in solving cases," he added, sarcastically.

"I may not be as quick as you'd like…Sir… but since I arrived here, there have been five murder enquiries and I and my team have solved them all. In fact, six cases, if you count the murders in Malaysia."

Charles realised that with the pause before he called Knox, 'Sir', he was getting as bad as Frank Selby had been at first when he had shown a reluctance to call Charles, 'Sir' and DS Macdonald, 'Ma'am'. Knox had bridled and had obviously noticed the pause. This was the man whom he had been persuaded to invite to his wedding, thought Charles.

"OK…OK…Well, if you haven't solved these two recent murders, how far have you got?"

"To start with, we thought that Martha Cowan, the first woman to die, had died of natural causes as she had a history of heart trouble but when Adele Stevenson died almost immediately afterwards, it seemed a bit too much of a coincidence, especially as she had no known heart problems. Martha Cowan left the bulk of her sizeable estate to the nursing home…"

"…which is called what?" demanded Knox.

"Tall Trees, but the second woman left most of her estate to her daughter, disinheriting her two sons."

"Did they know that they'd been left out of the will?" barked Knox.

"No but we heard from the daughter that her mother had told her she was informing the two men that she was sending for her lawyer to change her will."

"A will in which they were left an inheritance?"

"Yes."

"So, good God man, one or both must surely be a prime suspect in her murder!"

"Naturally, Sir, but what motive could either have had for murdering the first woman?"

"Coincidence, obviously," said Knox, dismissively.

"Oh yes, Sir, some coincidence that both died of arsenic poisoning. Happens every day!"

Knox's already florid complexion deepened and his piggy eyes seemed about to pop from their sockets.

"I will not stand for your insolence, Davenport. I…"

A buzzer on his desk sounded and just as his secretary's voice began speaking, the door opened and in came the assistant chief constable, Solomon Fairchild.

"Sorry, Grant. I know you're busy…hello, Charles. I've just had Roger Dickson in my office wanting to know if you've heard anything yet about application forms for the …"

"…not in front of another member of staff, Solomon, please," said Knox, reprovingly.

Charles got to his feet. He had the feeling that Fairchild with his uncanny sixth sense had come to rescue him and he took his chance now.

"I'll go now, Sir. I'll keep you informed with the progress of the case."

"Or lack of it," growled Knox but made no move to stop him leaving.

Fairchild smiled at him.

"Not long till the big day, Charles?"

This wrong-footed the chief constable who now felt obliged to thank Davenport for his invitation.

"Yes, thank you for the invitation, Davenport. "Who's the lucky woman?"

"Got his finger on the pulse as usual," thought Charles, wryly, as he replied that the 'lucky woman' was his DS, DS Macdonald. How different from Fairchild who had known about the engagement almost before him and Fiona!

Charles escaped.

# CHAPTER 24

Fiona rang Matthew Stevenson's home at around midday and found him at home and willing to stay there till she arrived. She commented on him having a good job if he could take time off as easily as this and he told her that his father had financed him in setting up a small travel agency which now specialised in very expensive short holiday breaks in Scotland.

"I didn't qualify as an engineer, unlike my brother who took over the firm when my father retired. Dad left him the company but neither Pauline nor I minded. I do very well and have two women who run the place very efficiently with or without me."

"What does Pauline do?" asked Fiona.

"She's never worked. Stewart was a surgeon till he retired and was well paid. When he retired early, they just seem to have rumbled along, Pauline with her painting and Stewart with his novel-writing. They'll never be famous but occasionally Pauline sells a painting and I think Stewart got his first novel published a few years ago and gets royalties from that, though not much. I've helped out sometimes, getting the girls things like Ipods, cameras, that sort of thing, for birthdays and Christmas."

"They'll be well-off now. With a third of the house sale and now Pauline being left your mother's entire estate," commented Fiona.

"Yes, and Stewart getting thirty thousand and my nieces the same."

There was no rancour in his voice, Fiona noticed so he was either a consummate actor or he really did not mind that he had been left out of the will. He offered her a drink and she accepted a cup of tea. He left her in the lounge and went into his kitchen. Fiona looked round the room which was tastefully furnished in a masculine style, like his study, where she had sat before. The suite was in dark brown leather with no cushions, the curtains beige with a pattern of brown circles and a wide screen TV sat in one corner with a state of the art music centre in another.

Matthew arrived with a small tray on which sat two mugs and a plate of shortbread. Fiona took her coffee and declined the shortbread. He sat down across from her in the other chair, lay back and smiled languidly, coffee mug in his hand.

"Now, DS Macdonald, how can I help you? Was this just a visit to see how well or how badly

I was taking being disinherited or do you have something else to ask me?"

"You don't appear to be upset, Mr Stevenson. Were you forewarned about the change to your mother's will or did it come as a complete shock?" asked Fiona.

"Put it this way. After we sold her house almost from under her, my brother and I were not exactly flavour of the month but I admit that I was surprised that she'd managed to get the will altered so fast."

"But she didn't tell you she was changing it?" enquired Fiona.

For the first time, Matthew showed some surprise. He sat up and placed his mug on an occasional table, placed strategically on his right.

"Tell us? No, she didn't tell us. Well, she didn't tell me. Maybe she told the others."

"She told your sister she was going to tell you, the day before she died."

"Did she? Well, either Pauline is mistaken or my mother changed her mind. I can see where this is leading. You think that either Robert or myself, or both of us, murdered Mother before she could change her will!"

"You must admit it looks that way, Sir, but it would help if you could prove that you didn't stay long that night...had another engagement perhaps."

"I've already told you that I came straight here, DS Macdonald."

"Yes, I know but your brother told us that you'd had to give up a prior engagement to visit your mother and I wondered if when you found out that you didn't have to wait and play bezique with her, you had managed to reinstate that engagement. That is, if you're sure that you didn't play the card game, Sir. Your mother's diary said that you did."

"I know. You told me that, at my interview."

"You must see that it would be better if you could prove that you came home right away or if you could produce someone who saw you that night."

Matthew Stevenson sat back in his chair and crossed one ankle over the other.

"I'm sorry. It was as I said. I came straight home. I live alone so no one can vouch for me."

"Not even a 'phone call, Sir, to you or by you?"

"No. Neither."

Fiona finished her coffee and, rising, put her mug down beside Matthew's. His coffee was untouched. She thanked him again for his time and was soon heading back to the station.

Matt closed the door and returned to his lounge. He sat for a while, as his coffee cooled, then he went into the hall and picked up his 'phone.

Salma sat in the waiting room of Browne, James and Knowles for some time. Magazines lay on the large coffee table in front of her but it was obvious that the lawyers brought in their own cast-off reading material, as her choice was between about six months' editions of 'Golf' or 'Which Car?' She had spoken to the receptionist, a young girl, but maybe her choice of magazine was not fit for a legal practice, thought the sergeant. She looked at her watch again. 12.30. Surely they timed their clients' visits so that they had a lunch break. She heard two voices and sat up hopefully on her Parker Knoll chair.

The door opened and a middle-aged man came in.

"Jonathan Knowles, Miss…"

"…Sergeant Din," replied Salma, getting to her feet and shaking the hand held out to her.

Mr Knowles led her into another room in the same corridor and they sat down, him behind the desk and her across from him.

"Sergeant Din, what can I do for you? I take it that this is about the death of my client, Adele Stevenson?"

"Yes, Sir, it is. You saw Mrs Stevenson quite soon before she died. Is that right?"

"Yes, that's correct. I saw her on the afternoon of the day she died."

"Would you tell me the circumstances of that visit, please," said Salma, pleasantly.

"Well, Mrs Stevenson's son, Robert Stevenson, told me that his mother wished to see me about doing a deed of covenant but when we got there, she seemed puzzled and claimed that she hadn't asked for me."

"Claimed, Sir? Did you not believe her when she said that?" asked Salma.

"I might have but her son told me that she had the start of Alzheimer's so I guess she simply forgot that she'd asked to see me."

"Did anything else happen while you were there, Sir?" Salma pressed him.

"It was rather embarrassing in fact. She accused her son of putting her into the nursing home without her consent, him and his brother, and asked me how she could set about having them both charged with selling what was in effect, *her* house."

"What did her son have to say about that?"

"He said that the house was left to him and his brother, to take effect after his mother died and he was only doing what was best for her. I think he said that the house had become too big for her," the lawyer remembered.

"Did you make an appointment with Mrs Stevenson to see her about this charging of her sons?" asked Salma.

"No, I didn't. I believed what her son said about Alzheimer's. She was after all ninety-four. I think I advised her to forget about contesting what they'd done."

Salma rose to her feet, thanking Jonathan Knowles for his time. She got back into her car which was parked a few streets away and sat inside for a minute or two thinking.

"Poor Adele, no one was prepared to listen to you, were they?" she said quietly.

Sitting in a large, yet cosy bedroom cum sitting room, Fraser was enjoying his chat with Frederick Graham.

"Call me Fred, please," said that man when Fraser had introduced himself, in the lounge. "And let's go to my room. Too many big ears here," he added, receiving a glower from his neighbour who was sitting knitting what looked like a baby's bootee, in white wool.

Fraser looked, as Adele had, at the photographs and as he had told Adele, Fred told him that the lady in the one which was not army-related was his late wife, Ethel. Fraser, who had a well-loved grandmother, spotted the signs of an imminent conversation based on either his wife or his army career and skilfully prevented this by commenting on the pack of cards, lying in a prominent position on the table by the window.

"So you are a card sharp too, Fred?" he queried.

"Yes. I play with my grandson, Bob, every time he comes to visit me and I had some good games with Adele...Mrs Stevenson... as she wanted to be called though she thawed out enough to let me call her by her Christian name, though we're not allowed to use that term."

"What term?" asked Fraser, puzzled.

"Christian name. We have to say, 'chosen name' in case we offend Mrs Mohammed though, personally, I don't think Mrs Mohammed would object. I think Matron is just being very politically correct."

"What did you play with Mrs Stevenson?" asked Fraser.

"We always played bezique. It's a difficult game to teach anyone but great fun to play and one of the few card games which two can play."

"I believe you played with her on the evening she died," Fraser said.

"I did indeed and soundly beat her. I don't think her mind was on it. She threw away a couple of silly cards."

"Did she talk to you at all then, Fred?"

"Yes, she did. She'd had a meeting with her elder son in the afternoon, just before dinner and she had decided not to give her two sons power of attorney. Do you know she actually said that her son looked as if he wanted to kill her!"

"Did she say anything about her sons coming up later that evening?" asked Fraser.

"Oh, yes. They were both coming up, though earlier she had told me that Matt who's the younger one, I think, wasn't coming up till later in the week and she said she was going to make them both play bezique with her though they didn't enjoy it. She told me earlier that her grandchildren didn't play and we talked about how nice it would be if my Bob and her Lucy could get together. No chance of that now," he added sadly.

"I don't imagine anyone in the home hated Mrs Stevenson enough to kill her," said Fraser.

"Apart from Claude who couldn't stand her being older than he was," laughed Fred. "He spilled coffee over her in the lounge, in the afternoon. Donny had spilled his over Mrs Mohammed and Tom Carew, Donny's carer took him away and Julia Harrison, another carer, came and took the two women away. Adele came to my room after she had changed. That's when she met my Bob."

"She had met Miss Cowan too, in Miss Cowan's room, I believe," said Fraser.

"Yes. I tried to ferret out what she had found out about our mystery woman but all she could tell me was that Martha Cowan was an avid reader, even read in French."

"Anything else, Sir?"

"No…wait a minute…there was something else. She said that Martha Cowan's daughter…no, sorry…her granddaughter…no, her niece, must have done something wrong because Martha had disinherited her."

"Done what wrong?" asked Fraser sounding interested,

"No idea. Sorry. In fact I've probably put that bit in myself," he said sheepishly. "Adele didn't mention the girl doing anything wrong. My grandson would be calling me an old sweetie wife."

"Was that the last time you spoke to Mrs Stevenson, Fred?" asked Fraser.

"No. I had a few words with her later or was that earlier, when she told me that she'd phoned her lawyer and he was coming up on Friday or was it Thursday."

Fraser saw that Frank's eyes were clouding over. His voice sounded weaker.

"She told me that she'd told her two sons that she was going to change her will."

"Are you sure of that, Fred?" asked Fraser.

"Yes, I think so. Pardon me young man but at my age and with this dratted Parkinson's, I get tired easily."

Fraser got up. He shook the old man's hand, warmly and thanked him for his very succinct information.

"Though I'm not sure, Sir, of the last part, about Adele Stevenson saying that she had told her sons she was seeing her lawyer on Thursday or Friday about changing her will. He was beginning to wilt then."

They were all once again in the incident room, everyone having returned from their various commissions and Frank having finished his report-writing.

"Well, it's worth thinking about. If it's true, then both sons thought that they had a couple of days to get rid of her so it must have been a nasty shock for them when the other will was read out," said Davenport.

"I can't help but believe that Matthew isn't at all bothered about being disinherited," said Fiona who had told them all about the man's attitude when she had gone to his house.

"I'm sure that if he had killed his mother that evening, he would have made sure that he had someone to bear him out about the time he arrived home," she added.

"As his brother had, you mean?" said Charles sounding cynical. "*He* certainly made sure that his wife would support his story."

"The lawyer seemed to think that Mrs Stevenson was in the first stages of senility," said Salma, "so maybe she invented what she said to old Mr Graham."

"Well as usual, the chief constable wants an arrest made yesterday. He's already assuming that the sons are guilty and that the fact that arsenic was found in the body of two elderly women is a coincidence," said Davenport.

"Mr Graham mentioned again that Mrs Stevenson told him that Martha Cowan had disinherited her niece, though he said her daughter, then her granddaughter," said Fraser.

"Which it couldn't be as she had an abortion and no child that we know about," said Fiona.

"We're getting nowhere," said Davenport dispiritedly. "Get off home and we'll meet again first thing tomorrow when I've had time to think of our next move."

# CHAPTER 25

A fter Charles had come down from heaven, after seeing God – "Though he should be downstairs and I could call him, "auld Nick" he confided in Fiona – he had waited in his room for his fiancée to return from seeing Matthew Stevenson. She had looked tired when she appeared outside his door and he had asked her if she wanted to go home and rest for the remainder of the day.

"And have them all saying that I get preferential treatment, Charles?" she had replied.

"Don't think Frank would use that word, love, though maybe Fraser or Salma might. Do you feel up to coming out for lunch or would you rather just brave the staff canteen?"

Fiona had opted for going out, asking him to take them to The Railway Inn which had been their favourite haunt for lunch until Charles had discovered that Solomon Fairchild had seen them there in the days when they were trying to keep their friendship a secret. She had declared that as it was no secret now, then they could return there for lunch and he had agreed with her.

When they were seated in a private little booth which had been easy to find as they were early for lunch, Charles remembered what it was that he had meant to tell her.

"Saying that about Frank not using a word like, 'preferential' reminds me of something that happened this morning," he said now, as she removed her jacket and laid it on the bench seat, next to her handbag. Charles looked at the bag. He had never seen Fiona with another bag and it was beginning to look the worse for wear. Certainly it was made of leather but it was wrinkled and battered-looking with almost bare patches on one side. It never matched her usual black or navy suits which she wore to work yet she was in all other matters of apparel, coordinated. He decided to question her about that after he had told his story.

"What was that, love?" she asked.

"I went up in the lift with Roger Dickson. You know, the DCI who's lent us Fraser twice," he added, seeing her bewilderment.

"Oh yes, I know who you mean now."

"He's really not very bright, academically. Roger, I mean, not our Fraser. He couldn't understand something I said and accused me of being a fancy, university type and …wait for it…he suggested that

I should swap Fraser for a less intelligent constable and send that constable to him instead of Fraser!"

"You're kidding?"

"No, I'm serious. Luckily the lift stopped and saved me answering."

"As if the lads are collectable items, not people!"

"My thought exactly."

They studied the menus for a while and then the waiter came up for their order. Talk turned to the wedding and clothes. Neither was prepared to tell the other what they were wearing on the big day but Charles had seen Pippa's outfit and commented on it now, telling Fiona that his daughter was delighted with it, telling him that the skirt was modern and the camisole had been made especially for her, to match the skirt. He did not tell his fiancée that he had bought his suit and shirt with Pippa's colours in mind. Talking about outfits, reminded him of Fiona's well-worn bag.

"Fiona, I keep meaning to ask you, why do you always bring the same handbag, even when it doesn't match your outfit?"

Fiona blushed.

"Trust you to notice a thing like that, Charles Davenport! I never have spent much on things like bags and gloves and this bag was my Mum's. It's one of the few things of hers that I kept. I feel as if she's with me when I carry this bag."

She picked it up and ran her fingers over it, lovingly.

"I won't throw it away, you know," she said defensively.

"As long as you don't carry it coming down the aisle," he laughed, and what could have been a small time bomb in their up-till-now peaceable relationship was diffused.

Their meals arrived and they tucked in, saying nothing for a while. They decided not to have any desserts and when their coffees were placed in front of them, the talk moved to the murders.

"I just can't for the life of me see why someone would want to murder Martha Cowan and Adele Stevenson," said Charles. "Adele Stevenson on her own or maybe even Martha Cowan on her own if Tall Trees is in difficulties and the Smiths saw an easy way to get a cool fortune but then why would they go on to murder Adele Stevenson?"

"Maybe she noticed something?" suggested Fiona. "She was in Miss Cowan's room the day of the murder. Was something said then to arouse her suspicions?"

They sat quietly for a few minutes then Fiona spoke.

"Or one of Adele's sons murdered their mother but what was Martha Cowan's murder then? A practice? A mistake?"

"Maybe the arsenic got into a cup in Martha Cowan's room...but how on earth could that happen?" said Charles.

Fiona clapped her hands.

"Got it! Someone put arsenic into Adele's cup on the Tuesday. She wandered, with her cup full of tea, into the other woman's room. Did she not invite Miss Cowan to her room for tea in the first place?"

"Yes but how did Martha Cowan get the poisoned cup then?"

"She made herself a cup of tea and somehow they got swapped."

"And neither woman realised that she had a different cup? Hardly. They wouldn't look the same. "

"Do you know that? Have you seen the cups?"

"No but..."

Charles hesitated. Funny things did happen and nothing else seemed to explain how these old ladies came to be poisoned.

"No, Fiona, that won't do. If that was how Martha Cowan came to be poisoned, how did Adele get poisoned the next day?"

"Well she didn't know it was meant for her and when her son or sons realised that the wrong woman had been killed, he or they struck again.

Charles was silent, considering.

"How else do you explain two unconnected people being killed, in the same way, within a day of each other?" demanded Fiona.

"Did anyone see the two women meeting at the door to Martha Cowan's room?" asked Charles.

"Well, who knew they'd been together?"

"Salma and Frank were told by Adele Stevenson when they went over after the first death. Salma told me and I remember later when she…Salma… went back to interview the residents, that the Asian lady, Mrs Mohammed, mentioned Adele getting into Martha's room and saying that it was unusual. She lived in the room between the murdered women. Perhaps she saw Adele going in. Let's get over to the home and check on this, love, while it's fresh in our minds."

Charles drove them to Tall Trees, where they spoke to Sandra Keith and Tom Carew and asked them if they had told anyone about Adele's visit to Martha Cowan and if so, how they had found out about it in the first place. Sandra informed them that Adele Stevenson had told her about going into the other lady's room. Tom said that Sandra had told him and Sandra supported that. Neither had heard of Adele asking Martha into her room first.

"She just said that she had knocked on the door and Martha Cowan had, reluctantly, I think was the word she used, invited her in," said Sandra.

"I think I told old Claude," said Tom. "It was such an unusual event and I struggle sometimes to make conversation with the old man."

Fred Graham was not in the residents' lounge so they went along to his room, directed by Sandra. He invited them in, looking frail. Charles remembered Fraser using the word 'wilting' to describe the old man when he had seen him the previous day and he thought that the word suited him now. He looked like a dying plant, hanging over his zimmer frame. The three of them sat down and this time it was Fiona who gently asked the old man how he knew that Adele Stevenson had gone into the room of Martha Cowan.

"She told me and Sandra about it. I teased her and said she could now tell me all she had found out about our recluse. Well, I said that to her later when she came into my room and met my grandson, Bob. Do you know he comes to see me every week?"

"How kind of him but then he must be fond of you," said Fiona, patting his hand.

"He is. Now where was I? Oh yes, we all knew by teatime. There's a good grapevine in Tall Trees you know," he said proudly.

"So how did the invitation come about, Mr Graham?" asked Charles, smiling at the man.

"Oh, Adele knocked on her door and asked Martha into her room first but Martha said no and asked Adele to come into her room instead."

"Have you any idea why Adele asked Martha to visit her? Didn't she know that the woman kept herself to herself?" asked Fiona.

"Oh, she knew that alright. I told her that, I think, or she would hear it on the good old grapevine. Goodness knows why she knocked on the door like that. It's not as if she wanted to get to know everyone. She'd made it very clear that she wasn't going to stay at Tall Trees...though I think she was beginning to like it here."

The old man looked suddenly sad and very tired. His shoulders had slumped. Charles nudged Fiona and she got to her feet, then sat back down, taking one of the old man's veined hands in her own.

"Mr Graham, was your new friend in the first stages of dementia?"

"Dementia? Adele Stevenson? No way! She was ...what does my grandson say these days...one of the sharpest tools in the box. Good God, you can't play bezique with dementia."

Fiona rose again, thanked the old man and she and Charles left the room.

They met Matron Smith who asked them if they were any further forward in finding out who had committed the murders and they told her that they wanted to see Mrs Mohammed

"Getting there," said Charles, non-committally. "Mrs Smith, would you say that Adele Stevenson showed signs of dementia?"

Matron looked a bit shame-faced.

"Her elder son, Mr Robert Stevenson, came to see me to tell me that he was going to arrange for his mother to come into Tall Trees. He'd enquired about vacancies the week previously, you see. He said she was in the first stages of dementia and showed me a doctor's letter confirming this. When Mrs Stevenson arrived, she didn't seem demented but then in the first stages there are often long periods of clarity…"

"…did you treat her as if she was demented, Matron?"

"I'm ashamed to say I did, on that first night, when she got upset. The doctor had recommended a slight sedative and I gave her that to help her sleep."

"And did these episodes of 'clarity' last, Matron?"

"They did, Sir. Looking back, I don't think she ever showed any of the usual signs of dementia."

"Thanks, Matron. Now, Mrs Mohammed, please."

"She's almost as recluse-like as Martha Cowan was, though she does come out for all meals," Matron told them. They went upstairs. She knocked on a door and Mrs Mohammed answered.

"Mrs Mohammed, the police would like to speak to you. Do you mind?"

"I can't think why but OK. You can come in," she said quietly.

The old lady sat down on her bed. There was only one chair in the room, in front of the TV set and Charles pulled it over for Fiona. He remained standing.

"We're sorry to intrude on you, Mrs Mohammed, but with you living in the room between the two ladies who were murdered, we wondered if you saw Mrs Stevenson going in to Miss Cowan's room or if you heard any of their conversation that day."

"I am rather hard of hearing so I heard nothing. I did hear knocking on the door but I probably thought it was Miss Cowan's carer bringing her tea or something. I'm sorry, I didn't see Mrs Stevenson going in or coming out."

"You did hear shouting from Mrs Stevenson's room the next night though, didn't you?" asked Fiona.

"Yes. I heard loud voices. They must have been loud if I heard them," she smiled.

Thanking the little lady, they left her room. They saw nobody on their way out but Charles stopped to look again at the visitors' book.

"I wish the two sons had signed as they left," he commented.

"Though they could have written anything," said Fiona. "And the fact that they didn't almost shows their innocence as they could have written false times."

In the car, Fiona asked Charles if they had ever asked Pauline Macartney about her mother's supposed dementia or if they had only heard about it from the two sons.

"After all, Charles, she asked her daughter to bring her a Camus novel, in French. That isn't really a request you would expect to get from a demented woman."

"Let's have a quick trip to the Macartneys. They don't work, so might be at home," said Charles.

"The 'team' will think we've eloped," laughed Fiona.

They were lucky to find Pauline Macartney at home, though Stewart was out getting her some picture frames. Asked if she thought that her mother had been in the first stages of dementia, Pauline had laughed. She repeated what her mother had told her after sending the lawyer away.

"She said that the boys were claiming that she was demented and she told me that she was going to get the lawyer up to do the deed of covenant that she had just claimed to know nothing about. If I remember rightly, she said something like, 'They want me demented: I'll give them demented.'

Does that sound like someone with dementia to you, Inspector?"

Charles and Fiona drove back to the station. Sounds of hilarity were coming from the main staff room and when they looked in, they were just in time to hear Frank saying, "I now pronounce you man and wife."

"New vocation plans, Selby? Notions of being a minister...sorry...a priest?"

"Maybe we could hire you for our wedding, Selby," said Fiona, matching the stern expression that Charles was managing to keep on his face.

Frank had gone scarlet. He turned to apologise but his two bosses had left the room, trying hard not to laugh till they reached the safety of Fiona's room where they burst out in peals of laughter at the constable's discomfiture.

# CHAPTER 26

It was Tuesday 26th of August, almost a week since the first murder and Charles was dismayed when he went to call Pippa to get up and she told him that she did not feel well. This left him in a quandary as his sister had got herself a part time job in her local newsagent's and Tuesday morning was one of her working times. It was so unlike Pippa to be ill. Charles sat on the edge of her bed and felt her forehead which was cool.

"What is you feel wrong, pet?" he asked.

"My tummy's sore."

"Is it your period again, do you think?"

"No it's not that kind of sore," said a small voice, from under the duvet.

"It might go away once you're up and have something to eat."

Silence.

"Can I just stay at home today, Dad? Please?"

"You can't stay at home by yourself, love and I can't take the time off right now to stay with you and Auntie Linda's working."

"I feel sick."

With that Pippa shot out of bed and made for the bathroom from where he could hear dry, retching noises. He went across the hall and put his arm round her. She turned a white face towards him and he had a sudden inspiration. He could phone Fiona. He could manage without her for one day and Pippa had felt reassured by her presence in Penang when her period had started.

"I'll try Fiona," he said and, leaving Pippa still holding on to the wash basin, he went downstairs to the hall 'phone.

Fiona agreed to play nurse this one time, though she told him that when they were married and had two children, it wouldn't necessarily be her who took time off if one was ill. Charles agreed that he would take his share of any responsibilities in the future and thanked her for agreeing to help out this time. Fiona arrived about half an hour later and he thanked her again and gave her a quick kiss before running out to the car.

Fiona made her way upstairs. Pippa was back in bed.

"Were you actually sick, Pippa? Maybe you got rid of whatever has upset your tummy and will feel better soon," she told her.

"I wasn't really sick, Fiona but I do feel a bit better," said Pippa.

"Well lie back down and try to have a sleep. You can get up later if you feel really better."

Fiona went back downstairs and made herself a cup of tea. Coffee was making her feel a bit nauseous these days. She had brought her Glasgow Herald with her and she sat down in an armchair in the living room and settled herself for a leisurely read. She enjoyed her work but this day off was actually quite welcome as she had been feeling rather sick herself the last few mornings.

She had read the paper, except the sports' pages which she never read and had started on the cryptic crossword when she heard footsteps coming downstairs. Pippa, fully dressed, appeared in the doorway.

"I feel heaps better, Fiona. Can I have some breakfast now?"

"Of course you can. Can you get it yourself or do you need me to get it for you?"

"I can manage thanks."

Pippa went into the kitchen. She came back through some minutes later and sat down across from Fiona who put down her paper. The young girl looked healthy now, her cheeks rosy as usual and Fiona asked if she felt well enough to go to school in the afternoon, saying that she could drive her there and go on into the station. Pippa thought for a minute, then said that she did feel fine and would go to school. Fiona switched on the TV and when Pippa seemed to get engrossed in the programme, she rang Charles at the station and told him their plans. He was delighted that his daughter now felt well enough to go to school and informed his fiancée that he had scheduled the team meeting for the afternoon so she would be able to attend that and not miss out on any information gleaned then.

Back at the station, having dropped Pippa off at school claiming that she did not need an absence letter till the next day for registration, Fiona made her way to her own room. The door to Charles's room was open as usual, so after dropping her faithful handbag under her desk and removing her jacket, she went in.

"She seemed fine, Charles. Whatever it was must have come out of her system."

"Thanks, my love. Did you manage to find something for lunch for both of you?"

"I made us some scrambled egg on toast. I'm not very medically clued-up but I thought that would be light for her tummy and my tummy is a bit delicate these mornings too."

"Well, I sincerely hope that my daughter isn't in your condition!" Charles said, pretending to be horrified. "It's almost time for our meeting. Will I make you a coffee...sorry...a cup of tea, to take along with you?"

"No, thanks. Don't start spoiling me or you might regret it."

As they moved towards the door, Fiona remembered something. She stopped.

"I forgot to tell you everything about my visit to Matthew Stevenson, yesterday. We were so busy going back to the home and then on to see Pauline Macartney."

" Did you find out anything new?"

"No but he looked genuinely surprised when I asked him if he'd known his mother was going to change the will, especially when I told him she had declared her intention of telling him and Robert. He seemed truly unconcerned about being left out of the will, Charles. I asked him about having no one to verify his statement about going straight home and he said that he did go straight home and he made no 'phone calls or received any either. I asked him that."

"Do you believe everything he's saying then?"

"Funnily enough, not the bit about going straight home. I sensed something when he said that nobody could vouch for him."

They made their way down the corridor to the Incident room where they found the others already seated. Fiona joined them and Charles took his usual position, sitting on the desk at the front beside the white board on which he wrote important things to do with the current murder.

"Right team," he began.

Frank turned his smirk into a wrinkled nose and scratched it, wishing that Penny was here to share his joke at their boss and his habit of calling them his team. He knew what would come next. Davenport would pull his left ear lobe, especially if he was puzzled or worried.

Sure enough, Davenport put up his left hand to his ear and gave a gentle tug.

"I want you all to consider this question. Why did Adele Stevenson go to Martha Cowan's room the day that lady was murdered?"

"Are you thinking that she murdered Miss Cowan?" asked Fiona, sounding surprised.

"No, I'm not. Of course not but I can't think of a reason for the visit and a lot came from it."

"What do you mean, Sir?" asked Frank. "What came from the visit?"

"You tell me."

"Well, Sir," said Fraser. "She must have been recommended the Gaviscon then surely, unless Matron suggested it, as Mrs Stevenson asked her daughter to get it the next day."

"And she must have got the idea of that book… what was it called again, Fraser?" asked Salma.

" 'The Outsider,' by Albert Camus," said Fraser. "That's right, she asked her daughter to get that too, after her visit to Martha Cowan."

"Did she eat something fishy while she was there, Sir?" asked Frank. "Something that upset her tummy?"

"No, there were only two used cups to be washed when her carer took them away, Frank, and anyway, surely she would simply have given Adele a couple of spoonfuls of her own Gaviscon if Adele had complained of indigestion while there."

"Yes, Sir and it takes about five hours for something eaten to cause problems, I believe," volunteered Fraser.

"Are you a bleeding doctor too, Hewitt," said Frank, moodily.

"Language, Selby," said Davenport mildly. "We're not in an episode of, 'Taggart', son."

"So, to get back to what you wanted from us, Sir," said Fiona. "You want us to come up with ideas as to why Adele went into Martha's room at all? Is that right?"

Davenport sent her a grateful look for diffusing the situation and, seeing it as a loving look, Frank fought a desire to make kissing sounds and looked more cheerful. Fraser who had a calm nature did not seem to have taken umbrage at Frank's remark.

"Yes, that's right. Come on then, folks. Put on your thinking caps."

"Out of nosiness, perhaps," said Salma.

There was silence.

Everyone looked baffled.

"Was she a particularly inquisitive person, I wonder?" said Davenport.

"She didn't intend staying, did she, Sir? So why did she want to find out about another resident?"

This came from Frank.

"Exactly, Frank," agreed Fiona. "If she didn't mean to stay, there was no need to try to get friendly with someone who didn't welcome company, was there?"

"Had she heard that Martha Cowan had a good supply of books, maybe, and wanted to borrow one?" was Salma's next suggestion.

"Well if she did, she didn't get anything or that would have been by her bedside or on her table because she wouldn't put another person's book in her own bookcase, would she?" mused Fiona.

"Who would want to borrow poetry books and highbrow stuff like that Camus one? I looked at Miss Cowan's books, remember and I didn't recognise one author," said Frank.

"But she did like that 'highbrow stuff' Frank, or she wouldn't have asked her daughter to buy Camus for her, would she?" said Fiona.

"It doesn't matter anyway as there wasn't a book lying around her room," said Davenport.

"Sir, I've thought of something else," said Frank, excitedly. "Did she not invite Miss Cowan into her room first?"

"Yes… so?"

"I thought that her daughter said she had to buy her mother cups and saucers when she was buying the other stuff. So she wouldn't have cups to give Martha Cowan a drink in." said Frank triumphantly.

"That rather knocks your theory on the head, Sir, the one you mentioned to me at lunchtime yesterday, about Adele wandering into Martha's room with an already poisoned cup of tea and somehow Martha drinking from it," said Fiona then she looked apologetic as if realising that Charles might not have wanted that suggestion aired at this meeting.

"True, Fiona. It was a bit ridiculous anyway as it would have meant the murderer having to have done a rerun of putting arsenic into Adele's cup again, the next day," said Davenport, smiling at her obvious discomfort. "This case is like that: it's making me invent daft theories."

"Well, Sir, there aren't any sensible ones that fit," said Salma." "As Frank said, how could she invite someone in for a drink if she had no cups?"

"But she did invite her. She told people that," said Davenport.

"Maybe she suspected that Miss Cowan wouldn't come and really wanted to be invited in," offered Fiona.

"So, back to square one! Why did she want to be invited in?"

Davenport groaned.

They heard a 'phone ringing, further up the corridor. Davenport, realising that it came from his room, went out, hurriedly. He returned with the information that Adele Stevenson's body was to be cremated the following Monday.

"That was Pauline Macartney. As she suspected, neither of her brothers was interested in arranging things. It's to be at The Linn at 9.30 on Monday. Fraser, I don't think you've tried attending a victim's funeral, have you son?"

"No, Sir. I've been at The Linn once, some years ago for my grandmother's funeral but that's all. Do you want me to go on Monday?"

"Yes and I want you to watch people's faces. Often the murderer attends the funeral and someone just might give something away."

"Mind you, we haven't ever spotted the murderer doing anything untoward at any previous funerals," said Fiona, laughing.

"But Fraser's so clever. He'll probably be able to come back with the murder all wrapped up," said Frank, but he said this with humour and not with any rancour so nobody was disapproving and everybody laughed, including Fraser.

"No problem. I'll come back and tell you it was Mrs Peacock in the conservatory with the candlestick," he said.

Davenport called the meeting to order.

"Right team; let's add what we now know. Martha Cowan left a lot of money to the nursing home and ten thousand to a niece we can't find."

Underneath Miss Cowan's name, he wrote:

'Estate left to Home and niece.'

Underneath Mrs Stevenson's name he wrote:

'Estate left to Pauline Macartney (daughter).

Legacies (large ones) to Avril, Lucy and Kim (granddaughters) & son-in-law, Stewart.

Legacy (even larger) to daughter -in-law, Margaret.

Both sons, Robert and Matthew, disinherited.'

"There were two small legacies to two former workers too, boss," said Frank.

"True but they were small beer in comparison. I think we can rule them out but you were right to mention them," said Davenport

"I'm going to get Matthew Stevenson in again," he continued. "He's till sticking to the story that he went straight home but both Fiona and I who have spoken to him, have the gut feeling that he's lying."

"Give him a ring first, Sir. He took time off yesterday to speak to me, so he'll probably be at work in his travel agent's business today," suggested Fiona.

Davenport duly did this, caught Matthew at work and asked him to come into the station on his way home.

# CHAPTER 27

It was like a rerun. Once again Pippa declared herself unwell and again asked for a day off school. As she had gone, willingly yesterday, in the afternoon, Charles did not suspect anything at first. All he could think of was that this could not have happened at a worse time, with the cases still unsolved and Knox breathing down his back. He could not simply take the day off so he would have to rely on his sister this time. He rang her at home and she declared herself willing to come to Newton Mearns.

She duly arrived and it was when Charles was explaining that it had happened the previous day and that Pippa had felt well enough to go back to school after lunch, that she set the alarm bells ringing by asking him if his daughter was unhappy at school.

"If she was unhappy why would she go back in the afternoon, Lin?" he asked her.

"Maybe it's one subject and it's been on both mornings. Is she finding one subject particularly difficult?"

"Well, in primary, she didn't find maths easy but she's too sensible to try to avoid it, surely?" asked Charles, anxiously. "That would make things worse as she'd get behind in maths to add to her problems and she's clever enough to realise that. I don't imagine she enjoys PE much. She's not sporty, like her friend, Hazel. What will I do, Lin? Should I tackle her about it or let her stay off again?"

"Let her stay off again and we'll see if she feels well enough to go back in the afternoon. You could sneak a look at her timetable tonight and see if anything leaps out at you."

Thanking her for her advice and her willingness to babysit Pippa, Charles left for work. He was slightly later than usual, even Frank getting there before him.

"It's OK, Frank. I stayed late last night to see Matthew Stevenson so I'll let myself off this time," he said, when he saw that young man grinning at him when he looked into the room used by his sergeant and constables.

Frank went a bit pink at being so transparent. He bent his head to his desk and the report he was writing up. There had been a number of 'phone calls when he had been left to man the fort and he had put off writing them up. Robberies were so common in this area of the city and he had had to deal with both of them the following day.

Fiona came into the room shortly afterwards. She and Davenport had both interviewed Matthew Stevenson the previous night, trying to persuade the man to, 'come clean' about his whereabouts on the night of his mother's murder. Matthew had resolutely stuck to his story but his manner belied his statement that he had gone straight home. It was as if he could not take seriously the fact that he might be suspected of his mother's murder.

"I don't think that Matthew Stevenson has ever had anything unpleasant happen to him in his sheltered life," Fiona said now. "I would guess that he saw some woman…"

"…or maybe a man. Remember Colin in our first murder case together?" said Frank. "Shirt-lifters are ten a penny these days."

"Homosexuals, Selby, please," said Fiona tartly.

"So, Ma'am, you think that he might have been seeing someone he shouldn't have been seeing," said Salma quickly. "Maybe a married woman?"

"Yes, Salma. That's exactly what I think and he thinks he's being chivalrous by not telling us."

Fiona turned to leave the room, then turned back.

"Will one of you boys go up to Tall Trees and bring us a cup belonging to both murdered ladies, please?"

"I'll go," said Frank, obviously keen to reinstate himself in his DS's good books and also wanting a change from writing. He took his jacket from its peg and his hat from his desk and went off, whistling.

"What's that he's whistling now?" asked Fiona. "He seems to have a whole new repertoire these days. Whatever happened to his Scottish songs?"

"Scottish songs!" exclaimed Fraser, incredulously. "Frank?"

"Think it's a song from a show, Ma'am," said Salma.

"It was "I'm Getting Married in the Morning," said Fraser, when Fiona had gone back up the corridor.

"I know, you clot but I wasn't going to tell her that, was I?" said Salma scathingly.

"Sorry, I wasn't thinking. Was Frank really into Scottish songs?" asked Fraser.

"Did we never tell you that we, or rather Frank, hoped for a station romance between the DCI and the DS and he likened them to Flora Macdonald and Bonnie Prince Charlie?" said Salma. "He kept singing and humming songs such as, 'Over the Sea to Sky' and 'My Bonnie Lies Over the Ocean'," Salma told him.

"That was clever of him!" exclaimed Fraser.

About half an hour later, Frank returned with two tea cups. He passed his colleagues on his way to DS Macdonald's room and came back down asking if anyone wanted to go to the cafeteria for a midmorning coffee.

"You two go," said Fraser. "I'll go when you get back."

Fiona took the two cups into Davenport's room and laid them on his desk.

"Not very dissimilar, Charles," she commented.

Both cups were identical in size and shape and both were mostly white, one having blue flowers and one having pink and yellow ones.

"It's possible that two old ladies, with failing eyesight, might get their cups mixed up, I suppose," said Charles.

"So, Adele Stevenson goes to Martha's door, cup in hand, a cup she didn't yet have, asks her to come through for tea, is invited in instead and puts down the cup… Martha brings two cups, puts hers down and picks Adele's up by mistake. She drinks the tea with the arsenic in it. Robert or Matthew comes up the next night and finds Mother very much alive and just having to have more arsenic on hand, poisons another cup."

"You're laughing at me, aren't you?" demanded Charles.

"Of course not, would I dare?" laughed Fiona. "It's just possible. Sillier things have happened… but only if Adele had her new cups and I'm pretty sure she hadn't."

"I think that we get the two sons in together. See if we can get them to contradict each other, if indeed they are both in it together. I'll 'phone both of them later and ask them to come in before work tomorrow. Better not presume on Matthew's good nature by getting him in two days in a row."

"Why not get them in tonight? If we rile Matthew, it might be productive and the days are going fast. Only ten days till the wedding, my love."

Fiona sounded anxious.

"I know but I really want to get back to see how Pippa is."

He explained that once again his daughter had claimed to be feeling ill and had asked to stay off school. He and his sister were wondering if she was trying to avoid a subject. At that moment the mobile in his jacket pocket rang.

"Hello…Yes… Lin…she has? Thank you."

He put the phone back in his pocket.

"That as you probably guessed was my sister. Pippa felt well enough to go into school again, after lunch."

"Surely she wouldn't have the same subject each morning," reasoned Fiona.

"That's what I thought so what could it be? A morning only bug?"

"What else could she be trying to avoid that's only mornings?" mused Fiona.

"Registration?"

"Seems unlikely. There's nothing scary about that."

"Interval?" suggested Charles.

"Don't they have an interval in the afternoon?"

"No, they don't. They have five periods in the morning and only three in the afternoon, so no break then."

They decided that Charles would have to sit Pippa down and ask her straight out what she was trying to avoid. This was the only way they could break the cycle of pretend illness, if that was what it was.

The afternoon passed without anything new transpiring. Fiona went down to tell the others about the cups, being careful not to sound derisory. Only Fraser seemed to think that the exchanged cup scenario was possible. He told them that his grandmother often picked up things that weren't hers wherever they went.

Charles left early, wanting to pick Pippa up from school as Linda had done her bit today. Pippa, Kerry and Hazel came out together, laughing. Charles had not had time to tell the Ewings that he would give Hazel a lift that day but she told him that she had just been going to walk home as her Mum's school got out later and her Dad was down in London for a few days. The three girls piled into the back, leaving Charles, like a chauffeur in the front. They laughed and joked and he could sense no tension in his daughter. They dropped Kerry at the top of Tassie Street hill and Hazel in Newlands. Pippa came into the front.

"Feeling better, love?" Charles asked.

"Yes, Dad."

She put her earphones into her ears and silence reigned from Newlands to Newton Mearns. Charles went into the kitchen to prepare their meal and Pippa raced upstairs, coming down forty minutes later when he called her. She wolfed down her meal and was about to dive off when Charles stopped her.

"Pippa. I want a serious chat with you. There's something you're trying to avoid at school in the mornings, isn't there?"

Silence.

"Pet, we've always been able to share everything. Please don't shut me out."

"If I tell you, will you let me stay off tomorrow morning?" she asked, looking scared.

"You know I can't promise that but I can promise that we'll solve the problem together," he told her seriously.

They sat across the kitchen table from each other and Pippa told her story.

Four third year girls had been grabbing first year girls at the interval.

"They take them into the downstairs toilet, Dad and force their heads down the toilet and flush it," she said, tears forming in her blue eyes.

"Does no one try to help them?" asked Charles, horrified.

"No. No one else is brave enough to go in."

"Pippa, they're bullies. If you all gang up on them, they'll stop. Remember how you sorted out Ronald in primary."

""But there was only one of him," Pippa reminded him.

"I need to think about this, darling but I promise you I'll come up with a plan. Get your schoolbag and do your homework."

Charles went into the lounge and, using his mobile, phoned Ralph Ewing. Ralph listened to what he had to say, then handed him over to Sally, his wife. She listened too.

"The important thing is to tackle the bullies, Charles. She mustn't let them think she's scared of them. How brave is she?"

"Pretty brave, Sally."

"I take it that she wouldn't just report them to a teacher."

"I doubt it as that would merely mean the toilets being policed and the girls would probably find another way to harass the first years and especially Pippa, if they found out who'd grassed on them."

"Right. Here's the plan," said Sally.

Charles listened.

"I wonder if she'll be brave enough to try that," he said. "Thanks, Sally."

He rang off.

# CHAPTER 28

Pippa tried to walk nonchalantly towards the girls' toilets. Inside, she was quaking and her tummy was doing somersaults. She had gone quickly out of the classroom when the History teacher had dismissed them, ignoring Kerry's shouts to wait for her. She knew that her friend would either try to dissuade her from doing this or would insist on coming along and she did not want either to happen. At the last set of swing doors, she hesitated, then took a deep breath and pushed through them. Two of the third year girls she had been dreading meeting this week, were standing outside the toilets.

Pippa went straight up to them.

"Oh, there you are. Good. Let's get this head-down-the toilet thing done with."

She pushed open the door and walked in, going to the first cubicle. She looked into the toilet pan, came out and walked to the next, doing this six times and returning to the first one. The two older girls watched her, saying nothing. Pippa knelt down and put her head into the bowl. Nothing happened, so she felt up and pulled down the flush handle, soaking her hair though she had been careful to twitch her pony-tail over the rim. She stood up.

There were now four, third-year girls standing watching her, open-mouthed.

"I hope I haven't spoiled it for you, doing it myself," said Pippa.

"You've got some guts, little first year," said the tallest of the four. She held out her hand.

"My name's Joan. What's yours?"

"Pippa," replied that young lady. "Short for Philippa."

They shook hands.

"Well, Pippa, short for Philippa, I wonder if you'll meet anyone brave like you when you're in third year and it's your turn to initiate the first years," said Joan.

"I won't, because I won't be doing it. I don't like doing things other people have done. I prefer to be myself," said Pippa, saying the first thing that came into her head and now totally unscripted by her father. She walked slowly to the door.

"Anything we can do for you?" asked Joan. "You've made my day, little'un."

"Yes, I would be very grateful if you would miss out on initiating my two best friends," said Pippa, holding her breath, scared in case she had pushed this too far.

"Right-o. Who are they?" asked one of the other girls.

"Kerry James in my class, 1C and Hazel Ewing in 1D," replied Pippa. "Can I have your word on that, please?" she added.

"You sure can, Kid. We wouldn't lie to you," said Joan.

"I'm getting a bit fed up doing this anyway, Joan" said another girl, the smallest of the four.

"We said we'd do fifty, Alice, and we've still got ten more to go, so stop moaning," said Joan who was obviously their ring-leader.

Pippa made her escape. Back through the swing doors, she stopped and took a deep breath, this time one of relief. Now that she had been through the ordeal and done it to herself, she realised that the actual act was not as dreadful as she had imagined. Her father had said fears were better faced than run away from and he had been proved right, as usual. She wished that she did not have to wait till after afternoon school to tell him that all was well and that she had saved her two pals as well. She could not wait to tell them!

She told Hazel in Ralph's car that afternoon. Her father was picking her up at the Ewing house, just after five o'clock. As it turned out, Hazel had not known of the ceremony because her timetable was such that she was seldom near that part of the school at the interval.

"If they were only going to do ten more, then I probably wouldn't have been done," she said nonchalantly, a different reaction from Kerry who had been very grateful and had thanked Pippa, warmly. Both girls had talked of nothing else since they had heard about the event, from a tearstained classmate. Kerry had managed only one morning off school, her mother being suspicious on the second day.

"Hazel! That's no way to thank Pippa. She went bravely through something and tried to rescue you from it," said Ralph, from the front seat.

Hazel looked shamefaced and tried to make up for it by telling her friend that she would be sharing her birthday cake the next day. Pippa would not have been human had she not enjoyed Hazel's discomfiture the next day, when she said that her friend, Vicky, had been dragged into the toilet at four o'clock. A teacher who was a bit late leaving school, noticed Vicky crying and got from her what had happened.

Things were not working out so well for her father. He had phoned the two Stevenson brothers and asked them to come into the station at lunchtime, knowing that both owned their respective businesses so could take time off. As usual, Matthew was obliging, though he sounded a trifle more irritated than previously. Robert, true to form, was angry but when Davenport said he would come to his place of work should he refuse to come to the station, he reluctantly agreed.

Davenport, asking Fiona to accompany him, saw both men together this time. He wanted to see if either would defend his brother or maybe give away something previously held back when they were interviewed, singly.

"Your mother claimed, in her dairy, that she played a card game" – he looked at his notes – "bezique… with both of you but you both claim not to have stayed long enough for this," he said, sternly, into the tape machine, after the usual preliminaries had been dealt with.

"Well, I can vouch for the fact that Robert was leaving when I came in," said Matthew. "You presumably have the time he arrived in the visitors' book, so by that you'll know that he couldn't have had time to play a complicated game like bezique."

"That's right," sneered Robert. "Satisfied now?"

"And who can vouch for you, Mr Stevenson?"

Davenport leant towards the tape machine.

"I am talking now to Mr Matthew Stevenson," he said, clearly.

"No one, I'm afraid," said Matthew, mildly.

Robert stood up and pushed back his chair.

"I'll be getting along now that you've had it proved to you that I couldn't have murdered my mother," he said.

Matthew looked surprised then rather hurt.

"Thanks, Robert. Nice of you to stay and give me your support."

"Well, I can't help you, can I? I don't know when you left Mother," blustered Robert.

"Oh, so you think I might have killed her?"

Matthew was riled for the first time. He stood up and faced his brother.

"Well, you might have. How am I to know?" said Robert.

"Matthew, you said that you didn't touch the playing cards, yet your fingerprints were found on some of them. How do you account for that?" asked Davenport.

Matthew looked puzzled and then his face lightened,

"I remember now. She knocked some of the cards onto the floor and I picked them up for her."

Robert gave a derisory laugh.

"That's how *my* fingerprints came to be on the cards. Can't you think up your own reason?"

"So, you're now accusing me of lying, Robert. I support you and you are only too glad to shift the blame onto me! Very brotherly!"

Matthew looked hurt, rather than angry, then his face took on a closed expression

"In that case, Inspector, might I suggest that you check up again with my sister-in-law, now that she is about to become independent and doesn't have to kow tow to my bully of a brother," said

Matthew vehemently. "He could easily have come back later that night and could have bullied her into giving him an alibi."

"I fully intend to do just that, after I have spoken with Avril Stevenson," replied Davenport.

"What do you need to see my daughter for? She wasn't in till later than night," said Robert, angrily.

"No, but I heard that she seemed very surprised at hearing that your wife made you a snack when you came in."

If Davenport had hoped to scare Robert Stevenson, he was disappointed. There was nothing for it but to let the two men leave, which they did, not speaking to each other.

Davenport and his DS left almost immediately for the Stevenson house. As they walked up the path, they could hear laughter and found Margaret and Avril working in the garden, side by side. They both got to their feet when they saw the visitors.

"Miss Stevenson. One question for you. Why were you surprised when your mother said she had made your father a snack for supper?"

"Was I, Inspector? Probably because my father isn't a snack person and it was hard for me to imagine him, sitting cosily in the lounge with a sandwich."

"Mrs Stevenson, have you thought again, carefully, about that night? Did you see your husband at about eight o'clock and another question – did he remain at home all evening?"

Margaret's face was set. She looked at her daughter, then began, "I can't tell you if Robert stayed in the house all evening, Inspector. I went to bed early."

"And at eight o'clock?"

They heard hurrying footsteps coming up the path and Robert Stevenson reached them.

"Have you been harassing my wife and daughter, Inspector?"

"No, Sir. Merely asking them a couple of questions."

Davenport smiled at both women then he turned and with Fiona, walked back down the path.

Once in the car, Fiona burst out, "Did you see that poor woman's face when he arrived? She looked terrified."

"Yes, yet she didn't give him an alibi for later in the evening. Did you notice that?"

"Yes, I did. I think the presence of Avril gave her some courage but that vanished when he arrived."

"Still, he's in the frame now that he has no one to give him an alibi for later."

"Both brothers are still in that frame, aren't they?"

No, Davenport's day had not gone as well as his daughter's!

# CHAPTER 29

"Are you going to report them?" asked Hazel. "Did you get any of their names?"

"I know two of them," said Pippa. "But I won't be reporting them. That would be kind of cheating, I think."

"How do you mean?" asked Hazel.

"Well, I soaked my own head and we were sort of friends at the end. I'm sure that Vicky will be able to point them out if she wants to but I hope she doesn't 'cos that will probably make them feel that they have to get her back for that."

"Oh she won't say anything else. She's too scared. She said to me that she told Miss Forrest she didn't get a chance to look at them properly though she described one of them quite well to me," said Hazel. "It was quite a big girl with fair hair, called…"

"…Joan," said Pippa.

"Gosh ! Did they tell you their names? They must have trusted you," said Hazel, awed.

"I'm sorry that I didn't think to add Vicky's name to the protected list," said Pippa solemnly.

Hazel went into the kitchen and got them both a glass of milk and a chocolate biscuit. They went upstairs to Hazel's bedroom and chatted about other school things. Hazel was in love with Mr Fraser, her English teacher, and told Pippa that he never gave them any homework. Pippa, grumbling, said that Mr Snedden gave them plenty but admitted that she had learnt a lot from him already.

"Did you know that Shakespeare wrote comedies *and* tragedies?" she said.

"What's a tragedy?" asked Hazel.

"It's a play where the hero dies because of a failing in his own personality," quoted Pippa from last night's homework. She had had to look that up for herself.

"Oh, Mr Fraser hands out wee play books and gives us parts and …"

"…does he take a part?" asked Pippa.

"Oh, no. He sits at his desk and just listens to us. They're funny plays."

"Comedies. So is, 'A Midsummer Night's Dream', supposed to be but to be honest I can't see what's funny about it – yet," said Pippa.

They went on comparing their teachers until Charles turned up, just after five o'clock, to take his daughter home. Pippa told him about Vicky.

"I liked Joan. I think she was the leader because she said they would stop once they'd done fifty girls. She shook my hand and said that I was brave and asked if she could do anything for me. That's when I asked them to not do it to Hazel and Kerry and they agreed but they got Vicky and a teacher found out and the headteacher, Mrs Martin, warned that if she found out who they were, they would be in trouble so maybe they'll stop at Vicky."

As usual, Pippa hung up her jacket in the hall and sped off upstairs to her bedroom. Charles got out the ingredients for his mince and carrots' dinner. He browned the mince, added the gravy and the chopped carrots, put the lid on the pot and peeled some potatoes. Going into the lounge, he picked up his Guardian newspaper and made a start on the crossword which was by a new compiler called Bonxie. When the kitchen timer announced that dinner was ready, he had not solved many clues. These days there were quite a few new compilers and he was finding it hard to get into their wavelength, just as Fiona was, with the new ones in The Herald. It would be good when they lived together and could help each other out, he thought now.

"Are you seeing Fiona tonight, Dad?" asked Pippa, sliding onto the kitchen chair.

She had changed out of her school uniform into her unofficial uniform of denims and teeshirt.

Charles would be doing the same after dinner and felt very overdressed, sitting in the kitchen in his working suit and tie. He removed the tie and slung it over the back of his chair.

"No. Not tonight pet. Fiona has some wedding things to see to."

"What? Does she not want me to help her? I *am* the bridesmaid after all," said Pippa. "Will I 'phone her and see if she wants me to go down?"

Thinking that the last thing his fiancée wanted was a thirteen-year -old girl turning up, Charles nevertheless decided to let Fiona tell Pippa this herself and was surprised when Pippa came hurrying into the lounge a few minute later to tell him that Fiona would be delighted if he took her down and left them.

"She knows I can't be long with school tomorrow, Dad, so maybe you can go somewhere to wait for me," said his daughter, nonchalantly.

"Fine by me, pet," said Charles.

His best man lived in Kilmarnock so he could not go to him as it was in the opposite direction but he knew that there was a pub near to Fiona's flat and he could hang out there for a while. If he turned up on Jean Hope's doorstep, she would probably get flustered, he thought.

An hour later, he dropped Pippa off in Grantley Street, outside Fiona's flat and as no traffic came down the street, he was able to wait to see the entry door open and Pippa skip inside. He drove round the block and, going into the main, Kilmarnock Road, he found a parking space not far from the pub.

It was quite dark inside and not very busy and he easily found a table for himself. He had brought the newspaper and settled down for a good read, something he rarely found time for these days. The pub filled up and someone asked if they could remove two of the chairs from his table. It got very busy and very noisy and he found it hard to concentrate. A sudden thought came to him and he left the pub, collected his car and drove across to where Penny was living with her mum and stepfather.

Penny seemed pleased to see him and Mr and Mrs Maclean were out, so he accepted a coffee and soon they were in deep conversation about work. Frank had told Penny a bit about the two murders, though no details and she asked if they were close to an arrest. Without mentioning any names, Charles told her about the people involved.

"I can't wait to get back, Sir," she told him.

"Any idea when that might be, Penny?" he asked her.

"I've got a line for another two weeks but maybe after that," she said.

"So you might come back while we're away," Charles informed her.

"On honeymoon, Sir?" she asked.

"Yes but if you see DS Macdonald, please don't mention it as it's a surprise for her."

In the flat, Fiona welcomed her soon-to-be-stepdaughter and told her that she was going to have a beauty- therapy night and would Pippa like to join in?

"I thought I'd be very busy soon and felt like a night to pamper myself. Do you fancy it, Pippa?"

Pippa was enthralled.

They spent the next half hour putting what Pippa called 'gunge' on their faces and trying not to laugh at each other. Fiona poured herself a glass of wine and got a coke for Pippa and they settled back to watch a short DVD, a girly one they both enjoyed. When that was over, each gently wiped the other's face clean and declared that they felt relaxed. Pippa told Fiona about her ordeal at school and Fiona congratulated her on her bravery. Charles had told her, of course, but she felt it prudent not to mention that. Fiona told Pippa that they were not getting very far with their murders but naturally did not give any details and Pippa knew not to ask for any.

Charles peeped his horn at about nine o'clock. A car had come up behind him so he had to drive round the block but when he got back to Fiona's close, Pippa was waiting for him and he waved to Fiona who was watching from the upstairs window.

"Important wedding stuff done then, pet?" asked Charles on the way home.

"Oh yes, Dad," answered Pippa, looking up at him, seriously.

# CHAPTER 30

"What did you tell that Inspector?" demanded Robert Stevenson of his wife, as soon as Davenport and DS Macdonald had gone out of earshot,

"I told him that I didn't know if you had gone out again that night as I was in bed asleep," replied Margaret, bravely.

"You fool," hissed her husband.

"Mother supported you coming in at eight o'clock, father," said Avril, coldly.

"I suppose that's something. You can always take back that bit about not knowing if I went out. Say you were thinking of the next night. You can say that we both went to bed early that evening, can't you my dear?"

Margaret looked frightened.

"What did you say we did when I came home?" he asked her.

"Oh, mother said that she made you a cosy bacon sandwich," his daughter informed him.

"That was a damn fool thing to say, woman," snarled Robert.

"Why, Father? That's the kind of thing a lot of wives would do, in a normal household," said Avril. "However, I may have thrown some doubt on that, with any luck."

"What do you mean?" asked Robert, sounding uneasy.

"I said I would have liked to have been in to join in the cosy supper and I think I managed to put a lot of sarcasm into that word, 'cosy'. I saw the Inspector looking at me rather peculiarly."

"You're a vindictive woman," said Robert. "No wonder you're unmarried. No man would have you."

"Do you think you've been a great example of a married man, Father? I certainly wouldn't want a husband like poor Mother's got!"

Avril went into the house, throwing a sympathetic look towards her Mother.

"I'll deal with you... later," said Robert, menacingly to Margaret, and followed his daughter. He would have been very surprised at the look that came upon his wife's face at that threat. He had not been privy to the conversation between his wife and daughter as they gardened that afternoon.

"Mum," said Avril, handing her Mother the trowel, "now that you have the promise of all that money, surely you'll leave Father?"

"Where would I go, Avril? It wouldn't buy me a house."

"No, but it would be a good deposit on a small flat and I'm sure the mortgage would be quite small and could be arranged for fifteen years. You could get a job. If you don't want a mortgage, I could lend you the rest of the money and you could pay me back in easy stages."

"A job at what?"

"Well, it needn't be anything marvellous. Did you not say that your sister asked you to help in her shop once?"

"Yes but your Father wouldn't hear of it and he still wouldn't."

"But if you left him, what he thought wouldn't matter, would it?"

Margaret sat back on her heels, the gardening forgotten.

"I would love to see Robert's face. Oh, Avril, you don't know how miserable I've been with him."

"No but I can guess."

The two women stood up and embraced each other, something they had seldom done.

"You called me, 'Mum'," said Margaret, tearfully.

"Well instead of despising you, this time I found that I felt so sorry for you and wanted to help but I suspected that every time I tried to help, you suffered even more."

"When I get the money, Avril, I promise I will fly the coop."

They went back to their weeding, kneeling side by side and Margaret had laughed, a carefree sound that infected her daughter and they were both laughing together as Davenport and DS Macdonald came upon them.

That night, Margaret went to bed. She knew that Robert would exact revenge on what she had said to the police and on the way that Avril had spoken to him but she felt strangely calm. It did not matter what he did to her now as she had her escape route. She had sat in the lounge that afternoon after Robert had gone back to work and thought over what her daughter had said. It would take time for the inheritance from her mother-in-law to come through but she could put up with anything, safe in the knowledge that it was not for ever.

The door opened and Robert came in. He went to his wardrobe and took out one of his belts. He swished it through the air and Margaret felt her flesh shrivel under the duvet.

"Get up and get undressed. I am going to punish you for your stupidity," he said slowly and with emphasis on the word, 'punish'. "Then we will rehearse what you are going to say to that

Inspector and then…if you're very good, I am going to sodomise you. You'd like that, wouldn't you, my dear?"

Margaret got out of bed.

"Come over here first. I want you to see what I'm going to do to you."

Margaret moved like an automaton to stand in front of the mirror. She put up her hands to remove her nightgown, then stopped.

"What's the matter with you?" asked Robert.

"Nothing's the matter with me."

Robert reacted as if a dumb animal had spoken. His face became more cruel that before.

"Did I ask you to say anything, Margaret?"

"No you didn't but I am going to say something. I am going to say, 'No. No, I won't get undressed. No, I won't let you beat me. No, I won't let you sodomise me. In fact I won't let you do anything cruel to me again because I won't be here! Do you understand, you fool? I am leaving you."

Margaret lifted her dressing-gown off its hook on the back of the door and was out of the room and at the door of her daughter's bedroom before Robert overcame his astonishment. He came out of their bedroom, just in time to see his wife go into their daughter's room and close the door. Furiously, he banged on the door, demanding that his wife come out.

There was silence, except for muted voices behind the door, then the door opened but it was Avril who stood there.

"Mum and I are going to a hotel. Don't try to follow us. She's told me what you threatened to do to her tonight and if you come anywhere near her, I will tell the police. I suggest that you spend some time thinking up another story for them, as I will persuade Mum to tell the truth about the night of my grandmother's murder."

Avril went back inside and slammed the door shut. About twenty minutes later, a taxi drew up outside the front door and Robert watched, furiously helpless, as his wife and daughter, with one suitcase between them, went downstairs and got into the cab. Going into the lounge, he rang his brother and told him what had happened.

"I suggest, Matthew, that we make up a story between us about where we were on the night of Mother's murder. You need an alibi and now so do I. I suggest that we say that we had arranged to meet up after your game of cards, that you got away from mother more quickly, as you said. You rang me on my mobile, before I reached home and I turned round and went to somewhere where we met and drank together all night."

There was silence at the other end of the phone so he continued.

"Margaret is going to renege on her story about giving me supper, so I'll say that I was a coward and thought that if I had her word, I would clear myself and I didn't think of you and presumed that you would be able to concoct an alibi. I thought that telling the police that we were together would make them suspect us. OK brother?"

He listened as the telephone went dead.

# CHAPTER 31

O n Friday morning, over morning coffee in his room with Fiona, Charles told her that he felt that he ought to take Matthew Stevenson into custody. He had made a call to Martin Jamieson to ask if he could be more definite about the time of death for the second victim and Martin had been about to call him. It would have taken Adele Stevenson's light supper three hours to digest and it had, so her death could now be narrowed down to between 8pm and midnight.

"There isn't anybody else who benefitted from Adele Stevenson being murdered, apart, obviously from his brother. Some of the other beneficiaries were not so well catered for in the first will and if they heard of a new will being drawn up, they had nothing to gain from stopping it, had they?"

"I would rather it turned out to be Robert Stevenson," admitted Fiona. "I know he has an alibi for earlier in the evening but couldn't he have come back?"

"What if Matthew had still been there?" queried Charles.

"He could have invented some excuse. At least after yesterday's little episode, we're almost sure that they didn't plan or do it together."

"Unless they're consummate actors, I agree with you there," said Charles.

"Don't arrest Matthew yet, Charles. We know that Avril was sceptical about the cosy supper her mother and father shared and it would be embarrassing to have arrested Matthew then find out some incriminating evidence about Robert."

Charles had agreed, saying that he was not usually in as much of a hurry to solve a case but with their wedding coming closer, he really wanted it wrapped up.

"I'm getting more like Knox every day," he laughed.

Fraser went to The Linn Crematorium and as advised by his colleagues, waited at the gates to see the hearse go past before driving up to the car park which was by now almost empty. Pauline had chosen the smaller chapel, no doubt thinking that, at her mother's advanced age, there would be few friends. Fraser slipped into the back seat which was empty and another man joined him. The service was short and soon they were back outside and it was only then that Fraser noticed Fred Graham, looking fragile and leaning heavily on his stick. He was with a younger man and woman. Fraser went over and introduced himself. Fred Graham smiled a bit mistily and introduced him to Victor Smith, "Matron's husband" and Sandra Keith, "Adele's carer".

The family group was standing a little apart, then Pauline detached herself and came across to them to invite them back to Tall Trees where Matron had offered to put on a light lunch. As she stood with them, talking to the old man, Fraser heard Robert's autocratic voice complaining that the funeral should have been held in the larger funeral chapel and it was ridiculous that the lunch should be in a nursing home and not a prestigious hotel.

"Well you could have offered to arrange it," said Stewart Macartney, mildly.

Fraser turned round in time to see him shake his head at one of the twin girls who looked furious. She ignored his look and said clearly, "Well Uncle Robert, you thought that Tall Trees was good enough for my grandma when she as alive so it's odd that suddenly it's not so great!"

"Well said, Lucy," said her twin and the other young woman in the group clapped slowly, bringing an angry tide of red to Robert's face.

The cars filled up and the short drive was made to Tall Trees. Inside the lounge, there were three groups of people, one group comprising Fred Graham, Sandra Keith and a young man, presumably another carer, thought Fraser. A second group was made up of the family, all seated. Fraser looked at the only woman he didn't know and assumed that she was Margaret Stevenson, as she sat side by side with the girl who had clapped who was obviously Avril, her daughter. They were both extremely smart in their black suits, Margaret wearing a chic little black hat on her hair which was stylishly set.

The third group comprised Robert Stevenson and Victor Smith who was trying to engage the ostracised guest in polite conversation. Fraser remembered that in the chapel, Robert had sat behind the others, in a row by himself.

"Now, let's pick out the murderer," Fraser said to himself and scanned the room once more. "Robert Stevenson, Matthew Stevenson, Victor Smith? Could hardly be the old man, Fred Graham. What had he to gain? The youngsters? Unlikely. Margaret Stevenson? Would have been understandable if she'd murdered her husband but why her mother-in-law? One of the carers? No way, as they didn't benefit in any way. Could they have killed Adele out of pity as that old lady was dying of a mystery disease that no one had heard about? Stop it, Hewitt, you're getting ridiculous now," he chided himself.

At that point, Margaret Stevenson got out of her chair and approached him.

"Excuse me. Are you by any chance from the police? I'm Margaret Stevenson, Adele's daughter-in-law."

"Yes, I am, Mrs Stevenson. I'm PC Fraser Hewitt."

"PC Hewitt, would you be so kind as to tell your Inspector that I'll be in to see him this afternoon, if you think that would be suitable."

"I will certainly do that," replied Fraser.

Margaret Stevenson returned to her seat. The lounge door opened and two elderly people entered with Matron Smith who guided them to two seats by the window. A couple of minutes later, a man and woman came in with trays of what Fraser would have called party food: sausage rolls, mini quiches, tiny sandwiches and chicken drumsticks. They were followed by another girl, carrying two large pots of presumably tea and coffee.

"Please everybody, help yourselves," said Pauline, rising from her seat. Her relatives stood but held back to let Fred Graham and the two elderly people go to the table first. As Fred finished putting food onto his plate, Fraser went up to him.

"Excuse me, Mr Graham."

"Fred, my boy. How can I help you?"

"Fred, who are the two elderly people who've just come in with Mrs Smith?"

"They're Claude and Claire, two other residents. Matron Smith invited all of us but I don't imagine Donny and Mrs Mohammed will join us. These two wouldn't miss a free lunch."

As Fraser was about to add himself to the end of the queue for food, the old man stopped him.

"I wonder if you would do me a favour, Constable. I meant to ask you the other day when we spoke together and forgot. Would it be possible for me to get hold of Adele's dissertation?"

"What dissertation is that Fred?" asked Fraser.

"Adele did a degree course in literature when she was in her seventies, Open University, I imagine and she wrote a dissertation on two of her favourite poets. She said I could read it and I would still like to do so."

"Who were the poets, Fred," asked Fraser with interest.

"I can only remember one, Sylvia Plath, because I know she was the wife of that other poet, Ted Hughes who was poet laureate and she committed suicide. I can't remember the name of the other one as I'd never heard of her, I'm afraid."

"I imagine that would be Anne Sexton," supplied Fraser. "Those two were always linked together. Both were confessional poets along with the one who was my favourite, Robert Lowell."

"That's right."

Fred's thin face lit up.

"She told me a wee bit about the confessional poets and it was interesting. That's why I asked her if I could read what she wrote and she said yes."

"She must have been a clever woman to do that at seventy," remarked Fraser.

"She was, son, and certainly not demented, that's for sure."

"Well, Fred, I think you'll have to ask Mrs Macartney, as I'm almost positive that all Mrs Stevenson's things were released to her," said Fraser.

He saw the old man walk slowly over to Pauline Macartney and he saw her smile and nod her head. When Fred had seated himself as far from the other two residents as possible, Fraser went across to Pauline and asked if he could also read the dissertation, after Mr Graham.

"I studied those poets too, at university, and I would be really interested in what your mother wrote," he told her.

"Mum would have been so pleased that two people thought that what she wrote was worth reading, Constable. Wasn't she marvellous getting a degree at seventy-two?"

Fraser agreed and going across to sit with Fred, he said that he would come up to the Home in a few days and borrow the dissertation.

"Pauline, is there to be no alcohol served?" a loud voice demanded.

"Robert, it's just late morning. No one wants alcohol," explained Pauline.

"I do. I can't think why you're penny-pinching with all that lovely money you've been left," he replied, nastily.

"Oh, Robert, do sit down and shut up!" said a woman's voice. "Why do you always have to make yourself look ridiculous?"

There was silence in the room and the family gazed in amazement as the timid Margaret berated her husband.

"How dare you!" he spluttered.

" I dare because I don't think you'd want me to tell all these nice people what kind of husband you've been to me," she replied, bravely.

"And for your information, Robert, the Home offered to pay for the refreshments," added Pauline, linking her arm through Margaret's.

"If I were you, I'd just leave, brother dear. You don't like it here and we don't like you," contributed Matthew.

Robert, his face red with rage or embarrassment, turned and went out of the room.

"Well done, Mum," said Avril. "Mum and I left home last night," she told the others.

"Where are you staying, Avril?" asked Stewart.

"At the Busby Hotel."

"Mum, Aunt Margaret and Avril must come and stay with us. Kim and I can sleep downstairs for a while," volunteered Lucy.

Avril reddened. She and her cousins had never been close. She had envied them their happy home life so had been distant with them and now they were showing her such kindness!

"Of course," agreed Kim, and Pauline laughed and said, "That's settled then."

As Fraser thanked matron for her hospitality and left the nursing home, he thought that he might not have found out who the murderer was but he certainly had some juicy news for his colleagues.

# CHAPTER 32

"Right, Davenport. Name me the murderer in this nursing home case," barked Knox.

"Sir, with my wedding coming up a week tomorrow, I'd be only too happy to see this case sewn up but at the moment it only appears that the younger brother of the second lady killed had the opportunity and, possibly, the motive for the murder of his mother. He has no alibi for the time of death but I can think of absolutely no reason for him to kill the first lady.

"Is there anybody who had a motive for the first murder?"

"Only the owners of Tall Trees Nursing Home. They inherited a lot of money but Mr & Mrs Smith had absolutely no reason to kill the other woman. In fact, if they did kill Martha Cowan, they would not have committed another murder because the first one was being seen as a natural death until the second one happened and shed suspicion on both deaths which were identical," said Davenport.

"Is it possible that the son heard of the first murder and decided to do a copy-cat killing?" Knox asked.

"Yes, that's possible, Sir. I've thought of that."

"So what's stopping you having him charged then, man?"

"He's actually quite likeable, Sir," said Davenport.

"So probably were many killers down through history," said Knox, dismissively. "If that's all that's standing in your way, get down there and arrest him!"

"And what about the first murder, Sir, the one that he's supposed to have copied? Am I to arrest the nursing home owners?

Charles tried to keep the sarcasm he was feeling out of this remark.

Knox picked up a folder from his desk and started to read it. Davenport, dismissed, went dejectedly downstairs. He called his DS into this room. She came in, shut the door and sat down across from him.

"How did it go, Charles?"

"Knox wants me to arrest Mathew Stevenson. He said that he could have done a copy-cat killing and that the Smiths could have killed Martha Cowan for the money she left the Home."

"So does he want Matron and Victor Smith arrested too?" asked Fiona.

"He didn't say but we can hardly do one without the other, can we?"

"Could Robert Stevenson not have done the same, copied the first murder?"

"There's the problem of his wife's statement that she saw him come home."

"I know but he could have gone back out."

"Yes but the time window is much smaller for him, isn't it?"

The 'phone rang on his desk as he finished speaking. He picked it up. Fiona got up to leave but he motioned to her to sit back down.

"Thank you, Joe. I guess you'll be printing that?"

He listened again.

"OK. 'Bye."

Davenport laid the receiver back on its cradle.

"As you probably guessed, that was Joe Harper of the Glasgow Herald. He wanted to let me know that our chief constable has just rung him to say that an arrest is imminent in, 'The Nursing Home Murders', as he called them. Knox has named Matthew Stevenson."

"So what are you going to do, Charles?" asked Fiona anxiously.

"I think we'll have Matthew Stevenson in. I can't make Knox look a fool…"

"…even though he is one," said Fiona, angrily.

Davenport went down the corridor and finding Frank and Salma together, told them to go and bring in Matthew Stevenson.

"He might be at home but if not he'll be at his travel agency, 'Bijou Travel".

Davenport gave Salma the home and business address of the younger Mr Stevenson.

Matthew was at work. He took the police into the back of the shop where Salma cautioned him. He looked dismayed but offered no resistance and just gave instructions to his middle-aged assistant, telling her that if he was not back by closing-time, she should simply take the keys home and open up the next day. He walked out to the car between Salma and Frank.

Once more in the interview room, Matthew sat slumped in his chair, looking despondent for the first time, while Davenport read him his rights once again. Frank Selby stood at the back of the room, his hands behind his back.

"I didn't do it. I'm not a killer," Matthew said, covering his face with both hands.

"Can you suggest anyone else who had motive and opportunity to kill your mother, Sir?" asked Davenport.

"No, only my brother and he has an alibi and if I had no motive, then neither did he. Neither of us knew that Mother was about to change her will. At least, if Robert knew, he didn't tell me and

I'm sure he would have done. We were partners in crime, before yesterday," he laughed bitterly. "Wrong choice of words, sorry. I just meant that we'd been partners in planning to get Mother into Tall Trees. I wish now that I'd never agreed to be part of that scheme!"

He bowed his head then looked up again.

"Why on earth would either of us kill that other old lady?"

"A mistake, perhaps. You slipped the poison into your mother's cup, she went into Martha Cowan's room and *Martha* picked it up by mistake. When you realised what must have happened, you did it all over again, the following night or you heard about the first murder and copied it."

"But I wasn't up there the previous night," said Matthew.

"And you have proof of that, Sir?" asked Davenport.

Matthew's relieved look was replaced by one of despondency which was all Davenport needed as his answer.

"Do you want your lawyer, Sir?" asked Davenport.

Matthew gave him the telephone number of a lawyer who was from a different firm to that of his mother, telling Davenport that Robert shared his mother's legal company but he did not. Davenport nodded to Frank who came forward and led

Matthew out of the room and down to one of the empty cells, in the basement. Matthew went in. He looked dazed as the heavy door clanged shut.

Davenport went back to his room, called Tall Trees and asked Mr &Mrs Smith to come in. He could hardly arrest them but he needed to question them thoroughly, for the first time.

Over at the Macartney house, unaware of what was happening to her younger brother, Pauline was welcoming her sister-in-law and niece. Kim had transferred a lot of her clothes into Lucy's wardrobe and drawers, leaving space for Margaret and Avril to put their meagre belongings, including the smart back suits which they had bought the day before for the funeral. Pauline took them upstairs and showed them which room was to be theirs, for the time being.

"Unpack, then come down to the kitchen and we'll have coffee," she said. "Stewart's escaped from what he kept calling, the 'monstrous regiment of women'," she laughed. "He's gone to Rouken Glen Garden Centre."

Over tea and coffee in the cosy kitchen, they discussed everything that had happened, not being aware that Mathew was languishing in a cell at that moment. They had all been fond of Adele and shared fond memories of her, talking about her determined but loving nature.

"A real matriarch," said Avril.

"What's that, Avril?" asked Lucy.

"Head of the family," replied Avril.

"You always were a clever-clogs," said Kim.

Avril blushed. Being about ten years older than her twin cousins, they had never been close and she could well believe that they found her distant and intellectual. She turned the conversation to their futures.

"I believe you've both finished with school," she said now.

"Oops, a tender topic," said Pauline.

"Why?" asked Margaret.

"I wanted Kim to come globe-trotting with me and she wants to settle down and be an old married woman," said Lucy, with no trace of bitterness.

"Not yet, Lucy," protested Kim. "Not till I'm qualified as a teacher."

"What subject?" asked Avril.

"A primary teacher. I couldn't cope with teenagers," said Kim.

"Will you still travel, Lucy?" asked Margaret. "I wish I was your age. I'd come with you."

They all laughed.

"Where were you thinking of going?" asked Avril.

"I want to go to The Far East, Malaysia, Indonesia, The Philippines, Japan," said Lucy. "Then maybe on to Australia and New Zealand. I could perhaps find work there to finance a longer trip. I don't want to spend all of Grandma's money in one go."

Avril looked interested.

"I'm going to The Phillipines. I have a job in Manilla, working with poor people who need medical aid. I'm sure I could get you work if you don't mind being quite poorly paid."

Lucy's eyes lit up.

"Oh, Avril, that would be great. I've always wanted to work with needy people but didn't know how to go about it. I thought you were in Russia."

"I was but I like to move about."

"I would be so much happier knowing that you were with Avril, at least at first," said Pauline, happily.

"And I'd feel less guilty," said Kim, also looking pleased.

Talk then turned to the murder. Avril asked her mother if she had meant what she had said about reneging on her alibi for her father. Pauline and the others were interested, so Margaret, the centre of attention for the second time recently, explained to the others that Robert had bullied her into saying that she had seen him come home and had made him supper.

"She said she made him a bacon sandwich," said Avril and they all laughed, knowing that this was not something that Robert would have appreciated.

"I think, subconsciously, that I must have chosen something ridiculous to…I don't know… make it seem like a lie, yet the police were not to know how silly it was."

"Where *was* Robert then?" asked Pauline.

"Probably with his latest fancy woman," said Margaret.

"How did you know about that, Aunt Margaret?" asked Lucy.

"Well let's just say that he flaunted her existence in my face at times," said Margaret.

Pauline asked if her two daughters and her niece would do her a big favour and go to Morrisons if she gave them a list, as she had only planned a meal for four and now there would be six tonight. The four left the kitchen, Lucy and Kim agreeing cheerfully to do the shopping and Avril being happy to go along. Pauline returned to find the mugs washed and dried. Margaret was back, sitting at the kitchen table. Pauline joined her.

"I sensed that there were things you wouldn't say in front of the girls," she said now.

"Thanks, Pauline. Avril knows a lot, or rather has guessed most of it but I wouldn't like to paint a picture that she might not be able to forget. However, I would like to tell someone. You'll think me an awful mouse…"

"...like Avril, I've guessed a few things over the years, Margaret and no, I don't think you're a mouse. A lot of women stay with difficult men for various reasons," said Pauline, gently.

"Robert often hit me and he was about to last night but he sexually abused me and mentally too. Until your mother left me that money, I was never able to escape, even once Avril left home and no longer needed me, if she ever did need me, that is. She was always so strong and stood up to her father. Things actually got easier when she left because he always took it out on me, if she argued or fought with him. She was so quick to leave home."

"Easier in what way?"

"Well he left me alone at nights, slept in one of the guest bedrooms... that's a laugh, we never had guests," said Margaret. "He was always quick to tell me when he had another woman. Recently, he compared with his latest one," she said, almost tearfully.

Pauline got out of her chair and gave her a hug.

"I wish that you could have confided in me before this," she said.

"I was so ashamed and what could you have done?"

"Well, it's over now," said Pauline.

"Yes and Avril called me Mum for the first time, yesterday," hiccupped Margaret. "Pauline, do you think he…Robert…could have killed your mother?"

"Well, it's more likely than Matthew doing it."

Matthew's lawyer had arrived at Shawbank and was being seen by Davenport in his room. Charles explained why Matthew was in custody and told the young man that his client could offer no explanation as to his whereabouts on the night of his mother's murder, other than saying that he went straight home, a statement which no one could verify. He told Mr Dunlop that his client had a possible motive for the murder, explaining that Mrs Stevenson had changed her will the previous day, disinheriting Matthew and his elder brother, Robert and that the police had been told that the old lady had informed her two sons about changing the will, a fact that both men denied. Mr Dunlop asked about bail for Matthew and Davenport told him that he wanted the man kept in custody in the hope that it this might encourage him to divulge his whereabouts, if indeed he was innocent, but that he saw no reason why bail would not be granted on Monday. He led the lawyer to an interview room and got Frank to bring Matthew Stevenson up from his cell and wait in the room while the two men conversed.

Frank could tell Davenport later that Mr Dunlop had tried to persuade his client to tell the truth about where he had been but Matthew stuck to his story that he had gone home alone. The lawyer had promised to try for bail the next day. Frank had taken Matthew back downstairs where he had been brought a simple lunch and the lawyer had departed, after telling Frank that he would be back on Monday.

"Matthew Stevenson looked so dejected, Salma," said Frank to his colleague.

"I hope it turns out not to be him," she replied.

Fraser arrived back from the funeral to find out that an arrest had been made. He also found out that Saturday was to be a working day.

"Sorry, team, no rest for the wicked…"

…or us," quipped the DS.

"Come in a bit later, say ten o'clock, to the Incident Room. Now I think a late lunch is called for and you can get off home early tonight to make sure you're fresh for tomorrow. Just make sure all reports are written up before you leave. I've got Victor Smith coming in later today. He and Matron are our only other possible suspects, apart from the Stevenson brothers."

As they filed out, Fraser held back.

"Sir."

"Yes, Fraser?"

"Mrs Stevenson, Robert's wife, asked me to tell you that she's going to come in and see you later today and the funeral was...interesting."

"Did you spot our murderer, lad?"

"I'm afraid not. Do you want me to tell you how it went?"

"If you haven't got important information that would lead to an arrest, we'll wait till tomorrow, Fraser. Now off you go."

Back in his room, Davenport sat and wondered what Margaret Stevenson would have to say to him.

# CHAPTER 33

Margaret Stevenson came in about an hour later, accompanied by her daughter. As it was not an official interview, Davenport saw them in his room. He offered them coffee and called for Fiona to join them.

"Now, Mrs Stevenson, what can I do for you?"

"It's what I can do for you, Inspector; I can tell you the truth now."

"You do know that it's a crime to lie to the police?" said Davenport, sternly.

"Please don't blame Mum," said Avril. "You didn't have to live with my bully of a father."

"Thanks, Avril but the Inspector is correct. It was very wrong of me to lie and I know that now."

More gently, Davenport asked her to tell them what she had lied about.

"I didn't see Robert come home at eight o'clock on the night of his mothers' murder. He told me to say that."

"When did he come home?" asked Fiona.

"I have no idea."

"And as I said earlier, I was out late, so I can't help you except to say that his car was there when I got back after midnight," added Avril.

"You were cynical about the cosy supper, Miss Stevenson," said Davenport.

"Yes. My father would never have had a bacon sandwich for supper."

"I think I said something that was out of character to kind of alert you, although I wasn't brave enough to go against him," said Margaret.

"Why have you decided to come clean now?" asked Fiona sounding curious.

"I've left Robert," said Margaret, proudly. "He has always been physically...and sexually cruel to me but last night, something snapped. I went for Avril and we stayed last night in a hotel. At the funeral today, Pauline invited us both to stay with them for the time being, so we are will be going there when we leave here. That is, if I'm free to leave, Inspector."

"Did the inheritance help in your decision?" asked Fiona.

"Of course! I never expected my mother-in-law to leave me anything. I didn't even visit her in Tall Trees because I felt embarrassed at being part of her being moved there or rather, not trying to stop it happening."

"I think Grandmother had had a taste of Father at his worst and for the first time sympathised with you, Mum."

"Maybe. I always thought that she despised me for being a wimp."

"Thanks for your honesty. You didn't lie under oath, so yes, you're free to go," said Davenport. "One more question. Do you think it's possible that your husband killed his mother?"

Margaret thought for a moment.

"Until last night, I would have said, no, but now I'm not so sure. Money means a lot to him, Inspector, money and position. I would say he is murderous now but whether he was that night, I'm not sure."

"Miss Stevenson?"

"He was never violent to me but he could never bear to be thwarted. I saw that when I lived at home, although for some reason he never crossed swords with me when I went against him."

"I think he was intimidated by your refusing to be afraid of him, Avril," said Margaret.

"Whatever… I do think him capable of murder, Inspector. There's a cruel streak in him and an utter selfishness that makes him only see his own position."

"What about your Uncle Matthew?" asked Fiona, knowing that this question was probably unprofessional but she was curious to see what this honest, young woman would say

"Uncle Matt is also selfish…"

"…Their Father brought them up to feel that they were important," interrupted Margaret.

"…but he wouldn't hurt a fly, I'm sure."

Avril agreed with he.

"Is he a bit of a loner?" asked Fiona.

Margaret laughed. Her face lit up and she looked happy, for the first time since they had met her.

"A loner? Matthew? Anything but. He always has a woman on his arm and he has lots of friends. A typical, carefree bachelor!"

Davenport took their empty mugs and thanked them both for coming.

Victor Smith and his wife arrived at Shawbank Police Station, at around five o'clock. Both looked very nervous when they approached the desk. Bob rang Davenport's office and was told to escort them to two separate interview rooms, downstairs, where Fiona and Frank went to see Mr Smith and Davenport and Salma went to talk to Mrs Smith. On hearing that the two were coming in, all the team had volunteered to stay on and Davenport had selected Frank and Salma to attend the interviews, sending Fraser off home with a reminder to be in at ten the next morning.

Now, facing Matron, he asked her for her first name and switching on the recording device, he said, in an official voice, "5.10pm on Friday August 29th. Present, Mrs Doreen Smith, with DCI Davenport and Sergeant Salma Din in attendance."

Salma sat back in her chair as Davenport leaned forward in his.

"Mrs Smith. Will you tell me please when it was that you first realised that you and your husband were to be beneficiaries in the will of the late Martha Cowan?"

"Not us, really. She wanted to leave money to Tall Trees," whispered Doreen Smith, nervously.

"I'm afraid that I will have to ask you to speak more loudly and clearly," said Davenport.

"Sorry, Miss Cowan left the money to Tall Trees, not to us."

"But as you and your husband own Tall Trees, it would in effect mean that both of you would have access to the money, surely?" said Davenport.

"Yes," she said. "I suppose so."

"So, when did you find out that you and the Home were to be beneficiaries in Miss Cowan's will?"

"About a year after she came to us."

"Was the Home in need of money?" asked Davenport.

Doreen Smith sounded relieved when she replied that the Home was not in financial difficulties now, nor ever had been since they had taken it over. She reached into her large handbag and brought out a buff-coloured folder.

"I thought this might be what you wanted to know so I brought our last year's bank statements, the ones for the running of Tall Trees and our personal ones."

"Mrs Smith is handing me a folder," said Davenport into the tape machine.

"I can give you the name of our accountant who deals with our business and private affairs," she said.

He took the folder and thanked her.

"You see, we have great difficulty understanding why anyone would want to kill Miss Cowan and you and your husband are the only ones to benefit from her death," Davenport informed her.

"But why on earth would we murder Mrs Stevenson? It's her family, I imagine, who will inherit her estate."

Salma had sat forward and Davenport nodded to her to speak.

"Mrs Smith, it is possible that Adele Stevenson saw something on the day or night of Miss Cowan's murder. She seems to have been in the garden that day, so could have seen you or Mr Smith coming from the shed where the arsenic was kept."

Doreen Smith slumped in her chair, then she looked up.

"Victor could have come and gone from the shed as he is our gardener but I was never in that shed. I couldn't even describe its layout to you."

"Or, being on the same floor, she could have seen either of you coming from Miss Cowan's room at an unusual time," said Salma who had obviously thought this out.

Davenport smiled at her.

"Victor never went into residents' rooms, unless on an occasion when something needed doing which neither myself nor one of the carers could do but that was rare. I am quite a handy person and Tom Carew is good at practical things."

"So, to sum up," said Davenport, "Victor could have been seen going into the shed, that day and you could have been seen coming from Miss Cowan's room?"

"It's possible, Inspector but I didn't go into Miss Cowan's room, until Sandra Keith came to tell me that she couldn't get in to Martha's room. I seldom enter the residents' rooms: the carers go in, not me. I tend to speak to them in the lounge area or at mealtimes. I don't like to intrude. As for Victor going into the shed, I imagine he must go in quite frequently."

Next door, Fiona had asked Victor when he and his wife had realised that they were to benefit from Martha Cowan's death.

"It's the Home which benefits really, not us personally but we knew not long after she arrived, maybe about a year or less. It's my wife who could tell you exactly. She's much better with times and dates than I am."

"Does the Home need money, Sir?" asked Fiona.

"I don't think so. Doreen keeps the books and she's never been worried or told me that there was cause for concern."

"You knew that there was arsenic in the shed. How many people knew this, do you think?"

Victor looked despondent. He ran his hands through his hair, before replying that he did not imagine that anyone knew, except himself and Donny who had had his wife bring the arsenic to the Home.

"I don't imagine that Donny will have a clear recollection of that either," he said, "so really only myself and Katy, Donny's wife would know that it was there, though anyone au fait with gardening wouldn't be surprised to find it in a garden shed."

"Is there any chance that visitors might go into the shed?" asked Fiona.

"I have to admit that it's extremely unlikely. Someone wanting, say a vase for flowers, would ask a carer who would get one from a store cupboard. I can't think of any reason why, unless they went out into the garden with their relative and for some reason they decided that they wanted, say a trowel, but that sounds daft, doesn't it?"

"Can you think of anyone who might want to murder either of the two ladies?" Fiona asked, not answering the man's question, deeming it to be rhetorical.

"Martha Cowan's only beneficiary, other than us, was her niece but she's never been here at all. I expect one of Adele Stevenson's children could have killed her."

"Thank you, Mr Smith. We'll get your wife to provide us with bank statements. Apart from that, you're free to go, Sir."

Fiona stood up and Victor Smith stood too. Frank escorted him upstairs and into a waiting room, asking if he wanted a tea or coffee, both of which were declined. About fifteen minutes later, he was joined by his wife and Davenport who told them that he would read through the bank statements and have them returned to them as soon as possible.

"Thank you both for your help. You will understand that because of you inheriting a large sum from one of the deceased, you remain in the frame for the time being but you are free to go now."

The Smiths left. Davenport thanked Salma for her intelligent questions, told both her and Frank to get off home and returned to his own room where he was joined by his DS. Together, they went over the accounts.

"Making a healthy profit each month, it seems," said Charles who had been reading the Home's accounts.

"And they're well in funds privately too," said Fiona who had scanned deposit and current accounts. They have an ISA each for £50,000 and their deposit account is healthy and gets added to quite regularly. Quite a large amount is withdrawn every September, probably for a holiday, I imagine."

"Matron offered to give me her accountant's name and address but I don't think that's necessary, do you?" asked Charles.

Fiona said it all seemed above board and they discussed what each had learned from the interviews. Charles told her about Salma's comment that Adele Stevenson could have seen either of them coming out of the garden shed or from Martha Cowan's room. He told her that Matron claimed never to have been in the shed and that she had said what was obvious, which was that Victor would often have come from the shed so that would not have been a remarkable event.

"Matron said that Victor very seldom went into residents' rooms," said Charles.

"So if he had gone into Martha's room, that would have been odd," said Fiona.

"Though not to Adele Stevenson who was new and, for all she knew, Victor often went in to do little jobs," commented Charles.

"Matron said she seldom went into residents' rooms either as she left that to the carers and talked to the old folk in the lounge or dining room, usually," he continued. "But same with her, Adele was not to know that so would probably think it normal for the matron to be in Martha's room."

"But, Charles, if either was guilty of the murder, they would probably not stop to think that out and would expect Adele to be curious," countered Fiona.

"So we're not much further forward, love," said Charles, putting the accounts and the bank statements back in the folder.

His desk 'phone rang and he picked it up.

"Mrs Stevenson, how can I help you?"

He listened, thanked her and hung up, looking despondent.

"That was Margaret Stevenson. She wanted to tell me that her husband always took delight in telling her that he had other women so he might have been with one of them the night of the murder."

"What will we do if the case isn't solved by our wedding day?" asked Fiona, looking anxious.

"We'll just have to take the Saturday off. One more day won't make much difference but hopefully it won't come to that," said Charles, putting his arm round her and trying to sound cheerful. He did not tell her about the short honeymoon he had planned. Maybe it was just as well that he had kept it secret, he thought now, as it might have to be postponed if the case had not been closed.

# CHAPTER 34

The team members were all sitting in the Incident Room by 9.55 on Saturday morning. Davenport and DS Macdonald had carried down three mugs of tea and some chocolate biscuits for the others as the session would probably be a long one and it was, after all, usually their day off. Davenport had drawn up a chair for himself this time instead of sitting on a desk at the front and had asked them to arrange their seats in a circle.

"OK, Fraser, you first, son. Tell us about the funeral."

"It was interesting, well not the funeral itself, except for the fact that the elder brother... Robert... sat by himself. It was in the smaller of the two chapels, St Giles I think it's called. When the family left, they all went in one large car and Robert drove himself. We went back to the nursing home for refreshments and when Robert heard the venue, he complained and one of his nieces said that if it was good enough for him to put her grandmother in alive, it was good enough for all of them to go back to and another young woman who turned out to be Robert's daughter, clapped."

"I don't think Robert Stevenson's exactly popular with his family," commented Frank.

"Only one resident came to the funeral, Fred Graham, but two others came for the refreshments. Mr Graham asked me if he could have Adele Stevenson's dissertation…"

"What's that?" asked Frank.

"Something that students write to get their degree. Something to do with their chosen subject, usually for honours," said Fiona.

"She did an Open University course, in her seventies," Fraser informed them. "In English literature."

"That explains all the weird books," said Frank.

"I told him to ask Mrs Macartney for it and he did."

"Anything else happen?"

"Just that Robert complained that there was no alcohol being served. He told his sister, rather nastily, that she had enough money now and his sister said that the nursing home had offered to pay for the refreshments. Robert's wife told him to shut up to the obvious amazement of everyone there and his brother told him to leave as he wasn't wanted…oh, his wife hinted that she could tell everyone about how he had treated her."

"Did he leave?" asked Fiona.

"Right away, looking furious."

"Well all that supports what we learned from Margaret Stevenson when she came in yesterday afternoon. She and her daughter are now staying with the Macartneys and she has left Robert. She did *not* hear him come in at eight o'clock on the night of the murder but he forced her to give him an alibi."

"Both Margaret and Avril Stevenson think that Robert could have killed his mother and Avril doesn't think that Matthew did," said Fiona.

"Victor and Doreen Smith were very nervous but adamant that they didn't kill Martha Cowan for her money and they brought bank statements and accounts to show that both they and Tall Trees are well in the black, financially. Matron especially, was quick to point out that they didn't gain from Adele Stevenson's death."

Davenport smiled across at his sergeant.

"Salma told them that either of them could have been seen by Mrs Stevenson, coming out of the garden shed with a bottle or out of Martha's room that night and that they could have killed her in case she told us that."

"What did they say to that, Sir?" asked Frank, eagerly.

"Matron said that she had never been in the shed and that Victor very seldom went into the residents' room. Victor, when asked, said that apart from him, only Donny and his wife knew of the existence of the arsenic."

"But you arrested Matthew, Sir," pointed out Frank. "Why?"

"Mr Knox pointed out that Matthew Stevenson had no alibi and at that time I couldn't tell him that neither had Robert, at least not the alibi he claimed to have...I'll have to get him in to check what he has to say now, in the light of his wife's new statement. Knox instructed me to, 'Get down and arrest him', I think were his words."

"Matthew couldn't tell us anyone else who might want to have his Mother dead, could he Sir?" said Frank.

"No, but then he also pointed out that neither he nor his brother had any reason to kill Martha Cowan," said Davenport.

"Isn't he correct, Sir?" asked Fraser.

"One or other of them could have poisoned his mother's cup the night before, she wandered into Miss Cowan's room, put down the cup, got a fresh one and Miss Cowan picked up the other cup," said Davenport.

"What did he say to that?" asked Fraser.

Frank, almost as eager as Penny Price in one of her enthusiastic moments, butted in here.

"He said that he wasn't up at Tall Trees the previous night but he had no alibi for that night either."

"Thanks, Selby," said Davenport, dryly.

"And anyway, as we keep saying, Adele didn't have her new cups by that time, unless Pauline came up twice with her mother's new things," Fiona reminded them.

"We must check that. Salma. Give Pauline Macartney a ring and ask when she brought her mother her new, flower-patterned cups."

Salma left the room.

"Odd, Sir," said Fiona. "Margaret Stevenson said that Matthew was anything but a loner and always had a girlfriend, yet on both nights he was alone, with no one to give him an alibi."

"Protecting someone?" suggested Fraser. "Maybe he's seeing a married woman and he doesn't want to get her involved in case her husband finds out."

"That thought had crossed my mind, Fraser," said his boss.

They sat silent for a few moments, all digesting what they had learned. Davenport rose to his feet but before he could say anything, Bob arrived in the room, waving The Glasgow Herald.

"Sir," he said, "Have you read the paper today?"

"I get The Guardian and only glanced at it over breakfast, Bob. Why?"

He stiffened.

"God, how could I forget? Joe Harper rang me yesterday with the news that Knox had informed him that an arrest was imminent. Is it in, Bob?"

"Yes, Sir."

Bob held out his paper and Davenport grabbed it. He read for a few minutes.

"Damn the man. We're going to look real asses if Matthew turns out to be as innocent as his family think he is!"

Fiona got up and took the paper from him. The other three stood too and read over her shoulder.

## "YOUNGER SON ARRESTED FOR MOTHER'S MURDER"

"Charles…Sir…"

Fiona felt her cheeks redden at her blunder. Charles smiled at her and she continued,

"Maybe this will smoke out Matthew's woman, if there is one. Surely she won't sit back and let him be arrested for a murder he couldn't have committed!"

"Possibly. It would be good if something came of this article. We forgot to tell you three about the other piece of information we gleaned yesterday from Margaret Stevenson," said Davenport. "She rang us later to say that Robert had other women so might have another alibi for the night of the murder."

"Why not just give us her name instead of getting his wife to lie?" asked Salma.

"Liked having his wife obey him? Didn't want to show he wasn't an upstanding pillar of the community? I don't know. I just hope his wife is wrong, otherwise we're back to square one with no solid suspects."

He sighed.

Salma came back in to say that Pauline had taken everything up the day after her mother had visited Martha and got the idea of having these things.

"Oh well, it wasn't much of an idea anyway. Come on, you lot. Let's go for lunch and cheer ourselves up. I'll ring Robert Stevenson when we get back, though he'll probably be on the golf course. I want to interview him again, now that he has no apparent alibi."

"And Matthew?" asked Fiona.

"Leave him where he is just now, as he still doesn't have an alibi. Come on, let's get out of here."

# CHAPTER 35

Back in their seats in the Incident Room, the discussion turned to the contradiction of the sons to their mother's assertion in her diary that she had played Bezique with both of them on the night of her death.

"How do you play Bezique?" asked Fraser.

"No idea," said Davenport.

"Is that relevant?" asked Frank.

"Probably not," replied Fraser equably. "I was just curious as that old gentleman, Fred Graham, plays it too. He told me yesterday that his grandson comes once a week to play and that he played a few times against Adele Stevenson. I'd heard of it but I'm sure nobody I know has played it."

"Pauline said that she hadn't learned it as if it was a difficult thing to learn," said Davenport. "However, as Frank so rightly said, it isn't important. What is, is why either Adele or both sons lied about playing it that night."

"Maybe Adele lied because she had told her old friend that she would be playing and didn't want to admit that her sons wouldn't spend the time after all," suggested Salma.

"But Mr Graham surely wouldn't be reading her diary!" said Fiona. "So she could have lied to him but why lie in her diary?"

"Neither Robert not Matthew had any reason to lie about it, surely," said Fraser.

"Except that it would mean that they'd still be there nearer to the time of death which must have at least been after 8.45 when Adele rang down to the kitchen," said Fiona. "From what she wrote about making Matthew wait till she finished playing with Robert, and all of them having supper together, they couldn't surely have left till about 9.30 at the earliest. Robert might have been earlier if supper came between the two games of cards."

"Martin said between 6pm and 10pm and we now know it must have been after 8.45, so the time has been narrowed and if they could have proved they weren't anywhere near the Home after, say 9 pm, they'd be in the clear," said Davenport.

He looked excited.

"If they are lying then about the time, surely that means that they know when she was killed!"

"Sir, what about the Gaviscon and the book? Are they just coincidences?" asked Fraser

"Things don't happen for no reason," persisted Fiona. "Someone is lying over the card games and the supper, and the tummy medicine and book were requested for some reason. The book might just have been a clever old lady wanting to keep up with another old lady but why the Gaviscon, especially when she didn't have a weak stomach?"

There was silence.

"Here's another question, Team," said Davenport. "Who would know about the presence of the arsenic in the garden shed?"

"Anyone with a garden who had had a wasp problem," said Fraser.

"Only a guess though, that it would be kept in the shed," said Fiona.

"Unless you worked in the Home's garden and used the shed," said Salma.

"So that leaves Victor Smith, possibly Matron Smith and Donny, the young resident," said Davenport.

"Maybe Donny's carer, Tom," suggested Frank. "Donny could have mentioned it to him."

"And Donny's wife," said Fiona.

"Now, why would Donny, Tom or Donny's wife want to murder those two old ladies?" asked Davenport, sounding exasperated.

"Tom said he'd never heard of a patient with dementia turning murderous," agreed Fiona.

"So that brings us back to the Smiths who had no reason to murder Adele Stevenson, unless she saw something suspicious on the night of Martha's murder."

"Surely a woman as astute as we are told that Adele was, would have mentioned it," said Frank.

"No, not necessarily, as the death wasn't seen as suspicious until after Adele died," said Fraser, earning himself a glare from his fellow constable.

Davenport got up and going to an unused section of the white board, he headed one column, 'Adele' and the other 'Martha'. Under 'Martha', he wrote the names, Victor Smith and Matron Smith.

"Anyone else who benefited from her death?" he asked.

"The unknown niece," suggested Fiona.

Davenport wrote, 'unknown niece', under 'Matron Smith'.

"We've ruled out the 'wrong cup' theory so we can't put the Stevenson brothers," he said.

"Now, what about Adele?" he asked.

"Robert and Matthew," said Frank.

"Pauline," said Salma.

"Motive?" asked her boss.

"She knew that she had benefitted hugely from the new will which she was told about and wanted to make sure that her mother didn't live to change it back," Salma added.

"But, Salma," said Frank. "She only knew the new will was to be written, she didn't know that her mother had hand written one, so surely it was in her interests to keep her mother alive till she saw the lawyer?"

"That's true. Sorry, Sir. Don't add Pauline to the list," apologised Salma.

"Certainly there was no reason for the Smiths to kill Adele because the second death would... and did draw attention to the first death which was being seen as natural up to that point," said Davenport.

He stood back and looked at the two lists.

"So to my mind, the only two suspects are Robert and Matthew Stevenson, though I suppose we should check the alibis of all the other family members. Frank and Fraser, would you get off right now and do that. See all the Macartneys, as they did all inherit large sums though they would have done under any will, and also see Margaret Stevenson and Avril although I don't think from what she said to me that Margaret expected to receive anything from her mother-in-law. You might be lucky and get them all in as it's Saturday afternoon."

"I don't imagine that you'll be so lucky getting hold of Robert Stevenson," said Fiona.

"Probably not, but I'll go and 'phone the house now.

Nobody answered the Stevenson's 'phone and there was no answering facility, Margaret presumably being always on hand to take messages.

Davenport returned to the Incident Room and interrupted the conversation about weddings which was going on between Fiona and Salma who had quite recently been to Penny's mother's wedding and wondered if her bosses' wedding would be at all similar.

"Not nearly as grand, I don't imagine. They had their reception at a posh hotel, didn't they?"

"Yes, The Brig O'Doon down in Ayrshire," replied Salma.

"Trust women! Let off the leash for two minutes and they forget the case in hand," joked Davenport.

Just as he sat down, his phone rang. It was Bob at the desk to tell him that a young woman had asked if he was available. Davenport listened and told Bob to bring her up to the Incident Room.

"Someone wants to see me and it's to do with our case," he said, sounding excited. Salma rose to her feet but he told her to wait and hear what was said.

The young woman who came in was in her late twenties, small, slim and blonde. She looked nervous. Davenport invited her to sit on one of the seats just vacated by Fraser and Frank and she sat down on the edge of the seat, twisting the strap of her black handbag between her fingers.

"I believe that you have some information for me regarding the two murders which we're involved in," Davenport said.

"Yes…the man who's been arrested…Matthew Stevenson…"

Her voice tailed off.

"Yes, what about him, Miss…?"

"Mrs Lawrence, Karen Lawrence. He's my boss. I work at his travel agent's in Clarkston."

"Yes?"

"Look, does this have to go any further? I mean…"

"Only if it comes to a court case, Mrs Lawrence, but if it does, I'm afraid your statement would become public knowledge."

The woman sat for a moment, rubbing her forehead with one hand. She looked, thought Fiona, as if she would have liked to have run off. Then she sat up straight in her chair and said, "Well, I'll just have to take that chance. I can't let Matt suffer for something he couldn't have done."

"Tell us about it, please, Mrs Lawrence," said Davenport, gently.

"I work part time for Matt, in his travel agency, 'Bijou Travel'. Over the last few months we've become …more than friends. I had arranged to see him on that Wednesday evening and he had cancelled because his mother needed him. Then it seemed that she didn't need him for very long, so he rang me on my mobile. John, my husband, is away for three months in Singapore…and we met up as planned earlier."

"Where did you meet and can anyone else vouch for both of you?" asked Davenport.

"We met in a quiet part of Simshill. I left my car and went into his. We can't go anywhere in case someone we know sees us. It sounds so sordid but I love Matt and John and I …we were never really a success together."

She began to cry quietly.

Fiona went up and switched on the kettle which was always ready in Davenport's office. By the time she had made tea and came back with the cup of steaming liquid, Karen Lawrence had composed herself.

"It was good of you to come, Mrs Lawrence. I appreciate that it couldn't have been an easy decision. One last thing, at what time did you meet Matthew Stevenson that night?"

She thought, briefly.

"It would be about nine o'clock. He was there first, waiting for me."

"You're sure about the time?"

"Yes, Sir."

"What made you decide to come to see us?"

"Well, I realised that Matt had obviously refused to involve me when I read of his arrest. You will let him go now, won't you?" she asked anxiously.

"I will indeed. In fact, you drink your tea and I'll go and get him right away and you can see him for yourself," said Davenport.

He left the room.

"He's very nice. You're lucky to work for someone like that," said Karen Lawrence.

"Yes I am and I hope he'll be good to live with too as we're getting married next Saturday, all being well," laughed Fiona.

She looked enquiringly at the young woman.

"Can you and Matthew not make a go of things? If you and your husband don't really get along any more, would it not be easier and better for you both if you ended it?"

Karen smiled.

"You know. that's what all this has taught me. I realised as I sat here. before I actually had the guts to tell you, that it wouldn't be the end of the world if John did find out!"

They heard footsteps coming along the corridor and Davenport came in, with Matthew Stevenson.

"I've just been giving your young man a row for not being honest with us. I'll be in hot water for having arrested him wrongly and now we have to begin all over again."

"Oh…and you've got your wedding next Saturday," blurted out Karen and Fiona reddened and looked sheepish. Salma smiled.

"Nothing will put that off," said Davenport. "Nothing!"

# CHAPTER 36

Davenport reached Robert Stevenson by 'phone later that afternoon and asked him to come again into the station. As expected, Stevenson complained and was told that a police constable would be sent to collect him from his home, if he did not appear within the next hour.

The team was gathered in the Incident Room, listening to Frank and Fraser's reports when Bob rang to say that Robert had arrived.

"Take him down to Interview Room 1, please Bob," said Davenport. "Ask if he wants tea or coffee and get it for him if he does, then leave him there."

"Making him stew, Sir?" asked Frank, appreciatively.

"Whatever gave you that idea?" asked Davenport and the rest grinned.

"Now Frank, you first. Who did you see?"

"Well, Sir, they were all in the one house so it made questioning all of them quite easy," said Frank.

"Oh that's right, I forgot that Margaret and Avril were camping out at the Macartneys! You needn't both have gone."

"Well, I took Mrs and Miss Stevenson into the kitchen and spoke to them while Fraser did the same with the Macartneys, in the lounge."

"Sounds like another episode of Cluedo, Selby. OK what did your two say?"

"Margaret Stevenson had no alibi. She watched TV and went to bed early. Avril met friends from schooldays in the West End. They ate out at 'Peter's'…near Partick, she said."

"So Avril has an alibi but her mother hasn't," said Fiona.

"Fraser, what about the Macartneys?" asked Davenport.

"Kim was with her boyfriend at his house. They had supper with his parents. Lucy was at Yoga classes in the local school from seven till nine."

"And their parents?"

"Pauline Macartney was at her art class, same time as Lucy's class and Stewart was out with a friend at 'The John Stirling Maxwell' which is a Wetherspoon's pub, Sir, in Shawlands."

"So, the only one of those six not to have an alibi, is Margaret Stevenson and we can't think of any reason why she would kill her mother-in-law and it's even more far-fetched to think that she would have murdered Martha Cowan," said Davenport, dejectedly.

"Now we know that Matthew Stevenson has an alibi too," said Fiona.

The two constables looked enquiringly at her.

She explained that not long after they had left, a married woman had come forward to say that she had been with Matthew Stevenson that evening, in his car in a quiet road in Simshill. Matthew had been allowed to go home and the two had left together.

Looking at his white board, Davenport sighed and getting to his feet, wiped Matthews' name from his, 'Adele' list.

"It would appear that the only suspects left are the Smiths, the unknown niece and Robert Stevenson," he said. "OK team, what's your choice?"

He sat back down.

"I'd plump for Victor Smith, Sir," said Frank eagerly. "He knew where the arsenic was and maybe he had plans, or they both had plans which involved having lots of money."

"And they killed Adele Stevenson, why?" his boss asked.

"As you suggested, Sir, she maybe saw one of them coming out of Martha's room carrying a bottle and although she obviously didn't see anything suspicious because she never said anything, the next day, they thought she might remember later."

"OK. Salma?"

"I agree with Frank, Sir, either Mr or Mrs Smith and for the same reason," said Salma.

"Fraser?"

"I'll go for Robert, simply because he's a nasty piece of work and I could see him not even being disturbed at another old lady dying by mistake and going on to repeat his poisoning of his mother the next night."

"DS Macdonald?" asked Davenport.

Fiona agreed with Fraser, claiming that Robert had lied about his wife seeing him come home early which, in her book, made him suspicious.

"What about you, Sir?" asked Frank, again taking on Penny's role of impulsive speaker.

"I know there seems to be no reason for someone wanting rid of Martha to also get rid of Adele and vice versa," he said, "but the explanation of the Smiths being seen seems to me to be more likely than that of Robert having a rerun murder, so I'll go along with Frank and Salma. Maybe Robert will come up with another alibi. I'll get down there now. Fraser, you come with me this time. Frank and Salma, you can get off home. I'll see you both on Monday. You too Fiona. See you tonight. I'll come down to you and bring Pippa, if that's OK."

"That's fine, Sir," said Fiona.

Robert Stevenson was pale. He sat drumming his fingers on the table top. He had obviously refused refreshments as no cup sat in front of him. Fraser took up his position at the back of the room while his boss sat down across from Robert. Davenport switched on the recording machine and made the preliminary statement. He sat back and crossed his arms.

"Mr Stevenson, you have not been honest with us."

"How do you mean?" the man said belligerently.

"You said that you arrived home early on the night of your mother's murder and that your wife saw you."

"Yes and she told you that she gave me supper," he persevered.

"Well, she has now withdrawn that statement. She did *not* see you and the first time anyone saw your car, was your daughter Avril who saw it quite late when she returned home."

"Well, she's lying!"

"Who? Your wife or your daughter?" asked Davenport.

"My stupid wife! Silly cow doesn't know her arse from her elbow."

"So are you saying that she is lying or being forgetful, Sir?" queried Davenport.

"I don't care which. I came home at just after eight o'clock and she saw me."

"OK, let's accept that for a minute. Can you prove that you did not go back out and return to

Tall Trees when you thought that your brother would have left?"

"I thought he was going to play cards with mother, so why would I do that?"

"You expected her to play cards with him when she hadn't done that with you?"

"He's the one you should be suspecting, Inspector, not me. He's the one with no alibi!"

"Oh but he *does* have an alibi, Sir. The woman he was with came into the station today."

Robert looked nonplussed for a minute.

"She's probably lying. Women do, you know. Misplaced loyalty!"

"Like your wife's, 'misplaced loyalty', Sir?" countered Davenport. "I need you to prove to me where you were between eight o'clock when you said that you arrived home, and ten o'clock. Your wife told my constable today that she went to bed very early."

Robert sat for a short time. It was clear that he was working things out in his head. Now that his wife had left him, he knew that he could no longer count on her support.

"OK, damn you to hell. I did leave the nursing home when I said I did but I went to see another woman."

"Her address please, Sir," said Davenport, and Fraser came forward with his notebook and a pen.

Robert Stevenson made a noise something like a growl. He grabbed the notebook and pen and scribbled an address.

Davenport turned the notebook to face him and read what was written which was 'Albany Hotel'.

"Does this woman work there, Sir?" he asked.

"It's the only address I have for her, Inspector. We meet there."

"A married woman, Sir?"

"No damn you, she's a prostitute!" Robert ground out through gritted teeth.

When Robert had flung out of the room, on being told he could leave, Davenport smiled and told Fraser that he thought that Margaret Stevenson would be pleased to know that her husband had had to pay for his other woman.

"I guess that being the type of self-centred, pompous man he is, he will have paraded his other woman in front of his wife, probably comparing Margaret unfavourably with her too."

"Will you tell Mrs Stevenson, Sir?" asked Fraser.

"I think I'll manage to bring it into my next conversation with her," replied his boss.

"Do you mind drawing the short straw, Fraser? I want you to go to The Albany before you go home. Talk to any 'ladies of the night' who are present in the foyer and try to find one who might have been with Robert Stevenson that night."

Looking rather reluctant, Fraser left. As he told Erin later it was not getting a late task to do that had bothered him, it was wondering how on earth he was going to spot what his boss had labelled, 'ladies of the night'.

In the event he asked the young man at the desk and he pointed out one young, very glamorous young lady sitting behind a potted plant in the foyer.

"I think she thought I was a prospective 'punter', Erin, till I took out my warrant card, then she seemed to think I was going to arrest her for soliciting. She wasn't the one who had gone with Robert Stevenson but when I described him, she knew who had and gave me her name and address. They shared a flat together as it turned out."

"Did you go to her flat?"

Erin sounded curious rather than annoyed.

"No, her friend said she was out 'working' so I just asked her to tell her friend to come to the station on Monday."

# CHAPTER 37

Fraser reported to Davenport first thing on Monday morning and told him to expect a visit from a young woman, that day.

"Though, Sir, if she works nights she probably won't come in till the afternoon."

Fraser left and went down to the room he shared with Frank and Salma. He told them about the prostitute who would hopefully be coming in that day. As they all realised, if she gave Robert Stevenson an alibi for the Wednesday evening, then they were left with only Victor and Matron Smith as suspects.

"Unless one of the residents did it?" said Salma.

""That'll be right," laughed Frank, then realised that his sergeant was looking serious. "Why would one of them kill two fellow residents, Salma?" he asked her.

"I can't think of any reason right now but they would all know about the garden shed and possibly all had been in – old people are quite nosy, at least my grandmother was. She knew everything about everybody who lived near us."

"So did my Gran," said Fraser. "She used to stand behind her aspidistra..."

"...What's that, Fraser?" asked Salma.

"A plant. I don't think people have them anymore," he answered her. "She stood hidden behind her plant and peered out of the window for most of the day."

"OK, so the old buddies might know about the arsenic but we need to think of a reason before we suggest this to the boss," said Frank.

"I think we should chat to them all again," said Salma. "Should I suggest it to the DCI?"

"See if he has anything for us to do first," suggested Fraser.

Salma however was oddly persistent about her idea and she went up to Davenport's room and knocked on his door. When invited in, she entered. DS Macdonald was sitting with him and Salma caught the end of her sentence,

"... but it would spoil the day, wouldn't it?"

Asked what she wanted, Salma apologised for interrupting them, then said that she had heard that it appeared as if Robert Stevenson might be in the clear and asked if she and the two constables might go back up to Tall Trees to chat to the residents again in case, by any chance, one of them could have used the arsenic.

"I mean, Sir, the problem we're having is with one person killing two old women who aren't connected in any way. The one thing that *does* connect them is that they were both residents of Tall Trees. They might all know that arsenic was kept in the garden shed," she added, defensively, when her request was met with silence.

"Well, another visit won't do any harm and we're certainly up against a brick wall at the moment. I'm expecting a call from Mr Knox any time now and it will be better if I can tell him that we're still engaged in trying to suss out the killer, rather than all sitting here doing nothing! OK, Salma, off you go but leave either Frank or Fraser behind in case something else turns up."

Salma hurried back down the corridor and asked the two men if one of them would come to Tall Trees with her. Frank seemed disinterested.

"I'll stay here, if you don't mind. I think you're going on a wild goose chase."

Salma looked puzzled.

"I haven't heard that phrase before," she said.

"It's called that because you can't catch a wild goose as it will simply fly away when you get close to it," explained Fraser. "So Frank means going up there won't help us at all."

"God, do you know everything, brain-box?" said Frank, sounding disgusted.

"Not quite and you needn't call me God, at least not till the afternoons," said Fraser, mock solemnly.

"Come on, let's get off," said Salma, smiling.

It only took them about fifteen minutes to get to Tall Trees. On the way, they had concocted their plan. Salma would tackle Mrs Mohammed who might open up to a fellow Muslim but then she would interview the men, leaving Frank to speak to Miss Williams, as being a young man he might be able to soften her rather stern manner and he would see Donny which might take longer if he was not rational today. They bumped into Matron Smith in the hallway and told her that they were there to interview some of the residents again. She looked worried but only reminded whoever spoke to Donny Bryant to try not to disturb him.

As it happened, Donny was rather vague. When Fraser asked if he remembered Adele Stevenson and Martha Cowan, he looked bewildered. Tom who was with him, reminded him gently that Adele had been the woman who was interested in the garden and suddenly Donny pointed his finger at Fraser and said, "You're the new gardener. I saw you in the garden one day. Tom, you said that I could still help Victor in the garden but *he's* back now!"

His voice was shrill. Tom led him over to his chair at the window and pointed out Victor who was pruning something down below.

"Look Donny. Victor is all by himself. This man…" he gestured at Fraser… "is a policeman.

He's not interested in the garden. He's not the same young man you saw before."

"No, I'm not interested, Donny," said Fraser, "but who else was interested in the garden and shed?."

Donny eyes were focussed on the garden.

"Everyone wants to nosy about in our shed. She said it was untidy."

Fraser's eyes lit up.

"Who's everyone, Donny?" he asked.

"What?" asked Donny, looking at him blankly.

"I'm sorry, Constable. You won't get any sense out of him now, I'm afraid. He's only having short lucid moments these days, poor sod," said Tom.

"Why would the residents be interested in the shed?" mused Fraser, almost to himself, but Tom had heard him.

"When he says 'everyone', he probably saw one person go in," he volunteered.

"Who might that one person be," asked Fraser.

"Well as far as I know, Claude and Claire never went outside except when Claire's teacher friend came to take her out for lunch, occasionally. Martha Cowan and Mrs Mohammed seldom left their rooms, never mind go into the garden though Martha did go to the shops about once a fortnight."

"Who does that leave?" asked Fraser.

"It leaves Fred Graham and of course Mrs Stevenson who was interested in the garden. Fred used to wander round, occasionally, often with his grandson who I suspect encouraged him to take some exercise in the fresh air when he came."

Thanking Tom and saying that he hoped that Donny would have more good times soon, Fraser knocked on Miss William's door. He had to knock three times before a stentorian voice told him to come in. The room was over-heated and quite dark. The TV was blaring away in the corner but Miss Williams looked as if she had just woken from sleep. She rubbed her eyes and squinted at him through the gloom.

"Who are you?" she demanded.

"I'm PC Hewitt, Ma'am. Do you want to see my warrant card?" asked Fraser, reaching into his top pocket.

"Haven't got my glasses on young man, so no point. As long as you haven't come to poison me."

She started to cackle with laughter at this witticism, then began to cough and demanded that Fraser fetch her a glass of water from her small bathroom. He noticed two cups on the window ledge and wondered who this old lady entertained. He handed her the water and she drank, her cough subsiding immediately, to his relief. He asked her if she had ever visited the garden shed to which she looked at him in disbelief and informed him tartly that she had lived all her young and working life in the city and was not in the least interested in gardens and their old sheds. Fraser thanked her.

"Have you not found out our murderer yet?" she demanded as he rose to leave.

"I'm afraid not," he told her, wondering if he should have lied and said they were near to solving the case.

"I think it was Victor," she said. "He's got shifty eyes."

Thanking her for this insight, Fraser said cheerio and left her to the withering comment, "Goodbye, young man, not cheerio!"

He went into the hallway. It was deserted. Idly he flicked through the Visitors' book, noting that there had been no more entries since Matthew Stevenson's on the night of his mother's murder. The magazines on the hall table were not to his liking so luckily it was not long till Salma arrived, looking despondent.

"Mrs Mohammed never appears to even look into the garden. She watches TV all the time and is a fan of antique and cookery programmes and all Soaps and quiz shows. Mr Ferguson is across the hall and can't see into the garden, though he claimed that he had offered to help in the garden but been turned down. Seeing the time it took him to get out of his armchair and answer his door, I don't think he's fit for any physical exercise. He kept repeating that he was the oldest resident, at ninety-three."

"What about Fred Graham?" asked Fraser.

"He likes to stroll round the garden, occasionally. It appears that his grandson, Bob, encourages him to do that. He's been inside the shed but said that he didn't know anything about arsenic though when he heard through the Home grapevine which he proudly claims is wonderful, that the two old ladies were poisoned by arsenic, he felt sure that arsenic would be kept in the shed. He told me that it's used for getting rid of wasps though he didn't know of any wasp infestations recently."

"My lot aren't gardeners, apart from Donny and I don't think he could plan one murder let alone two and the only thing that recommends him is that there is no apparent connection between the two murders and he might have killed twice, randomly."

"But we were told that although dementia patients can become violent, there's no history of it with Donny."

"So we've really learned nothing new," said Salma despondently.

"Well, we could rule in Donny and Fred Graham, I suppose," said Fraser, consolingly. "Look, I want to see Mr Graham for a few minutes anyway. I'll see what I can ferret out. Do you want to head back without me or wait? I'll only be about ten minutes"

Salma opted to wait and sat down with the Hello magazine so despised by Fraser just recently.

Fraser was invited into Fred's room when he knocked. The old man looked frail, sitting by the window but seemed pleased to see the young constable.

"Ah, Constable, have you come for that dissertation? I didn't finish it I'm afraid. I found it too depressing, especially in the light of Adele's death."

He got slowly and painfully to his feet and, with the aid of his stick, crossed the room to his bedside table on which lay the large, hard-backed folder. He picked it up and handed it to Fraser.

"One thing did strike me. One of the poems she mentioned, "Two Sons", reminded me of Adele herself because she had two sons and she liked to play solitaire though Adele called it by its English name, patience."

"Are you sure, Sir, that she said that she would be playing bezique with her two sons that night?"

"Yes, I'm sure, as she said that they didn't enjoy it and that was why she was going to insist, to pay them back in a small way for bringing her to Tall Trees against her will."

"She must have hated them for that," said Fraser.

"You know, that's reminded me of something I'd forgotten, Constable. I caught a look on her face when she was talking about what they'd done. I couldn't quite place the look but I realise now from what you've just said, it was hatred, pure hatred."

Fraser asked him if he and Adele had ever discussed dying.

"Did she want to die, Sir?"

"Why? Because she was ninety-four? She had more life in her than some young'uns I know."

"So she wouldn't have asked anyone to…help her out, then?"

"Me, you mean, young man? I was her best friend in the short time she was here. If she had wanted that, I was the one she would have asked but she didn't, I can assure you. Anyway it would take a brave person to ask someone to poison them when they didn't know how they would suffer while waiting to die!"

Fraser apologised if he had upset him and prepared to leave.

"Only doing your job, Constable, only doing your job. I hope you enjoy your reading."

Fraser was almost at the door when he thought of something.

"Can I have a look at your bezique cards, Sir. I'm a nosy person and these cards keep being mentioned and I've never seen them. Are they very different from ordinary cards?"

"I can't lend them to you as Bob will be up either tomorrow or the next day to play with me but if all you want to know is the difference, I can tell you that. There are two packs used together and there are no threes to sixes in the packs."

They made their way back to the station. Davenport and DS Macdonald were out for lunch so they let Frank know that they were back, and, finding out that he had been for lunch, they went off to the canteen.

By two o'clock, they were all back in the Incident Room, discussing the Home visit, when word came that a young woman had called to speak to either a Constable Hewitt or a DCI Davenport. The DCI left the room. They heard footsteps going past their room and they returned to their discussion. Salma had been apologetic about what she saw as a waste of their time but Fiona consoled her, telling her it was possible that one of the residents had committed the murders.

"As you said, Salma, there's no logic to the two murders so it could be a case of two pointless killings, therefore it's possible that one of the elderly residents could have done it with all of them having recourse to the shed and therefore the poison," Fiona comforted her sergeant.

"But the only two credible ones are Donny and Fred Graham and Donny seems so placid..."

"...but he can get agitated."

Davenport had come back in and added this last statement.

"Remember that Tom was calming him down a few days ago because he had got so upset over seeing two cups of coffee. Maybe one of the ladies, probably Adele as Martha didn't come out of her room often, upset him in some way."

He thought for a moment.

"Are there any similarities in the two dead women; in how they look I mean?"

Nobody knew what Martha Cowan looked like, having only seen Adele Stevenson. Davenport took out his mobile and rang Martin Jamieson. He spoke and listened, switched off the phone and told the others that both women had short, white hair and both were of medium build.

"Could Donny have been annoyed for some reason by Adele, gone into Martha's room, poisoned her then seen Adele the next day and realised that he had killed the wrong woman?" said Frank, excitedly.

Although it had been Salma who had first ventured the idea of a guilty resident, it was she who found the holes in this argument.

"I can't see Donny having the presence of mind to plan a murder," she said. "Different if it had been a spur of the moment thing but this had to have been planned."

"I wondered if Fred Graham might have assisted Adele in killing herself, Sir, a mad idea but worth a try but he said she didn't want to die and had more life in her than many young people he knew," said Fraser. "He told me that Adele hated her two sons and I guess she wouldn't have given them the satisfaction of ridding them of her. Another good point he made in his defence was that she would have been very brave to ask to be poisoned when she didn't know how much she would suffer before death."

There was silence as they digested all that had been said, then Davenport spoke.

"Well, that was Joanne Frew. She works from The Albany Hotel and Robert Stevenson was a regular customer. She described him perfectly and he was with her that evening, from just before nine o'clock so he can be ruled out. I had a call from Mr Knox's secretary while I was with her and I've to see him in half an hour."

Davenport sounded really glum and Fiona sent him a sympathetic look. Frank, seeing the look, coughed and caught Salma's eye, grinning at her.

# CHAPTER 38

Davenport went off upstairs for his meeting with the chief constable. The rest of the team dispersed to wait for his return. They had plenty to mull over. Fraser sat at his desk, immersed in Adele Stevenson's dissertation, entitled, 'A Disturbance in Mirrors'.

"A good title for a piece of work on a confessional poet," he murmured to himself.

Salma walked up to his desk and asked what he was saying and he told her that he had made a start on reading Adele's work and that as it was about two poets who attempted suicide, one successfully. It was an appropriate title as the two women had distorted views of life.

"How do you mean, Fraser?" asked Salma, interested, looking over his shoulder at the title.

"Well, Sylvia Plath wrote happy poems about her two kids but felt guilty about what her father could have done to Jews in the war and after trying a few times, killed herself. The other woman, Anne Sexton, was in and out of mental homes and tried to commit suicide, unsuccessfully. They obviously had different views of themselves, therefore the mirrors they looked in were 'disturbed'.

Salma went back to her own desk and sat, lost in thought. Even the ebullient Frank was sitting at his desk, staring into space. Up the corridor, in her own room, Fiona Macdonald was scribbling furiously on a notepad.

Davenport returned about half an hour later, looking quite tense. He called to the others and they joined him in the Incident Room once more, Fraser clutching the dissertation to his chest.

"I've promised to go back up later once we've had a chance to discuss the latest events, so let's sum up once again, Team.

Robert Stevenson went to see his mother on the Wednesday evening. He left when he said he did, just before eight o'clock but instead of going home, he went into town to the Albany Hotel where he met a prostitute. Matthew Stevenson also left when he said he did, not long after he got to Tall Trees. He realised that he could still see his female friend and they met around nine o'clock. Both have not got alibis. That leaves us with Victor and Doreen Smith."

He saw three pairs of eyes looking at him intently.

"I know, but we'll come onto the timings after we've dealt with these two. The Smiths could have realised that they were in for a lot of money when Martha Cowan died. OK they weren't in the red, either businesswise or personally, but they could have been greedy and wanted more and soon, but, and it's a big but, they had no reason to kill Adele Stevenson, unless she saw one of them coming out of Martha's room. Would she have seen anything suspicious in Mrs Smith being in a resident's room? I don't think so as she hadn't been there long enough to know that Matron seldom went into the rooms of the residents. She might have wondered why Victor had been in, in the event of the murder but she didn't know that the Smiths inherited from Miss Cowan. In spite of the grapevine that Fred Graham seems so proud of, I don't imagine that any of the residents knew that so she would not be suspicious."

He stopped for breath.

"Would the Smiths, if guilty of the first murder, not realise that, and in any case, would it not be Matron who slipped the poison into Martha's cup as no one would ever suspect her. Matrons do visit residents in care homes! So...."

He paused.

"We are left with no suspects as we now know that Adele Stevenson was killed after 8pm when both sons were elsewhere."

At that dramatic moment, Bob appeared at the door, to say that there was a call for Davenport from

Tall Trees and, apologising, he left the room. Fraser returned to his reading while the others sat silent, staring at the white board. When Davenport returned, it was to tell them that Miss Cowan's niece had been found. She was quite agreeable to go along with what the Home had planned for her aunt's funeral, it being a burial. She had not been disinherited, as Adele had told Fred Graham she had been

"We knew that. She received quite a large sum," commented Fiona.

"Yes and she isn't at all annoyed at the Home getting the lion's share. She expected nothing as she and her family had disowned Martha when they heard about the abortion! The niece, Mary, heard about that from her mother before her mother died. They are all Jehovah's Witnesses and so had Martha been originally."

"So Martha Cowan must have told Adele that she'd been disowned, not that she'd disinherited," said Salma.

"That's more likely as she might have felt obliged to explain why no one came to see her, though even that seems out of character."

"Didn't Adele tell Fred Graham that Martha's sister lived in Russia?" asked Salma.

"Yes, why?" enquired Davenport.

"Well, Adele's niece, Avril, lived there for a while too so maybe that triggered off an unusual burst of confidence," replied his sergeant.

"Well, it doesn't matter now, anyway. It just threw a wee spanner in the works. We might have got round to wondering if the niece had murdered her aunt if she'd come up and been told she was getting nothing in the will," laughed Davenport.

"So a genuine mistake on Adele Stevenson's part, do you think, Sir," asked Fiona.

"Well in the light of what I now think, Mrs Stevenson seems to have made a lot of…mistakes," said Davenport.

He could see that all his team were waiting for him to finish. All, except Fraser who was still reading, seemed to want to speak.

"Ok, I'll let you have your say now but if it's what I think, we'll all be thinking the same thing. Fiona, ladies first."

Frank's look of disappointment was almost comical.

"Ok, I'll say a bit and the others can chip in," said the DS.

"Who has done all the lying in this case? Adele Stevenson, it seems. She lied about when her two sons left. She even wrote it in the diary. Do we put that down to dementia? I think not. I think the dementia was a ploy of her sons to get her accepted for Tall Trees. Fred Graham claims that she was very astute…"

"…and she lied about playing that weird card game," interrupted Frank.

Before anyone else could contribute, Fraser intervened.

"Sir, would it be possible for me to ring Mr Goodwin just now?"

Three pairs of startled eyes turned to him and he flushed.

"It *is* relevant, Sir."

Davenport took out his mobile phone and pressed the digits before handing it to Fraser who got up and went into the corridor. He seemed to have stopped the flow of speech because when he returned it was to a silent room. He handed back the phone.

"Thank you, Sir. It was in reference to that weird game that Frank mentioned. Mr Graham at the Home told me that bezique cards are different from ordinary cards. There are two packs and no threes to sixes…"

"… and this is relevant why, Son?"

"I've just asked Mr Goodwin about the cards found strewn about in Mrs Stevenson's room the day her body was discovered and which had the fingerprints of both sons. That seemed to suggest that they *did* as she said play bezique but she was lying, Sir. The packs found in her room had threes, fours, fives and sixes in them!"

"So she lied about that and she lied about when they left," said Davenport. "Well done, Fraser. They didn't stay long because they didn't play the game."

"And she made a 'phone call to the kitchen saying that her two sons were still with her when they weren't and saying that they were all going to have supper together when they'd both already left," said Salma, excitedly.

"She made sure that both sons came up that night…"

"…she'd already made provision for the two family retainers in the new will, so she didn't need to have Robert back up. Did she want someone to hear them arguing…?

"…she asked both sons to get her a cup of water, so that their fingerprints were on the cups…"

"…and she dropped the cards while each son was there to get fingerprints on the cards. Remember that Robert was scathing of his brother giving the same excuse for his prints on the cards!" reminded Davenport, having to interrupt, like the rest, to get himself heard.

"Sir, does that mean that she killed herself and also Martha Cowan?" asked Salma.

"With the weedkiller? Did she have a chance to get it from the shed, in a wheelchair?"

Fiona was scribbling again in her notebook.

They were silent. Expressions of disbelief were on every face.

"Why on earth kill another old lady?"

Frank obviously put into words what the others were thinking as no one answered him.

"I often wondered and Fred Graham did too, why Adele went to Martha's room. As the old man said, why try to get to know someone if you were determined to leave?" said Charles.

"So she went on purpose," added Fiona.

Fraser had been silent but he spoke up now.

"I think she went to kill Miss Cowan and I know this sounds unbelievable but I think she decided, quite cold-bloodedly, to practise on the other old lady."

"Surely not! And why Martha? She wasn't the eldest," said Salma.

"No but she was the loneliest. She seemed to have no relations who would grieve for her," persisted Fraser.

"Let me sum this up," said Davenport. " Adele Stevenson wanted to die so killed herself…"

"…she maybe wanted to see if Martha suffered first," said Fiona. "Sorry, Sir," she added.

"But why all the lies about when her sons left and whether they stayed long enough to play bezique and have supper, was what I was going to ask," said Davenport.

"I think she wanted them to be blamed for her death, Sir," said Fraser. "And she maybe killed Martha because two deaths would look suspicious whereas one could be taken for a heart attack," he added.

"Why, Fraser, do you think she wanted them blamed?" asked Fiona, with interest.

"You haven't explained the bit about wanting her sons blamed," said Frank, dismissively.

"I've only read part of Adele Stevenson's dissertation but it's about poetry written by two poets who wanted to kill themselves. One was successful. One of the poets, Anne Sexton wrote a poem called 'Two Sons'."

He opened the dissertation at a place he had kept open with his finger and read:

" 'I sit in an old lady's room… You make a toast for tomorrow… I'll be playing solitaire'. I think she hated them for putting her into Tall Trees. She hadn't begun to settle down …"

"…as her daughter thought. Remember, Fiona, Pauline sounded really surprised?" said Davenport.

"Yes, I remember."

"The poem shows the old lady in an old lady's room, as Adele was in Tall Trees. Adele's sons were celebrating getting money for the house sale and did someone not mention her playing patience or solitaire, as the Americans call it? Oh, I remember. Ma'am it was Robert Stevenson when you interviewed him in here."

"That's right, Fraser. I remember him saying that she insisted on calling it patience," said Fiona.

"So, let's get this straight. Adele Stevenson, to get her own back on her two sons, poisoned herself after practising on another old woman to make sure the police were called, as two sudden deaths, one after the other, would be suspicious and she wanted her death looked into. Also she might find out if the other lady suffered a lot…"

"…and was probably told by matron who I believe went in to see her, that Martha died sitting in her chair," commented Fiona.

"Sir, what about the Gaviscon and the French novel?" said Salma.

"I think that Martha Cowan must have had it lying out when Adele visited her and she was obviously reading the Camus novel, so Adele simply added two things to make us sit up and take notice: see similarities in the two deaths so that again we would suspect foul play."

"Gosh, she certainly wasn't demented!" exclaimed Frank.

"Another thing, Sir. That old man, Fred Graham told me, today, that he had surprised a look on Adele's face once when she was talking about her sons and he now realised that it was pure hatred," said Fraser.

"I've thought of something else, Sir," said Salma. "The cups were badly washed in Adele Stevenson's room because she had washed them badly to leave fingerprints on them. It wasn't Robert or Matthew."

Not to be outdone, Frank also put in his two pence worth.

"Fred Graham told me that Mrs Stevenson had told him that she thought her two sons would kill her for her money, if they thought they could get away with it."

"She thought of everything," said Davenport, in admiration. "Any other loose ends anyone wants to tie up?"

"One more thing, Sir," said Fraser, to a groan from Frank.

"When I spoke to Donny today, he said that everyone wanted to, 'nosy in our shed', I think were his exact words. Tom said that probably meant that he'd seen one person going in and Donny also said, '*she* said it was untidy'.

"I don't think we'll be able to rely on Donny for a statement but it does seem to confirm what we now suspect," said Davenport. "Right, if there's nothing else, I want you, Salma to go and see Pauline Macartney. Ask whether or not she brought her mother a new pack of bezique cards which were asked for. Ask her if her mother was more mobile than she appeared to be. She couldn't have wheeled a wheelchair into a shed that size."

He looked at them all in turn.

"Anything else, folks?"

Fiona looked at her notebook.

"Yes, Sir, we need to know if anyone saw Adele in the garden of the Home. "

"True. Frank, get over to Tall Trees and try to find out if Victor ever saw Adele in the garden. Ask Fred Graham if she ever showed an interest in the garden, too, while you're there."

"Sir, do you think she did ever tell her sons that she was going to change her will?" asked Fiona.

"Probably not but she planted that idea in her daughter's head, certainly."

Davenport laughed.

"I'm going to have the last word before I go off upstairs, with a happy heart. Adele risked her sons not signing out that night but she had probably worked out that we would suspect them of forging the times if they did."

The meeting broke up with much laughter. As Davenport made his way to the lift he heard Frank's, "Glad she wasn't my mother. Vindictive old hag!"

# CHAPTER 39

Pauline Macartney was out when Salma called at the house but Stewart told her that his wife had said that she would be back in an hour and had been away almost that long. He offered her a tea or coffee and Salma gratefully accepted, as she'd had nothing to drink since lunchtime. Pauline duly arrived about quarter of an hour later and confirmed that her mother had asked for two lots of cards, a bezique set and two packs of ordinary cards for playing patience but that she had only been able to buy the latter.

"It was so cruel of Robert and Matthew to not only put Mum into a home against her wishes, but also to throw out so many things which she valued," she told Salma.

"I ordered the bezique cards," she said sadly. "I'll probably give them to that old man at the home, the man Mum played bezique with. I might see if he'd like my Father's blue cardigan which Mum loved to wear as it had pockets for carrying things about. I'm sure Mum would have left things to people if she'd had time to think about things like that. I don't think that she got close to anyone else though,"

She asked Salma if they were any further forward in discovering who had killed both ladies and Salma told her that some new things had come to light but that she was not at liberty to tell them what these were.

"My DCI will be in touch whenever he knows for sure," she said. "One other thing, Mrs Macartney, did your mother need the wheelchair to get around or could she walk quite well and just use it for convenience?"

"I was surprised to see Mum using the wheelchair so often when I got home from Cornwall. She refused to use it much at all when at home but I thought that she was just making it easier for her carers. No doubt in her own room, she still walked about."

Salma thanked her for her help and Stewart for his cup of tea. She told them that the funeral of the other woman, Martha Cowan, was to be held on Thursday, that her niece had turned up and was only too pleased to go along with the burial that the Home had planned. The short service was to be at the Cooperative funeral parlour in Pollokshaws Road, across from Shawlands Primary School. Pauline said that she might attend as she felt a bond with Miss Cowan who had died in the same way as her mother.

When Salma got back to the station, Frank had just arrived back from Tall Trees and the team met in the Incident Room to await the return of the DCI from his interview with Chief Constable Knox.

"It's hard to believe, Ma'am," said Salma, "that Adele Stevenson hated her two sons enough to poison herself and another innocent woman."

"I know, Salma, I feel like that too," sympathised the DS.

"In the days of hanging for murder, she would just have sentenced two innocent men to death," contributed Fraser.

Footsteps coming along the corridor, heralded the arrival of Davenport who came into the room, smiling broadly.

"Well, that went OK. Mr Fairchild was with him and both congratulated us on the solving of the two murders."

He looked at the amazement on all their faces and laughed.

"Mr Knox will be able to inform the press of a satisfactory outcome which should help Joe Public to forget that he made a mistake. I'll have to inform the family of Adele Stevenson, before they read about it in their newspapers. Now, Salma, how did you get on with Pauline Macartney?"

"Sir, she was asked to get bezique cards and ordinary cards but had to order the bezique ones so only brought her mother the ordinary playing cards and she was surprised to see her being wheeled about in the wheelchair so often as she walked about when at home."

"Thanks. Frank?"

"Victor Smith saw Adele Stevenson quite often in the garden in her short time there. She told him about being a keen gardener and he had promised to give her a small bed for her own use. She had talked to Donny until he had become a bit confused. I asked if Mrs Stevenson ever went into the shed and he said he hadn't seen her go in but she had wheeled herself round the garden and had been out of sight. He looked at me a bit oddly, Sir, and asked if we were now suspecting the old lady of stealing the poison. He had laughed and said jokingly that she certainly could have carried the bottle off in the huge handbag she always had with her. He said the bag had slipped off her lap once and he'd picked it up for her, Sir."

"Sir, that reminds me. Pauline Macartney mentioned a blue cardigan with pockets that her mother liked to wear so she could have put the arsenic in there, especially if she'd transferred some into a small container before putting the bottle back in the shed," said Salma, excitedly.

"All it needed was for someone to have mentioned the wasps' nest to Adele Stevenson for her to have thought about arsenic and the possibility of it being in the garden shed," said Davenport. "However, we don't need proof of that, neither do we need to know how or when she returned the bottle, wiped of fingerprints, into the shed. She had time to pour some into some other receptacle, and go back into the garden."

"So what happens now, Sir" asked Fraser.

"Well obviously, there doesn't have to be any arrest but I will have to inform both Robert and Matthew Stevenson that their mother set things up to make them prime suspects. It won't be nice for them to know how much she hated them, in her last few days though the new will might have shown them a little of that hatred. Someone will have to attend Martha Cowan's burial and then we can all look forward to a certain wedding…which reminds me, Fraser, you and your other half, what's her name again?"

"Erin, Sir."

"Yes, Erin. You and she have been added to the guest list for Saturday if you haven't anything planned for that day."

"Thank you, Sir. We'd be delighted to come," said Fraser, beaming.

"Right folks, time to go home. I'll go tomorrow morning, to inform the Stevenson family about the outcome, so I'll be in quite late. Spend tomorrow getting all interviews and reports up to date. Mr Knox was kind enough to remind me that he still doesn't have all our previous cases written up and in his hands so get that done in what remains of the week. Your DS and I are being allowed Friday off."

Fiona looked startled but pleased. She drove over to Grantley Street to change into casual clothes and then made her way up to Newton Mearns to join in dinner with Charles and Pippa. Pippa was still full of her experience in the school toilets and insisted on regaling Fiona with the story after which she disappeared upstairs.

Settled in the lounge, Charles with a Scotch and Fiona with a glass of orange juice, he loosened his tie and told her about both visits to Knox that day.

"The first time was fraught, to say the least. He was furious about the fact that Matthew Stevenson now had an alibi and had been released. He was in full flow, blaming me of course, when I suddenly realised that if I let him continue, I was in effect letting myself be bullied, after telling my daughter not to let that happen to her!"

He laughed.

"I heard this voice saying,' Oh no, you don't, Sir. It was *you* who made the press statement and *you* who told me to arrest Matthew Stevenson."

"What happened, then?"

"There was what seemed to be a long silence, then he actually told me to sit down, rang his secretary to make us coffee and apologised. Admittedly, it wasn't a very gracious apology but he made one, Fiona, and somehow I don't think he'll be so quick to state someone is guilty without concrete proof again. I promised him some results today, then wondered if I'd been rash to do that."

"Was that why you looked so tense when you came back down?" she asked.

"Yes, it was. I'd have hated to have had to go back up and confess to still being stumped."

"What happened when you did go back up?" she asked, slipping off her shoes and wriggling her toes.

"Solomon was with him, so more coffee and I got to sit down ...again. I told them what we had found out, about both sons having alibis and that we'd turned our attention to the Smiths, then realised that Adele Stevenson had been lying all the time and when we went into that, we knew that she had tried to frame her sons and had in fact killed herself and poor Martha Cowan was a scapegoat. Solomon commented that we'd had a hundred per cent success rate in the murder cases we'd had since I had arrived, so Knox had to be complimentary as well, though no doubt he'll be quick to forget that when the next murder case comes along..."

"....which will hopefully not be until after our wedding!" exclaimed Fiona.

The talk turned to Saturday. Fiona was to collect her outfit on Wednesday and hoped that she would fit into it as she was thickening round the waist slightly. They discussed when they would tell the others about the coming baby and Fiona still wanted to wait until about the four month stage although she said that she did not mind if Pippa knew before everyone else. She had already admitted to telling Caroline. At ten o'clock she declared that she was exhausted and got up to go home.

"Keep their noses to the grindstone, till I get there tomorrow," he called after her as she went down the path to her car.

# CHAPTER 40

Saturday dawned grey and wet. Fiona, lying awake in her single bed, in her top flat in Shawlands, listened to the rain pattering on the windows and was surprised that she did not mind the poor weather. She was just so happy that her wedding day had come at last and she wondered why lots of couples planned their wedding about a year ahead. She looked at her outfit hanging from her wardrobe door. It had still fitted when she had tried it on on Wednesday. Her fair, wavy hair always looked neat so she would just be washing it herself and she was not a fan of lots of make-up so could manage that herself too.

Pippa was having her blonde hair pinned up, with tendrils of waves framing her face, at her local hairdresser's at one o'clock, then she was being driven down by George, the best man, for about two fifteen. Her long skirt and bodice top were hanging in Fiona's hall and her shoes were sitting alongside Fiona's, in the bedroom.

Fiona gave a contented sigh and snuggled further under her duvet. Once the wedding was over, they were having five days off to transfer Fiona's things to Newton Mearns and find homes for them in Charles's house. Nearly all the furniture was her mother's so she would get rid of it to charity if possible and ornaments, bedding and crockery which were mainly her mother's too would go to the church Nearly New sale. Charles had packed a case with unwanted clothes so the church men's clothes' stall would be benefitting also.

Both were looking forward to telling Pippa about the expected baby and after that they could decorate the small third bedroom, for the new arrival. It would be a busy five days, she thought now as she drifted back to sleep.

Charles was lying awake too. In his jacket pocket were the plane tickets for the surprise honeymoon. He was feeling nervous. What if this marriage went the way of his first one? He smiled to himself. Fiona was so completely different to Anita and with her being in the police force too, she understood his unsociable hours and would sympathise with him rather than shout at him, if he had to stay late at work. He knew that Fiona did not like his best man, George, who, unmarried, could be a golf bore but he had warned his friend to keep his speech short and devoid of golf stories. He had written out his own speech last night and was keeping it short too. He tried to go back to sleep but sleep eluded him now, so he got up and quietly made his way downstairs.

Pippa had been sworn to secrecy about the honeymoon and knew that she would be spending the coming week at Hazel's which she was looking forward to as they had not had any sleepovers since starting their new school in August. She hugged herself under the covers, thinking of her new outfit and the grown-up hairstyle she would be getting soon. The photographer had only been thought of quite recently and had come along a few weeks ago to show them samples of his work. Pippa was looking forward to seeing herself with her Dad and Fiona in their photographs. She looked at her bedside clock – 8.10 – still too early to get up, so she turned over and was soon fast asleep again.

The bell of Fiona's control-entry door rang just before 2.15 and, still in her dressing gown, she went to press the button to let Pippa come up. She opened her flat door and soon the excited teenager was with her, looking much older with her hair swept back and up. They hugged each other, excitedly. In the bedroom, Pippa got out of her denims and slipped on her long skirt in peach-coloured satin then Fiona helped her lace up the bodice which was in darker shade of peach. She stepped into her delicate shoes which we were in cream silk with a tiny peach rose on the front of each.

"I've bought us both fascinators for our hair," Fiona said. "But you help me into my dress first, please."

Pippa helped Fiona step into the dress which was in cream and swept the top of her shoes which were a larger replica of Pippa's. The dress had a large artificial rose in peach on one shoulder. The other shoulder was bare. Fiona looked in the mirror and prayed that she wouldn't blush today. She picked up a small box from the dressing table and opening it, took out two wispy fascinators, in cream and peach. She pinned one to the side of Pippa's head, just above one ear, and then did the same for herself. She looked in the mirror, got out her lipstick and touched her lips lightly.

"Would you like a little of this, Pippa?" she asked.

"Oh, yes please," said Pippa and stood still while it was applied.

They stood together in front of the mirror and gazed at themselves,

"Fiona, you look beautiful," Pippa whispered. "Dad will just love your dress."

"And you look like a princess, my soon-to-be stepdaughter," was the rejoinder.

The sound of a horn startled them. Pippa looked out of the window and shrieked, "Fiona, it's our car and I need to go to the toilet."

"On you go and don't get the skirt wet. Lift it carefully," warned Fiona.

She went to the window and waved down to the driver and when Pippa was ready, they picked up the little bouquets of freesias which had arrived before Pippa, and went carefully downstairs. The rain had stopped and there was a little knot of bystanders on the pavement, alerted by the beribboned limousine. Fiona smiled at them and Pippa scrambled into the car first. Fiona told the chauffeur that she didn't want to be early and he promised to drive slowly.

The car wound its way along Coustonholm Road, past the library and the empty spaces where multi-storey flats had once stood and arrived at the church. Fiona saw George standing outside with his video camera and a few people from the remaining flats were hovering to see what was happening. The car stopped and she got out carefully, reaching in to help Pippa alight. They negotiated the few puddles in front of the church and were soon in the foyer. They had asked John to be their only usher, insisting that they didn't want a 'them' and' us' seating arrangement. He handed them both an order of service which came as a surprise to Fiona as they hadn't requested this.

"I'll get in and let the organist know you're here," John whispered and Fiona smiled at him, feeling suddenly completely calm. They heard the music change to Handel's Water Music and, smiling at Pippa, Fiona set off down the short aisle. Pippa followed her, trying to keep in time with Fiona's steps which were unhurried. At the front, Charles turned round, looking very smart in his charcoal grey suit with pale grey shirt and a peach-coloured tie which had been very difficult to find. Fiona arrived at his side and Pippa moved up to stand beside Fiona, with George on Charles's other side, the small camcorder in one hand.

The service went without a hitch, Fiona and Charles both repeating the vows though the minister had said that they could merely say, "I do" after she had said them. Charles duly kissed his bride and they left the church to sign the register, Fiona causing a laugh when she tried to sign the part for Charles.

"You can see who's going to be the boss in this outfit," Charles said, laughing, to the minister.

"Quite right," she laughed.

That over, they made their way out through the church, Pippa behind them with George who put her arm through his. They stopped for a few photographs, then got into their cars for the short drive to the golf course. Once at the golf club, the sun having come out, the four important people were taken in a golf buggy to a picturesque part of the course and the guests went inside for pre meal drinks.

The reception was informal, the few short speeches being made while everyone stood round the cake which the bride and groom cut, traditionally. The top table was for Charles, Fiona, Pippa, George and the minister and the guests found their named places round four tables. Anita, Charles's ex-wife had chosen not to attend but his ex mother-in-law, Rachel, was there and sat with Caroline and Paul, Linda and Joe, Jill, Fiona's best friend and John and Jean, their bridge friends.

Frank, with Sue, Fraser with Erin, Penny with Gordon and Salma on her own, were seated round one table and looked relaxed. Their boss had promised them that they would be nowhere near their chief constable and assistant chief constable who were seated at a table with their respective wives and Ben Goodwin and Martin Jamieson with his wife, Kath.

Finally there was a table for four people and this held the Ewing family and Fiona's cousin from Tarbert. Ralph and Sally were friendly people and Fiona knew that they would make her cousin feel at ease. Hazel had been put in charge of their camera and was even now trying to snap Pippa as she sat down at her table. Pippa, seated, caught sight of her friend and waved to her.

The meal progressed without any setbacks and then the tables were cleared, the seats set out on the carpeted area and the wooden flooring left clear for dancing. Charles took Fiona onto the floor, to cheers from the guests. He and Fiona had practised their waltz and although neither was an expert dancer, they managed to look regal as they danced slowly round the floor, joined by Pippa and George, both looking a bit embarrassed. Hazel took more photographs, as did the official photographer who had been told not to take too many pictures, either at the church or at the reception as both Charles and Fiona had had experiences of being bored stiff at weddings while they waited hours for photographs to be taken.

After their dance, they walked round their guests, thanking them for their presents. Charles introduced Fiona to Rachel, Pippa's grandma and Fiona introduced him to her cousin with whom she had spent some holidays as a child. Both stayed for some time with Caroline and Paul, congratulating them on their forthcoming baby. No mention was made of their own baby, as Fiona had reminded Caroline that nobody yet knew and Pippa especially might be upset to find out that she hadn't been told first. Linda and Joe told the happy couple that their daughter, Alice, would be sorry to have missed the wedding, being on her gap year in the

Far East. Solomon Fairchild congratulated them both on their wedding and on the solving of their last case:

"Just in time, Charles. Good timing."

Knox had smiled a bit thinly but his wife's congratulations were warm, as were those of Ben Goodwin and Martin Jamieson whose wife, Kath, warned Fiona that she would never see her husband were she to give up police work.

"I think that my wife enjoys her freedom from her workaholic husband," said Martin, in his precise way and Kath grinned, good-naturedly.

The last table to be visited was that which seated their 'team'.

"What's with all the tartan, you lot?" asked Fiona, noticing that all were sporting small tartan flashes.

"Long story, Ma'am," said Penny.

"Right, we have plenty of time," said Charles, pulling across two chairs. He and his new wife sat down.

"Frank, you tell them. It was your idea in the first place," said Penny.

Frank looked a bit red in the face but Charles smiled at him.

"Come on, Frank. Why are you so obsessed with Scottish things? It used to be songs, now it's tartan."

Frank launched into his explanation.

"When you arrived, Sir. I thought of you as Prince Charlie. Then I sort of decided that the DS who was Fiona Macdonald could easily have been Flora Macdonald, so I kind of imagined a romance between you."

He looked carefully at his bosses but both were grinning.

"Very clever, Frank. So I guess that you brought out the Scottish tunes every time we did something together."

"That's right, Sir and got sent to a Scottish Night for my pains."

"Me too," said Salma. "I went with you, remember?"

"So he's taking all the credit for you getting married," piped up Penny.

"Well if that's the case, you deserve a big thank-you," said Fiona.

"Erin, see what your boyfriend has got himself into?" said Charles, to bring the shy-looking girl into the conversation.

"It's awful, Erin," said Gordon Black, Penny's boyfriend. "They're all mad!"

Everyone at the table laughed and then Charles and Fiona got up and moved back to their own seats.

Charles put his hand into his jacket pocket and pulled out a small envelope, handing it to Fiona.

"A wee, extra present, my love," he said.

Opening the folder, Fiona found two return plane tickets to Madeira.

"Charles! You shouldn't have. How long for?"

"A week. Wasn't it fortunate that we closed the case in time?"

"What about Pippa? Is she coming?"

Fiona rifled through the tickets.

"No. She's going to have a long sleepover with Hazel. They need some time together and she's looking forward to it," he answered her.

"I love you, Charles Davenport," said Fiona, mistily.

"That's convenient as you're lumbered with me for life. You heard the minister: 'Till death do us part.'

The evening ended at eleven o'clock and the guests dispersed, after thanking their hosts. Pippa gave her Dad and Fiona a big hug each and went off with Hazel and her parents, carrying the wedding cake which she and her friend were going to cut and parcel up for sending to friends and family.

"You've to keep some for your first baby's christening," she laughed, as she waved to them.

"It won't have time to get stale," muttered Charles, looking down at Fiona. "Did I tell you you looked beautiful today, my love?" he added.

"And you were so handsome and so colour-coordinated with us. Did Pippa's outfit give you a clue?" she asked.

"It did and the trouble I had getting this tie," he laughed.

They drove off to spend the night in Newton Mearns, as planned and jetted off to Madeira the next day, unaware of the final thread which was about to be woven into the tapestry of their double murder.

# CHAPTER 41

Charles and Fiona arrived home the following Sunday. They unpacked, had a cup of tea and went down to Newlands to pick up Pippa who was full of her stay with her friend. Charles thanked Ralph and Sally for looking after her and handed over a wee souvenir from Madeira. Hazel had had some of her photographs developed, although most would merely stay on their computer and she handed them over for them to look at, once they got home.

Declining more tea, they set off back to Newton Mearns, Pippa chatting ten to the dozen in the back seat but it was not till they had arrived and she had unpacked, that she remembered to ask them if they had had a good time.

"Yes, but strangely enough we missed you," laughed Fiona and Pippa grinned happily.

"Pippa, we have some news for you. You're getting it before anyone else and we want you to keep it to yourself, for a few weeks, pet, said Charles.

"What is it? Are we moving?"

"Well yes, probably, eventually, but that's not it," he replied, sounding a bit anxious.

"Well, what is it? Hurry up. I want to go upstairs and sort out my stuff for tomorrow," she informed him.

"You're going to have a wee baby brother or sister," he told her.

"Already! That was quick work!"

She grinned at them both.

"You don't mind, Pippa?" asked Fiona.

"As long as you don't want me to feed it at night, I don't mind," she told them. "Does no one know except me?"

"I told Caroline," said Fiona, honestly. "She told me that she was pregnant and I sort of blurted it out. Sorry."

"That's OK but let me tell Aunt Linda and my friends, when you're ready for folk to know, will you?"

"Of course," said Fiona, sounding relieved.

"Will you tell the folk at work tomorrow?" was the next question.

"No, not yet," said her father.

The station was quiet when they arrived the next day but even Frank arrived on time. Salma came up to Davenport's room, looking excited.

"Sir, before you tell us all about your holiday, we've got some news for you both. Will you come down to the Incident Room?"

She left and he heard her footsteps going down the corridor.

"Did you hear that, Fiona?" he called across to his wife's room.

"Yes. I'm coming."

The others were seated as they went it. Salma was holding a letter.

"Listen to this," she said. "It's a letter from Adele Stevenson to her daughter, Pauline. Pauline brought it to us on Friday."

She cleared her throat and read:

"Dear Pauline

When you receive this, I will have been dead for about two weeks. As you will now know, I did as I told you and disinherited Robert and Matthew. They have enough money already from the sale of my house. I hope that Margaret will break out of her marriage to my stuffed-shirt son. I suspect that he has treated her harshly, if not cruelly, during their marriage. To that end I have left her a considerable amount.

I know that you and Stewart and the girls will enjoy using the money I have left you, as will Avril. Lucy will no doubt travel but I suspect that Kim will save for her wedding! I wish I could have arranged for Lucy to meet my new friend Fred's grandson, but it was not to be.

I have no idea what stage the police will have arrived at, in solving the double murder of myself and Martha Cowan but I hope that your two brothers will have been suspected and arrested.

Maybe you will have begun to guess what I am about to say, my dear. Yes, I took my own life. I had begun to enjoy my life in Tall Trees but things could only go downhill at my age and I so wanted to get my revenge on Robert and Matthew!

I was scared, naturally, about how I would die, not having a wide understanding of arsenic, so I quite callously practised on poor Martha Cowan who did not keep well, had no life to speak of and had no one to miss her. I was glad that she appeared to die quite peacefully, after what appeared to be a bout of indigestion. I took arsenic from the garden shed and returned the bottle, after keeping enough for myself. I removed all fingerprints, of course.

I asked you for the Gaviscon and the Camus novel to draw attention to both 'victims'. I didn't want both deaths to be taken as natural so I did this and also lied about Robert and Matthew playing cards with me, in the hope that the police would assume that they were lying when their fingerprints were found on the cups they claimed never to have used. I rang down to the kitchen after they had both left, to say that they were still there.

Did they sign themselves out? I would have loved to know. Did Fred Graham remember that I told him they would like to murder me? Did you help me out by telling the police that the boys knew that I was going to change my will?

Please forgive me, Pauline. I think that Stewart and Lucy will not blame me too much but you and Kim might find it harder to take. I wanted Robert and Matthew to suffer but I did not want to risk either or both being put away for life, hence this letter.

Please pass this on to that nice, Sergeant Din. I didn't meet her superiors who hopefully would be called in when two deaths had taken place. I certainly hope so, as I went to a lot of trouble to make the deaths seem suspicious.

Don't think too badly of me, darling. Enjoy life to the full.

Your loving Mother."

Salma smiled as she finished reading.

Davenport was looking satisfied. He too smiled.

"I'm delighted to get this. What I learned of Adele Stevenson made me admire her. The only blot on the landscape was that she had to end the life of an innocent woman. Will Pauline Macartney let us copy this for our records, Salma?"

"Yes, Sir. I asked her that."

"Good. Make a copy and I'll take it up to God."

Made in the USA
Charleston, SC
09 February 2016